No Longer Mine
By
Shiloh Walker

41/2 Stars eCataRomance

"This gripping story kept me reading long into the night. Nikki and Wade's tragic past was so well written that my emotions were engaged right from the start. I felt their pain and devastation and at times wanted to slap them when they kept hurting each other. Shiloh Walker writes a heart-rending story of love and betrayal and the road to forgiveness. If you like an emotion packed story, you'll love ***No Longer Mine****. I know I did!" – Donna*

5 Stars Recommended Read from Fallen Angel Reviews

"From the very beginning, *No Longer Mine* will captivate readers. Within the first chapter I'm thinking to myself, "No way did that just happen!" You know you've gotten a great book when it starts with that much emotion and heart. ***No Longer Mine*** isn't just about Nikki and Wade's attempt to be together again. There's also a family element that is all too plausible. Having parents not always there as they should be and the responsibility of her younger brothers has shaped Nikki in to the person she's become. The same is true with Wade. The decisions he made and the outcome of those decisions made him into the man he is now. Not only that, but Wade isn't the only one affected by what he's done. **Shiloh Walker** writes all of this so well, that the ripple effect shows throughout the entire book. ***No Longer Mine*** is the type of book that you'll stay up reading until 3 in the morning because you can't put it down. I loved this book because not only did it touch my heart but also because the story is so compelling it makes you want to read other books by **Shiloh Walker** just so you can read more of the same. *No Longer Mine* is just an awesome read and therefore justifies a Recommended Read!" Jaymi, Fallen Angel Reviews

From the very beginning, NO LONGER MINE captured my interest and held it until the very end. The first chapter brought tears to my eyes and had me saying to myself "I can't believe that just happened!" I knew I had started to read a great book when it started with such enormous emotion. As an avid reader of Shiloh Walker novels, I can honestly say that she has out done herself with NO LONGER MINE. This well-written, magnificent novel is not an erotic saga; in fact, it is a loving romance story that will touch your heart and pull heavily on your emotions. This book is definitely a keeper and I would recommend this amazing read to all!" Contessa, Romance Junkies

"This story is so captivating that you won't be able to stop reading it till you are finished. It will keep the reader glued to the PC / PDA. From the beginning onward the emotional writing draws the reader into the story and you can feel with Nikki and Wade. No longer mine is a wonderful story of love, betrayal and forgiveness. Both Nikki and Wade were emotionally wounded in the past, but when they get a second chance for their love they finally find the happiness that they deserve so much.

I recommend to have a few Kleenex near you when you read the book, because Shiloh Walker wrote this book so real that you will fear Nikki and Wade's pain and sadness that will need them."

Danny, MonBoudoir

Published by Triskelion Publishing www.triskelionpublishing.com
15508 W. Bell Rd. #101, PMB #502, Surprise, AZ 85374 U.S.A.

First e-published by Triskelion Publishing
First e-publishing January 2005

ISBN 1-933471-53-0

Cover art by Triskelion Publishing

Chapter One

Nikki strode out of the grocery store with Jason perched on her hip as Shawn pushed the cart behind them. The scent of rain hung heavy on the air. Grim, overcast skies had been hovering over them for days, while everybody hoped for rain.

"Looks like the farmers are going to get the rain they wanted and then some, Nikki mused as she secured the straps on the baby's car seat. With a muttered curse she said, "I knew damn good and well that if I washed the truck it would rain."

As Shawn unloaded the groceries into the back of the truck he smirked at her and asked, "Then why did you do it?"

"Because we needed the rain," she replied drolly. "There's been a drought, or haven't you noticed?"

How could you not notice? All around, the normally lush Cumberland Lake area showed signs the dry summer, browned grass, dying crops…farmers suffering.

"Why couldn't this rain have come a few months ago?" she asked absently as she handed Jason his stuffed mouse. Casting Shawn a quick glance she said, "Hurry up and get in already."

As she slid into the driver's seat, flattened drops of rain splattered the hood of the truck.

An eerie silence fell as Nikki prayed silently the worst would hold off until they got home. The radio came on as she turned the ignition; just in time to hear the DJ warn of severe weather conditions. "Now you tell me," she muttered. "Always a day late and a dollar short."

Then Nikki glared at the skies as the clouds burst, dousing the parking lot under a deluge of water.

"Don't sweat it, Nik," Shawn advised. "We can just wait it out at Dad's."

With a sigh she said, "I guess we'll have to. I'm not driving thirty miles in this."

From the backseat, she could hear Jason jabbering to himself. Dogs, dogs, over and over again while he played with a tattered stuffed mouse. He chewed busily on the remaining ear. Flicking Shawn a glance, she ordered, "Put your seat belt on, will ya?"

Rolling his eyes he fastened the lap belt and drawled, "Yes'm." He gave Jason a look in the mirror, circling his finger at his temple. The baby laughed and clapped his hands before launching into a long and detailed monologue with his friend, Mouse.

With hazel eyes squinted to better see the rain-blurred landscape, Nikki stared through the windshield, blocking out the noise of the rain and her son's jabbering. Even though she drove with the lights on and blocked out everything but the road, she could barely see anything.

Twenty minutes passed and she still wasn't near her dad's. The store was ten minutes from his house, but that was under normal driving conditions.

Growling with frustration, she snapped, "I can't see a damn thing in this!"

The rumble of thunder edged closer. Lightning flashed

"You're almost there, Sis. It's just up there"

She spotted the turn off as Shawn spoke. "Almost there, fella," she said as Jason started shrieking, "Eat! Momma, eat!"

"Just a few minutes, Jas—"

Nikki was thrown forward. A blinding pain struck her head while a loud crash filled her ears. A blaring noise rent the air but, above it, she heard her baby's panicked startled cry.

From the passenger seat Shawn swore viciously, reaching for the door handle.

"Jason!" she tried to scream, but her voice was garbled, choked. Blood filled her mouth and a red haze clouded her vision.

Instinctively she slammed on the brakes, wrenched the steering wheel to the right, towards safety, away from that deep drop off to the left—

Another jolt struck her truck, throwing her back, pinned against the seat as the world started to spin before her. Above the roaring in her ears, she heard thunder and the screeching sound of metal against metal. Then all was silent.

It was less than a minute before the Blazer came to rest at the foot of the thirty-foot embankment, upright, but totally destroyed.

Nearly a half an hour passed before Nikki regained consciousness, wakening to the sound of birdsong. The air was clear, the sky blue, and rain drops sparkled under the sun as it dripped from emerald green leaves.

She came to slowly, something warm and wet trickling down her face. The air bag lay like a grayish-white blob in her lap. The air bag. Her vision loomed in and out of focus as she tried to force her body to move. It didn't want to but slowly, awkwardly, she lifted her hand to her brow. Under her fingers, she felt torn, wet flesh and, numbly, she pulled her hand away, staring down at the blood that stained her fingers.

"My God," she whispered, her voice shaking, hoarse.

In the seat next to her, Shawn lay unconscious, a large swollen knot on his temple. She touched him, sighing in relief when she felt the movement of his chest under her hand

Her baby. *Oh, God, please,* she prayed as she fought and struggled to free herself.

Please God, please.

The emergency release on the seat belt gave and she twisted to see in the back seat, hardly able to get her head high enough above the seat to be able to see. Everything was blurred, out of focus.

Where are my glasses? she wondered numbly

She couldn't see her baby. She shoved and pushed at the driver's side door, but it wouldn't move. Panic set in. She shifted until she could use her legs against it. She thrust her legs against the door again, and again. Jammed tight, it didn't want to open but finally, with a hideous grinding sound, it gave way. The back door came open surprisingly easy, simply pulling away when she jerked on it desperately.

Something was wrong. Jason's neck...

He was so still.

"No," she whispered, her voice soundless. Gently, lovingly, she reached for him. His sweet smelling baby flesh had already started to cool. A tiny bit of blood had dried beneath his right ear, another dried track below his left nostril.

Somehow, she freed him from his car seat, the seat that was supposed to help keep him safe. Stumbling away from the wreckage, she made it only ten feet before her knees gave way and she collapsed. Tiny whimpering noises filled her ears, but she didn't realize they came from her.

Jason was gone. Skills learned long ago were useless as she tried to breathe life back into his tiny lungs. Compress, compress, compress, breathe. Over and over. She huddled there, hoping against hope, praying. Agonizing moments later, she realized the futility of her efforts. His neck was broken. Even she could see that.

Jason was gone. His precious little face was still, peaceful. Thick soft black hair fell over his forehead and gently, she brushed it back, praying her touch would startle him out of his sleep.

He didn't move.

Her head fell back and her unseeing eyes locked on a clear blue sky.

The storm had passed. Rainwater continued to drip from the leaves. The forest floor around her was wet. Birds were singing and the air was clean and fresh. Squirrels were chattering in the background and leaves rustled as various forest creatures rooted around. There had rarely been an afternoon this picturesque. This beautiful. Beneath the trees, she rocked him back and forth to a tune she could only hear in her mind as she held him cradled to her breast. A thousand pictures flashed through her mind, each one causing a shard of pain to lance through her. He couldn't be gone.

Christmas was only a few months away.

And his second birthday.

She never had the chance to teach him how to swim.

Never taught him how to ride a bike.

She had promised to take him to Disneyland.

She never had the chance to tell him about his father.

He couldn't be gone.

An inhuman wail filled the air, startling the forest around her into silence. Her throat burned, her chest ached and before she realized she had made that god-awful sound of denial and desperation, her head fell back and she cried out a second time.

And then, mercifully, a black curtain fell over her eyes and she remembered nothing else.

Chapter Two

July
Three Years Later

The house was silent, save for the monotonous clacking of fingers hitting the keyboard. Eyes racing over the screen, tongue darting out to dampen her lips, Nikki painted a scene for her readers with words and twists of phrase. Her eyes narrowed and she bit her lip once in sympathy as her hero took a slice from an enchanted sword in his unprotected side.

And when Daire of Dien conquered yet again, against all odds, she smiled with him in shared victory.

But now that the ideas were put down on paper, her daze left her, and she realized...*she hurt.* The headache had been brewing for some time, but she ignored it in favor of the story.

Nikki hit save, her mouth stretching wide with a yawn. Updating the CD copy, she finally shut down and gave into the urge to bury her head in her hands. The demon headache throbbed behind her eyes, nausea churning in her belly. Her hands were shaking.

"Idiot," she mumbled. "Deserve what you get for trying to ignore it."

She fumbled in the drawer for a familiar bottle and downed a pill dry before she stumbled over to the couch in the corner. She buried her face in her arms to cut off the fading light and prayed for oblivion.

When she woke, it was after midnight. Even though the headache had subsided, a million other body parts protested as she sat up. Stiff shoulders and back screeched and her stomach growled loudly.

Damn it, how long ago did I eat? she wondered.

She shuffled and stumbled her way to the kitchen, much like a man after a few drinks too many. With a scowl, she rubbed her elbow after she bumped into the wall a second time.

Tomorrow, she promised. *Tomorrow, I'll take a break.* She silently vowed not to go into her office even for a second, not even to proofread today's work.

Her refrigerator was bare, except for a nearly empty gallon of expired orange juice and a plate of chicken her dad had made her bring home three days earlier. In the corner was something on a plate that reminded her of her science experiment in ninth grade. The store was a definite must for the upcoming day off.

Wrinkling her nose, she pitched the juice, the science experiment and what was left of the chicken before heading for the stairs. She'd skip dinner and eat a big breakfast once she got to town tomorrow.

She paused by the huge floor-to-ceiling windows that graced the landing of the stairs. She never tired of the view, not after spending the first eighteen years of her life in a concrete jungle. Outside stars shone brightly down, huge, diamond bright and looking close enough to touch.

Heavy eyes and drifting mind refused to allow her much time to appreciate the view now. Her nights of catnaps and the migraine had caught up with her and she was ready to *crash,* but the bed would be a lot more comfortable than the couch.

As she walked through her bedroom, she stripped down to her skin. She didn't notice the svelte figure, even though she had dieted and exercised religiously through her teenage years in an attempt to lose that extra twenty pounds.

It was ironic, now that the weight was gone, Nikki couldn't care less. After all, she hadn't a soul to impress, now did she?

Her thick auburn curls floated around her face as she pulled off her shirt. A pleasant round face was set off by wide hazel eyes and a full generous mouth. A lone dimple was visible beneath the left corner of her mouth when the rare smile appeared. Though she was only five foot three, she had a strong athletic figure, her shoulders slightly broader than normal for a woman, a bust of bigger than average size and full hips. Her waist had slimmed down over the years as her appetite faded to nothing, giving her the longed for hourglass figure that she hid now in baggy jeans and even baggier shirts.

She paused by the sink long enough to open the medicine cabinet and down a small yellow pill dry before she turned on the water.

Within minutes, hot steamy water fogged the air and she sighed with relief as her sore muscles stopped yelling at her.

While she rinsed off, though, her blissfully blank mind turned traitor, and memories rose up, rushing at her like freight train, unstoppable, unasked for. *Unwelcome.*

Time wasn't healing her wounds. Wasn't it supposed to?

God, she pleaded silently. *Will it ever get any easier?* Some days were better than others, passing with not even thinking of him. But then there were the days like this, when she was worn out, tired, without defense, the memories just lying in wait for her to be off guard, so they could lunge out at her.

The pain was just as shattering now as it had been then. It clawed at her, filling her chest, then belly with hot lancing little darts of pain. Her throat constricted until crying was punishment, but she had no control over the tears that swam in her eyes, the sobs that filled her throat.

With the water pounding down around her, she slid down the shower wall to huddle in the corner, wrapping her arms around her shivering naked body. She thought wildly, *it has to get better. It has to. Sometime.*

Then…

Peering out the window, she saw him. Less than an hour ago, the guy had climbed out of an electric blue Thunderbird, a grin on his mouth as he called out to the guys lounging on the porch.

Her gaze fastened on the naked back that gleamed under a sheen of sweat, the muscles that flexed and moved under skin the color of teak as he carefully backed away from the rental truck. Hands gripped the underside of a ratty couch, biceps bulging under the strain. As she watched, he tossed his head, sending a sweaty hank of hair out of his eyes.

Oh, he was gorgeous.

She was fifteen years old and he was the first guy to really catch her interest, right from the start. One look at him had her young heart fluttering.

He laughed a lot, worked hard. From the look of

it, he was Native American, with blue-black hair, high cheekbones, and dark smooth skin. He wore his longish hair in a loose queue, and a flashing white grin lit his face often.

But she didn't know his name.

And she probably never would.

To her surprise, and embarrassment, she found out that night while ringing up groceries. Without registering who he was, she quickly rang up his items, flashing him a polite, impersonal smile as she asked, "Did you find everything you needed?"

He answered, but she didn't hear a word. Even before she had even looked up, that low, smooth voice had her shivering. And when she looked up to take the offered money, words froze in her throat. Her cheeks flushed red and she shifted from one foot to the other as he studied her with quizzical eyes.

A six-pack of beer plopped down on the conveyor belt, and she jumped. Another voice intruded on her mind as somebody loudly said, "Hey, Wade, get this for me. I'll pay ya back later."

Wade. His name was Wade. Still in a daze, she rang up the beer, totally forgetting the little law that said minors couldn't sell. She later doubted he was old enough to drink. Nevertheless, she added it to the bill, took his money, dropped change into his hand all without speaking another word.

Chocolate brown eyes, a voice quiet and smooth, with a soft southern accent...He was absolutely beautiful. And she thought with disgust, he thought she was some kind of retard.

*****

"Sonovabitch!" she screeched as she went flying through the air. Landing hard on her back, she gasped for air, laying on the ground, panicking, unable to move a muscle, unable to breathe.

Oh, God, no. I'm paralyzed... Blood roared in her ears and her head spun dizzily the minute she tried to raise it. Distantly, she heard tires squeal and a door slam shut, but it hardly registered. Black dots danced in front of her eyes and a black cloud rolled over her.

She came to immediately but her thoughts stuttered to a halt at the face that was just inches from her own. *I've died and gone to heaven,* she thought. Either that, or she was dreaming. She tried to speak, but couldn't.

Instinctively, she tried to get up and move, but a gentle, firm hand held her still by pressing on her shoulder.

"Hold still, kid," he murmured. "You forgot to use your wings when you took that flight."

Finally her throat unlocked and she croaked out, "What happened?"

A new voice said, "Some kids were joyriding and ran you clear off the road. Do you remember?"

She turned her head and met the eyes of one of the movers. Closing her eyes, she forced herself to think. It hurt to do that "Yeah. I remember." She remembered, all right. A loud engine coming entirely too close as she turned her head to look. She panicked. She must have jerked the wheel to the right.

She also remembered the gleeful grins on two very

familiar faces.

"Don't worry. Wade here got the license plate." The older man smiled, a kindly face with a voice just as quiet as Wade's. "We'll be sure and let the cops know."

Again, disoriented, she tried to move once again, but that hand still held her shoulder. "Lie still," he ordered. "The ambulance will be here any minute. You shouldn't move."

It was easier just to obey, so she did. "My bike?"

Somebody grunted, bones popping as the older man moved away. Then he called out, "Flat tire in front. Rim's warped but the bike is okay. What about you?"

"Dizzy." Sirens were moving closer and it made the roaring in her ears louder. Her dad was going to throw a fit. Maybe she could get these guys to leave and just tell them an ambulance she didn't need them…

But they didn't leave. Soon, she was lifted into the ambulance, and *he* ended up in the back with her. How he managed that, she didn't know. A loud buzzing echoed in her ears and although she was hearing words, they didn't quite make sense. And she was cold.

"…kind of shocky…"

"…that flight she took…be shocky, too…flew twenty feet…"

"…name…parents…"

She couldn't make heads or tails of the conversation, not with her head pounding the way it was. Man, I'm gonna be sick…

Black dots loomed in front of her eyes. Her belly churned.

She tried to focus on the hand somebody held up in front of her, but it just wavered in and out of focus.

"...many fingers...?" a decidedly female voice asked. Her glasses. She couldn't see without her glasses.

She turned her head aside, or tried to, considering they had it secured in a brace. "I don't wanna go to no hospital," she muttered, her voice slurred. She tried to sit up without success. They had her strapped down and trussed up, like a Christmas turkey, her dad would say. "My dad's gonna freak."

A deeper more masculine voice said, "Chances are he will be madder if you wake up in the morning and can't move from the neck down." She rolled her eyes in that direction. *Jeez, it really was him.* His hand slid into hers and squeezed reassuringly. "Lori here needs to know how to get a hold of your parents."

"Just m'dad. Mom's dead." Her eyes filled with tears.

"How do we get in contact with him?"

"At work," she mumbled, her tongue feeling thick, clumsy. "Number in my bag. Head hurts." The fog was clearing from her brain - but that only made her more aware of the sickening pounding within her head.

"Close your eyes, kid, that might help," he told her.

In the background, she heard a woman...

"Concussion... bones... lacerations...pretty... bruising..."

A tinny sounding voice in the distance replied, but she could barely understand it.

"Yeah, lucky, all right."

Lucky wasn't exactly how she felt when the doctors insisted she stay overnight. Her father, eyes red rimmed from another marathon drinking session, surprisingly agreed without any argument.

"You're sure she's okay?" Jack Kline asked, his voice rough from years of whiskey and smoke.

"Fairly certain, but we need to watch her. Sometimes injuries don't make themselves known until later. It sounds like she took a pretty bad fall. She's got a moderate concussion, and she's going to feel like hell..."

Already do, she thought petulantly.

"Damn good thing that kid got the license plate number," her father grunted, turning away to stare out the window.

Nikki rested her on the pillow, keeping her eyes closed. The bright evening sunlight made her nauseated. Her head was throbbing. Her bike would need new rims, at the least.

Damn it, she didn't have money for that.

And what had happened to her glasses? Hell of a way to end the day. Things couldn't get worse.

*****

"How's the head?"

Cautiously, Nikki turned her head, her eyes squinting to accommodate for the old glasses her brother, Dylan, had brought up, handed to her, and left, all without saying a word.

The stupid things were three years old easy, and she couldn't see too clearly. Fortunately, she was getting new ones within a week, courtesy of Dion and his insurance.

Wade stood in the doorway, a sympathetic smile on his face.

"A little better," she said, straightening in her chair, laying her book on the side table "I think they are going to let me go home today, after all."

They had ended up keeping her two days, unsure if her blurred vision was the result of the crash, or something worse. All the tests were normal, so *finally*, they were letting her leave.

Two days in the hospital...because of a damned bike wreck.

"Mind if I sit down?"

"Go ahead," she offered, shrugging. Within her chest, her heart was dancing a nervous jig. "Thanks for your help the other day. I doubt I was in any shape to say so then, but I appreciated it."

"Not a problem," he said, flashing an easy smile. "Know what's going to happen with those guys who ran you off the road? Is your dad pressing charges?"

"Their insurance has already offered to settle. I get a new bike, new glasses, and my hospital stay is covered," she said dryly.

"That's it?" he asked, his voice disbelieving.

"Dad is pretty easy to please," she said blandly. "I'd rather the jackass go to jail for a few days, but nobody asked me."

He opened his mouth to speak, but shut it without saying anything.

He stayed a few minutes, surprised her with a single rose in a vase from the gift shop, then he left.

*****

"I see you got some new glasses."

Startled, Nicole looked up from her book. "Hi," she said, her heart pounding in her throat.

"Some colorful bumps and bruises you got there," he noted, squatting in front of her. His hair was damp, sweaty, pulled back in a loose ponytail. The neck of his tank top was dark with sweat.

She eyed the purplish blue bruise on her right shoulder with dislike before glancing at the various bruises and scratches that marred her right leg. The worst was a large blackish bruise on the back part of her right hip. Nearly a week, and it hurt so bad at night she had a hard time sleeping without the pain pills.

"Yeah. I figure these are my battle scars," she said, one corner of her mouth quirking up in a grin. She'd attempted the day before to return to work, bumming a ride from a neighbor - less than two hours later, she was driven back home by her boss, who scolded her for even trying.

He chuckled, moving to sit on the step next to her. His face sobered and he ducked his head. "A friend of mine lives across the street… and well, he says the guy who almost hit you lives around here."

"I know," she said quietly. "He also happens to be

a friend of my brother's. He's not very happy about being caught. His insurance canceled his coverage and his license was suspended. He's had more than his share of 'minor' violations. Not too mention he's in big trouble with his parole officer. He's running his mouth off a lot."

"What if it's more than talk?" Wade asked, turning to face her. "This uh, well, this isn't exactly the nicest part of town..."

Oh, man, wasn't this cute...he was blushing. Gone and embarrassed himself, had he? But doggedly he continued, "And I know there's some pretty rough kids around here."

She smiled slightly, tucking her book under her hip and leaning forward carefully, trying not to aggravate her bruised body. "I know. I would probably be considered one of those rough kids," she said, grinning slightly at the disbelieving look in his eyes. "I've lived here for eight years, you know."

"You don't look like you belong here," he replied.

With a sad smile, she said, "That's weird...because this is the only place I've ever been."

But I'll be damned if I stay...

She wanted to be normal, to walk to the library instead of working her ass off for money under the table. Wanted to go to football games and know if she walked home at night, she wouldn't have to worry about trouble.

Trouble was a permanent resident here. She'd learned how to fight at an early age, learned how to avoid the cops if she had to leave home late at night. Knew how to pacify those same cops who showed up at the door when her father went a little wild after a few too many drinks.

No, she wasn't the shy naive little girl she suspected he saw in his mind. She doubted she had ever been naive.

He didn't respond to that directly, but she could see the disbelief lingering in his eyes. "About that kid…"

"I'm not worried. Dion isn't much more than talk. That's all he ever really has been. Besides, he can't do anything more than talk unless he wants to end up in back in juvie. He's on probation and his P.O. is pretty strict"

"That's no guarantee."

Nikki grinned now and said, "There are no guarantees, especially not in this part of town."

Her eyes skimmed over familiar sights, broken down cars, fans whirring in open windows, women walking around in their nightgowns, hair still in rollers, overweight men with their beer bellies hanging over their jeans. Cigarette butts, broken bottles, and God only knew what else littered the sidewalk.

The sounds were just as pleasant, squalling children, parents who screamed and shouted at the least offense, loud music blaring from cars, stereos and TVs. Under the brutal summer sun, the trash dumpsters were baking, leaving the air clouded with the underlying stink of garbage.

I'm getting out of here, she thought to herself. For easily the thousandth time.

*****

Neither of them would have admitted, or even thought, that what was happening between them was a romance. Both were two lonely souls who had befriended each other. While Nikki might have dreamed for more, friends were too far and few between, therefore, more precious than anything else.

It started with Wade just dropping by for a few minutes when he visited his friend Mike across the street. Then he started asking her if she wanted to go with them out to get a bite to eat. A friend was having a barbecue and she was welcome to come. Before much time had passed, rarely more than day went by without them seeing each other, even if just for a few minutes.

For the first time in her life, she had somebody she could talk to, about anything. The hot humid days of summer passed quickly, her morning spent working, and her afternoons spent studying. She spent evenings with Wade and his friends, either at Wade's house or at other friends, usually the EMT Lori who had taken Nikki to the hospital. She was much younger than a lot of them, but they seemed to kind of adopt her, especially after learning of her plans to go to nursing school in less than a year.

Before she knew it, those lazy days of barbecuing in Wade's backyard or swimming in Lori's pool were over. And it was time for school. Her senior year. She had crammed enough during the past three years that she would graduate midterm this year. She had started high school early, when she was only twelve, having skipped a grade in elementary school.

Come next fall, she would be starting college at U of L on a full scholarship, and she'd get her Bachelor's Degree in nursing

For the first time, she had somebody there to encourage her, to help with the study sessions and quiz her on Spanish. Granted, Wade's accent was worse than hers, but he tried. Besides helping her study, he helped her keep her unruly brothers under control as best as could be managed.

Nikki had no idea why was he always there, but he was. And she was afraid if she asked, he'd get offended and not come around so much.

Early one morning she locked the door behind her, resolving herself to one more hellish bus ride. Dion was in the front seat of the low riding Monte Carlo, riding shotgun with one of his friends, Dylan slouching in the backseat as they pulled away.

There was a cruel glint in Dion's eyes as he looked at her, but Dylan's presence in the back kept him quiet. Dion had learned how little Dylan cared to hear his sister getting bullshit—so he saved it until he was away from Dylan before mouthing off.

She supposed she could fill her twin brother in on it, but what was the point? Dylan would still hang around with that bastard, after he beat the shit out of him again. All that would come of it was possibly Dylan getting in trouble with the cops again.

So she just ignored the bastard.

As she headed down the steps, a low hum caught her ears and Nikki looked up as a familiar Thunderbird came around the corner.

Wade didn't even glance at the souped up

lowrider Monte Carlo that drove past him as he parked. Climbing from the car, he smiled at her, but it didn't really show in his exhausted eyes.

Even after three weeks of working the graveyard shift, it looked like he still hadn't adjusted.

A grin tugged at the corner of his mouth as he met her on the sidewalk. "You two want a ride?"

Shawn had already headed for the car, but Nikki hesitated. "Wade, you just got done working a twelve hour shift." From the looks of his uniform, it had been a rough one. Wrinkled, bloodied. Eyes were shadowed and grim. She wondered what had put that look there. Then she remembered what part of town he worked and decided she didn't want to know. He had been transferred to one of the few areas that made Portland look like a nice middle class suburban neighborhood. "You live on the other side of the bridge."

"Yeah, but I work less than twenty minutes away from here. If I go home, I'll just sit around. I have to be too tired to see before I can sleep."

Nikki slid into the seat, eyes closing with bliss. Better than riding that damn bus any day. Better than riding in a Ferrari, in her opinion. The car smelled of him, of soap, of the slight musk scent that came from only him.

She had drifted back to sleep before she even knew it, worn out from studying for a calculus test.

They were officially dating by Christmas.

And Nikki was head over heels in love.

Now…

Nikki's eyes flew open, and she lay alone in her huge king size bed, facing the floor-to-ceiling windows. And that had been it. At one time, Wade Lightfoot had meant everything to her, more than her books, her writing–her dreams to leave her poor childhood behind her. He had been her entire life.

And then he had gotten another woman pregnant.

New Albany, Indiana

The hot summer sun shone brightly down on the little house. A 'For Sale' was in the yard, tópped by a bright red sign announcing to the world that this house was sold. Toys dotted the closely cropped lawn, and a crop of wildflowers bloomed under each window. Freshly painted shutters gleamed under the noonday sun.

He had taken care of the house, even though it hadn't ever become the home he had wished for.

Shoving the door open with a booted foot, Wade Lightfoot walked out of the house, three boxes precariously stacked in his arms.

A gleefully laughing child darted in front of him, a yapping puppy at her heels. Wade stumbled and the box on top, one covered with dust, fell to the ground, falling open as it hit the concrete.

A familiar picture fell out–one he hadn't looked at in years. But he hadn't ever forgotten it, either.

Automatically, he diverted his eyes and started to reach for it without looking, intending to pack it away with the rest of his memories. But then his hand slowed, stopped, and he turned his eyes back to the smiling faces looking up at him.

Damn, we looked so innocent back then…

It was Nikki and him at her senior prom. He had worn a monkey suit, had even gotten his hair cut. Her shy grin, tousled hair at odds with the flirty black dress she had worn. He smiled, remembering how she had dieted for two months, exercising like some aerobics instructor from hell, losing fifteen pounds, to fit into that dress.

He looked up to check on Abby as she shrieked. Her uncle Joe had caught her up in a bear hug. Slowly, knowing he shouldn't, he righted the box. Photographs, notes, souvenirs from some local amusement parks jumbled inside as he reached in, pulled out a picture at random.

Their first real date. Lori's Christmas party.

The day he realized just how *right* it felt to be with Nikki. It was more than friendship, and that was a little scary. This girl was from the wrong side of town, but worse, she was only fifteen and had more problems than he had ever imagined anybody having.

She was five years younger but, in her mind, she was far older than he would ever be, after growing up around some of the ugliest things a girl could see. He saw pieces of the ugly side of life, drive by shootings, victims of gang violence, domestic abuse. But he only saw it in his work. It touched his life, but it hadn't shaped him.

She had lived in that. Had lost friends to sick random violence. Lived in a home where some sort of domestic abuse was the norm. At the age of thirteen, she had come home from school to find her mother lying dead on the living room sofa, dead from an overdose of sedatives a doctor from a local clinic had prescribed.

She had that grim look around her eyes that was familiar in such a rough part of town. The look that came from seeing too much of the dirty side of life, and not enough of the good side. But she hadn't had any of the callousness, the desperation, or the wildness.

He stared at the picture, at Nikki in her red dress, her eyes laughing, as she stared at the camera. If he closed his eyes, he could still remember the smell of her flesh, how she felt in his arms…

Then…

He found her out in the backyard, head tipped back, arms wrapped around her body against the cold night air. He wrapped his owns arms around her and told her, "If you'd go inside, you wouldn't be cold."

"No. I'd be hot. Too many people in there," she said, slowly relaxing against him. "Besides, it's pretty out here. Are you spending tomorrow with your parents?"

"Yeah," he said, distantly. The friendly hug he had offered didn't feel as friendly as it used to. Good, maybe too good. Tension spread through him until he was standing stiff as a board.

"—okay?"

"Huh?" He looked down, realizing that she had been talking to him.

"I asked if you were okay," she repeated.

He didn't answer then, either. Instead, he studied her upturned face as if he had never seen it. Before Wade had even thought about it, he dipped his head, pressed his mouth to hers. He had to know if she tasted as good as she felt. She couldn't. No woman could. But she did. He traced her full lower lip with his tongue, using his hand to arch her neck, angle her face to his. Then he deepened the kiss. Her breath caught, drawing him deeper as he shifted her body, turning her to face him fully. Burying one hand in her hair, he used the other to mold her against him.

When he raised his head, he was breathing hard. She tasted every bit as good as she felt. This fifteen-year-old girl had his heart pumping a mile a minute. And he wondered if he hadn't been expecting this. Why else would he have spent so much time around a girl still in high school who was neck deep in more problems than he had ever encountered in his somewhat charmed life?

She stared up at him, eyes hazy and somewhat bewildered. He started to let her go, to move away. Then her tongue darted out, tracing the curve of her lower lip, eyes fluttering closed as though to hold on to the kiss a moment longer.

With a groan, he lowered his head again, shoving the matter of her age out of his mind.

Wade knew that if he was completely honest, he had fallen for her practically from the first. It had probably started when he had seen her huddled in an uncomfortable vinyl chair in the darkened hospital room, her eyes closed, her face sad.

But he kept it buried. For two years, he squashed

it down inside him, until her seventeenth birthday, then he lost control of the needs she awoke within him.

Wade hadn't meant for anything to happen even then, but he had downed one beer too many and Nikki had ended up driving him home from the restaurant.

She had all but carried a happily grinning drunk into the living room, laughing as he all but poured onto the couch. He had tumbled her down on top of him, easily, for she was more than eager.

Hot kisses, fast hands, and low whispers replaced the laughter and silliness. It had always been Wade who stopped things before and he was drunk enough, needy enough to ignore the quiet voice of conscious.

Nikki's plan to call Lori for a ride fell to pieces and she woke up in his bed the next morning.

And after that night, there was no going back, not for him.

Now…

"Daddy?"

He started, looking up into dark eyes so like his own. Abby. "Yeah, darling?" he asked, amazed his voice could sound so calm after spending heaven only knew how much time lost in memories.

"I'm hungry." She flashed him an engaging grin and held up her stuffed cocker spaniel puppy and added, "Skip's hungry, too." So was Tigger, the real life cocker spaniel that sat at Abby's heels, staring up at him with soulful brown eyes.

"So is Joe," his older brother said, mounting the steps.

He nodded, ran his hand over the picture, feeling a familiar ache in his chest. And then, he tucked the picture back in the box. She was no longer a part of his life.

That was that.

Chapter Three

Morning found Nikki at a tiny hillside cemetery, the old-fashioned kind that had a little white chapel in front of it. A white picket fence surrounded the cemetery and a tiny stream ran through it.

It was one of the loveliest sites she had ever seen. Peaceful and quiet. That was why she had chosen this site.

Her entire world lay six feet below in a tiny coffin, clad in his Easter Sunday suit, his precious Mouse tucked under his arm.

JASON CHRISTIAN KLINE
BORN MAY 11, 1995 DIED SEPTEMBER 2, 1996
Beloved Son
'I Am With You Always, Until The End of Time.'

Closing her eyes, Nikki's mind drifted back to that time of brief consciousness in the ER when she had awakened after the accident.

"Jase..."

She didn't know where that weak whisper had come from. Licking her lips, she tried to call out louder so he would hear her better. When he was playing, it damn near took an earthquake to get his attention. "Jason..." the second pathetic whisper was only minutely louder than the first.

She tried to open her eyes, but couldn't. Reaching up, she encountered gauze. Searching fingers roamed her face. The gauze bandages covered the top half of her head. What in the hell...

"Ms. Kline? Are you awake?"

She turned her head in the direction of the voice. "Where am I? What's happened?"

"I'm Dr. Lawrence, Ms. Kline. You're in Wayne County Hospital. Do you know where that is?"

"Yes. It's in Monticello. What am I doing here, Doctor?" she asked, telling herself not to worry. Jason was fine. He had to be. She reached up to shove the bandages off her head and another voice intruded.

"You need to leave those bandages be, now," the soft cool female voice said. "You had some trauma to your face and we have to careful."

"Who are you?"

"Leanne Winslow. I'm a nurse. How are you feeling?"

"I hurt. Will you please tell me what happened?" she asked, reaching out, encountering a soft gentle hand. Another hand rested comfortingly on her shoulder.

Above her head, she didn't see the glances exchanged between nurse and doctor or how the doctor compressed his lips and nodded.

"Honey, you were in a car accident. Remember?" Leanne said. The bed dipped beneath added weight and the soft voice was closer.

"The storm…"

"A tornado passed through two neighboring counties. It was a pretty bad storm. Then a drunk driver hit your truck. Do you remember any of it?"

The prodding made her try to recall what the nurse just told her. The sluggish black curtain that obscured her mind wouldn't let her think too clearly. "Not much. My son?"

The hand on hers tightened. "I am so sorry," the nurse said, her voice sounding odd. "Ms. Kline, your son is gone…"

She heard those last words and the black curtain suddenly cleared and she remembered. Jason's tiny little body gone cold, his eyes sightless. Pain roared up through her, biting, slashing, and clawing until she wanted to scream with it.

She couldn't, though. Her throat was tight. Whimpering noises came to her from far off as she drew her knees into her chest, shrugging off restraining hands.

He couldn't be gone. He was all she had left…

Again, darkness clouded her mind and she remembered nothing else.

In a cool hospital room that hummed with machinery, the young woman lay on a hospital bed. She had been comatose for a week and five days, ever since awakening in the ER to hear her son was dead. During that time, she hadn't so much as flickered an eyelid. The doctors were unsure whether or not she would snap out of it. They had found no physical reason for the coma, certain it had been caused by the trauma of losing her son.

They couldn't say whether she would wake. It could happen any minute. It could happen never.

The room was dark and quiet, save for the steady beep of machinery in the corner

She gained awareness slowly. First, of the sheets beneath and above her, then of the faint itchy feel of her skin. She shifted her hips and noticed another oddity, a tube strapped to her thigh. A catheter.

She swallowed, her mouth dry, her throat tight. Her nose, the area behind it felt strange. Slowly, she lifted a hand and with tentative fingers, she probed her nose. Another tube. They had put a feeding tube down her nose, inserted through her left nostril.

When her eyes opened, she squinted automatically,

prepared to not be able to see clearly. Instead, she saw a gauzy white light. Bandages. Her searching fingers found the end of the bandage, peeled back the tape and unwound it. Clarity. She could see everything clearly, from the clock on the wall, to the drab painting, to the room number on her open door. Outside her door, one nurse was bent diligently over paperwork while two others stood at the desk, speaking quietly.

Nikki plucked the little rubber probes from her body, dropping each one over the rail before seeking out another. As the machine attached to those little probes began to beep steadily, she plucked the third one from her breast.

The nurses were rushing in as she reached up for the tape that secured the feeding tube. Before they could reach her, she had already pulled it out and dropped it on the sheet next to her. She barely blinked at the sharp pain it caused

A familiar voice stayed her hand as she was reaching beneath the sheets. "Easy, Ms. Kline. That won't be quite so easy to remove," one of the nurses said. This one was clad in baggy blue scrubs. A nametag at her breast read Leanne Winslow.

Nikki recognized that name.

Her hand fell from her thigh, catheter forgotten as she leaned back. Reaching out, her hand was caught in a soft strong grip. She squeezed it, closed her eyes, and whispered, "My son's dead, isn't he?"

"I'm afraid so, Ms. Kline." Her soft pretty blue eyes were filled with distress and she sat on the bed next to Nikki for the second time.

Biting her lip, she turned her head away. "What about Shawn? My brother?" Her voice was calm, abnormally so.

"He's fine. Just a concussion and some bruises. He went home the next day," another nurse said softly, glad she

hadn't been the one to break the news.

"But Jason didn't make it," she whispered quietly. "He's gone."

This time, Nikki turned her face into the offered shoulder and started to cry silently.

Nikki returned to the present at the sound of gravel crunching several hundred feet away.

Just like that, he had been gone. One minute he had been playing happily with his plastic keys and Mouse, and now he was buried under six feet of cold earth, all alone.

Nikki had spent nearly two weeks in a coma. The very day she awoke, she had walked out of the hospital, against medical advice. Her eyesight was suddenly perfectly normal, the intense pressure that had caused her nearsightedness relieved when glass had cut her retinas.

She had left the hospital in better shape than she had entered it.

Jason had left it in a body bag.

Thankfully, Nikki didn't remember him being taken away. The time after the wreck was a blissful blank.

Now, she sat quietly in the cemetery by her son's grave, reflecting on the things they would never do. Not exactly therapeutic thoughts, but Nikki wasn't in the mood for therapy today. Her depression weighed down on her shoulders and she knew realistically, that this wasn't normal; that she needed to be talking to somebody about this.

But even after three years, she wasn't ready to let go of her grief. It seemed it was all she had left of him, and once she stopped grieving, he'd truly be gone from her.

A gentle breeze drifted past, ruffling her hair and bringing with it the scent of wildflowers. The scent of honeysuckle teased her senses and she remembered taking Jason for a walk on the hillside very close to where he rested.

It had been only two months before the accident. They had had a picnic and he'd toddled after butterflies and returned with a fistful of honeysuckle, which he had shared with her before trying to eat it.

They had waded in the stream, the very same stream that ran through the cemetery. Jason had laughed in delight as tiny fish no bigger than her little finger had darted around their feet.

"You're going to be old before your time if you keep this up, sis," a voice said softly, jerking her out of her reverie.

She turned her head and squinted up at Shawn. "G'morning," was all she said, not responding to his words.

"I saw your truck on my way to work," he said, kneeling beside her. His left eyebrow was neatly bisected by a thin scar. That, and the scars he bore inside, were the only reminders of the accident.

There were scars inside, though. She sensed it, wished she could help him…but she couldn't even help herself.

Jason had been like a little brother to Shawn, she knew. He'd adored the baby from the first and talked about how he'd teach him to wrestle, to go fish…all the cool boy stuff.

"Y'know, you're going to be late for work," she told him, turning back to study the headstone.

Shawn shrugged. "I doubt they'll mind." And even if they did, he didn't care. How could work be that important when he looked at her and all but saw the dark cloud she had wrapped around herself? He settled on the grass next to her, uncertain of what to say to her. When he had been little, he had always run to her when he had been hurt. Nikki had always made the pain go away. And even when he had been nothing more than a street punk, causing trouble and raising hell, when he was in trouble, it had been Nikki Shawn had gone to. She had always fixed it, in some way.

It didn't seem fair that after so many years of patching him up and kissing away his tears that he had not be able to take away any of her pain.

"Jason is probably the sweetest angel in heaven, Sis," he said, looking at his feet as he spoke. He could feel himself turning red to the roots of his hair and he had no idea where those words had come from.

"I bet he is," came her soft whisper.

And looking over, he saw the beginning of a smile on her face.

The words, wherever they had come from, had been the right ones.

*****

Before Nikki got out of her truck, she donned a dark pair of sunglasses and forced her unruly hair into a stubby ponytail. She hadn't really thought she would be recognized when she had decided to use her own name on her books. She really hadn't thought that far ahead. She had only wanted them to sell.

When they had sold, it was right after she had just seen Wade for the last time and her grief had kept her somewhat distant from the kind suggestions and advice her newly gained editor had offered.

And if she lived in a larger town, she'd have more anonymity than she had in Monticello. But in the past few years, it had come to where she couldn't go much anywhere without somebody hailing her down to talk about books

...my little girl wrote this...isn't that something...

I got a book...can you help me...

And lately, total strangers who were just in town to fish were recognizing her. Nikki wasn't ever going to let another picture be taken of her, and her website master had taken down the one they'd conned her into putting up. Now if she could just get it off the back of the books...

For a while, she hadn't minded the attention, but as time passed, the more she craved solitude. People and questions were coming to grate on her nerves something bad. So she avoided the attention when she could by doing her shopping in the nearest half way large town simply for the anonymity it gave her.

Today, though, she hadn't the energy to drive the extra forty minutes, so she simply hoped for the best as she headed into Monticello's lone supermarket. Halfway across the parking lot, she wished she had made the effort when the local Romeo accosted her.

David Ellis, son of the mayor, fancied himself a

reporter. He mailed off resumes by the dozen on a weekly basis, hoping to get out of the 'one horse hick town' but until his big break came, he lowered himself to write for the local weekly paper, just to keep his skills up to par.

He stood just at six feet, not overly tall, but the way he hovered over her made Nikki feel claustrophobic. He had a decent enough body, Nikki would admit, if she was held at gunpoint. He kept it that way by working out religiously in the personal gym he had set up in his basement. All paid for by his doting papa. Thick carefully styled blond hair glinted under the sun. Even though the day was windy, not a strand of hair moved thanks to a healthy application of mousse and gel.

His smile, which he practiced regularly at his mirror at home, could be sly, kind, sympathetic or cold. The one thing it couldn't be was real. His teeth, straight as a ruler, were blindingly white, and kept that way by regular trips to the cosmetic dentist in Louisville.

He fancied silk ties and shirts, linen suits in the summer, wool suits in the winter. He wore polished loafers for three months, and then tossed them out. He worked out in designer sportswear and used only products bought at a salon for men in Lexington.

If other people thought half as much of David Ellis as David Ellis did, he would already have secured a lifelong spot on prime time TV.

All in all, he was as fake as a cubic zirconia masquerading as a diamond. He had the depth of a rain puddle and as much substance as cotton candy.

And just simply by breathing the same air she did he irritated the hell out of Nikki. His favorite thing to do, it seemed, was follow Nikki and pester her like mad.

Her regular refusals to his dinner invitations, which she assumed would no doubt be followed by bedroom sessions, had earned his enmity. So he had tried to repay her by spreading nasty little rumors, only to have his aquiline nose broken by a coldly furious Dylan Kline. Then one Shawn Kline had threatened him within an inch of his life.

So for about six months, she had peace. But lately, he seemed to have regained his courage and was once more dogging her every step.

"I was thinking of trying a new Thai restaurant in Louisville," he said. "It's a bit of a long drive, but we could get hotel rooms and maybe see a play."

She shrugged off his hand, cold and dry, and refused.

"Now, I know that you must be missing some culture in your life," David said, dogging her footsteps. "Living in this one horse town is hard on people like us."

"Your idea of culture, Ellis, is using the Holiday Inn in Somerset instead of that pile of bricks on the highway that some people call a motel," she said coolly, moving away a second time from his snake like hand. "Don't consider us the same kind of 'people,' Ellis. I moved here remember? I stay here because I like it. You were born here and stay here simply because you can't hack it anywhere else."

Ignoring the glint in his eyes, she slung her

cavernous bag over her shoulder and snagged a cart from the corral. Tipping her glasses down her nose, Nikki aimed a chilly stare at him. "I'm not interested, not now, not tomorrow, not in this lifetime," she informed him, probably for the fiftieth time. "Now, if you will excuse me. My brothers are expecting me at my dad's soon. We're having a cook out...of course, you can come to that if you..."

And Nikki made good her escape, smiling at the way he had paled.

Some twenty minutes later, she was still smiling. Insulting that jackass just seemed to do it for her. She tossed frozen orange juice concentrate into her basket before heading to the dairy aisle, humming absently under her breath. She added a carton of yogurt and some cream cheese to her cart then promptly ran into somebody else's cart. "Damn it," she muttered, but her voice was lost under the sound of baskets crashing together and groceries tumbling to the floor.

A sheepish smile crossed her face and she said, "Sorry about that." She would hit somebody whose cart was beyond full. Kneeling, she picked up a carton of cookies and Donald Duck orange juice. She placed them in the basket before stepping away.

The guy had knelt in front of a dark child of four or five, his face hidden as he scooped up items from the floor. "No problem," he said, his voice belying his words, sounding slightly irritated.

Nikki was about to make a quick get away, but then he stood up. And revealed his face.

She saw a familiar face, one that haunted her dreams on a regular basis. His hair was shorter, cut at his nape, and his face had thinned out just a bit, the dimples at the corners of his mouth now slashes in his lean cheeks. But the eyes were the same, deep bottomless pools of brown velvet

"Wade," she whispered, her eyes stricken, then landed on the child's face. A little girl, a little mirror of her father.

And of Nikki's son. The girl wore a red T-shirt, decorated on the front with a sketch of a bright-eyed puppy. A baseball cap in that same candy apple red sat on top of thick black hair that fell razor straight to her tiny shoulders. She held a stuffed cocker spaniel, a mirror image of the way Jason had carried his precious Mouse.

A knife slowly imbedded itself in Nikki's heart, started to twist.

For a moment, Wade's face was blank and then his eyes narrowed. She was unable to move as he slowly reached up, tugged her sunglasses off. "Nikki," he breathed, his eyes lighting, as though from within. He took a step closer and brushed her cheek with the back of his hand.

That gentle touch shattered her like glass. Flinching, she grabbed her purse and took off running down the aisle. She had her keys before she was even out the door. Swallowing a sob, she dodged around an elderly couple who glared at her with censure in their eyes.

As she dove into the dubious safety of her truck, Wade came striding out the main doors of the grocery store. "Nikki!" he shouted, his little girl perched on his hip.

She spared him only one glance as she started the engine and threw it into gear. The little girl was staring up at her father in confusion, her dark hair streaming around her face

The sight of it sent tiny daggers plunging into her heart.

Dear God, she thought.

And unable to go home where she'd just sit and brood and cry, she ended up making the forty minute drive to town, tears streaming down her face the entire time

*****

What in the hell…

Wade stood there, dumbstruck, as Nikki peeled out of the parking lot in a Ford Explorer, leaving a bit of rubber on the pavement as she went.

His mind was a total blank. He didn't know what to think. Nikki was here.

She had run from him.

The look in her eyes had reminded him of the way a doe trapped in the headlights of an oncoming car. Scared to death, knowing the end was near, unable to do anything about it.

"Daddy, who was that?"

Blankly, he turned his head to look at his daughter. Abby was staring up at him, her small dear face puckered with confusion. And his silence didn't help. "Daddy, was she a friend of yours? Do you know her?"

"Yeah, sweetie. I know her," he finally said,

discovering talking not exactly easy, considering how his vocal cords seem to have frozen.

"Why did she run away?"

"I guess maybe she had somewhere to go," was all he said, casting one last glance out at the highway, eyes following the path the black truck had taken.

So what was he supposed to do now?

*****

Later that night, Nikki stared dully into the freezer, eyes unseeing as she put away half-melted ice cream and nearly warm chicken breasts. She continued to stand there, staring woodenly, until the cold air on her already chilled flesh snapped her out of her daze.

Finally, she realized she had been putting canned goods and dishwasher detergent in the freezer as well.

After removing what didn't belong, she shut the freezer and dropped exhausted to the floor. "What's he doing here anyway? Whatever happened to Texas?" she asked the empty kitchen. "He was supposed to have moved to Texas."

Folding her arms around her middle to ward off a very real pain brought on by her misery, she leaned forward as a sob built in her throat.

Why now? I'm just starting to stand on my own two feet again.

Remembering the beautiful little girl drove a dagger into her already bleeding heart. A healthy beautiful, alive little girl. The pain was more than she could bear.

Then…

"Nikki?"

She looked up from her keyboard, eyes bloodshot and weary.

Shawn was slumped against the doorframe, hands shoved deep in his pockets. "Your boyfriend's at the door. Want me to tell him you ain't here?"

Wryly, she thought, I must look worse than I thought. Shawn was almost acting protective. Then she turned her mind to the matter at hand. She had to see him sooner or later. "He can come on up, Shawn. But, thanks."

He only shrugged and walked away. She swiveled in her chair to face her mirror. Yep. She looked like hell. Bloodshot eyes, face pale and strained, hair messily shoved into a ponytail. Her ripped sleeveless sweatshirt had certainly seen better days, and her cut off shorts weren't much better. Not only that, they bagged slightly at the waist, evidence of her lack of appetite in the past week.

She turned back to her keyboard as footsteps echoed on the steps, tapping away at the keys, putting half-formed ideas into words. She worked a few minutes more, even after Wade slowly entered the room.

Still too still too angry to make the first move, she continued to work.

Finally finished, Nikki skimmed the rough draft and then she saved the file on the slow word processor. What she wouldn't give for a computer…

She spun around in her seat and found Wade staring out the window, his posture slumped, head bent. Finally, he voice sounding rusty, he asked, "Did you make it home okay?"

He was, of course, referring to the night a week earlier when he driven away from the store in a fury unlike anything she had ever seen in him. Cocking her head, she coolly said, "It looks that way."

He sighed, looking even more miserable, if possible, and flung himself on her unmade bed, his arm over his eyes, hand clenched so tightly, his knuckles were bloodless. He looked utterly dejected, Nikki thought with mild amusement.

If she didn't know better, she would think he was feeling guilty for picking a fight over nothing. And he damn well ought to. However, Wade never felt guilty about anything. Feeling guilty meant you had done something wrong, made some sort of mistake. Things like that were below him.

She couldn't gloat for too long, though. He looked too awful. "I caught a ride home with Connie," she said, diplomatically declining to tell him that Jared McNeil had offered her a ride home. Dinner, a movie. And more.

Wade's lower lip was still puffy.

Nikki still couldn't believe she had hit him. But, damn it, the way he had acted…

Wade's hoarse voice broke the silence when he said, quietly, "I'm sorry. I had no right to do that, no right to jump all over you. I don't know what in the hell came over me."

"Don't you?" she asked, her voice remote.

With a sigh, he lowered his arm and sat up in bed, swinging around to sit on the edge of it. Looking her right in the eye for the first time since entering the room, the corner of his mouth quirked in a grimace. His skin was unnaturally pale, dark blue circles under his eyes. "I was jealous," he said simply "And worried that maybe you might be curious as to what it felt like to actually date. You and I've been together so long, you didn't have a chance to play the field the way your friends did. You would have every right to wonder."

"I never have wondered," Nikki said quietly. "The girls my age think I'm damn lucky to have found myself somebody. The guys my age aren't worth the trouble. But that's beside the point. You came in with guns blazing and attacked me simply for talking to a guy I work with."

"He'd like to do more. I know what a guy looks like when he's interested. And he's definitely interested."

Sighing, he scrubbed his eyes with the heels of his hands. "But that's not the point either. You weren't encouraging him and that's all the matters. I should have had more faith in you." Then he stood up abruptly.

Startled, Nikki was slack when he pulled her out of the chair and into his arms. Wade then yanked the rubber band from her hair and buried his face in it, breathing deeply. Silently, she locked her arms around his waist and stood there, feeling vaguely as though something was wrong. Something else was going on, but what it was, Nikki didn't know. Her internal radar was sending out signals.

He began rocking back and forth, and instinctively, she tightened her arms. Turning her head, she pressed a kiss to the side of his neck, cuddling against him, trying to ease some of the tension that was rolling of him in waves.

She gasped out a breath as Wade swept her up in his arms and went to the bed, cradling her in his lap.

Her internal radar was screaming now. They'd fought before and he hadn't acted like he was afraid she would slip away.

"Wade, what's going on?" she asked, cupping his face in her hand and forcing him to look here. Nikki searched his eyes for some clue but all she saw was torment and guilt. She was almost afraid to ask, but knew she had to. "Is there something that I need to know about?"

He closed his eyes and Nikki felt her stomach drop. She waited for him to tell her, but all he did was bring her hand to his lips and kiss it. "I just don't want to lose you," he said, raising his head and staring at her intently

"I'm not the one who left," she reminded him softly. Then she shrugged. "It was a fight. It's not the first, and it won't be the last. I…I shouldn't have hit you"

"You've got a mean right hook, Nikki," he said, a ghost of a smile on his face. "But I deserved it. I'm sorry. The entire thing happened because I'm an ass."

With a forced a smile, she replied, "Yes, you are an ass." Then she forced aside her misgivings. Everything was okay. "It's all right, Wade. It's over."

"It's not all right," he insisted, cupping her face in callused gentle hands. "It's not, baby. I'm sorry for everything I've done that hurt you. I'm sorry for things I said and did and thought that weren't fair to you."

She only tucked her face against his shoulder, looking away from those intent eyes. Meeting them only made her vague feelings of wrongness return.

Nikki had to bite her lip to keep from asking, "What things?"

*****

A month had passed since that day. Buried in her writing and studying, Nikki was also preparing for classes to begin in just a few weeks. On top of that, she was taking an additional college course on correspondence. She was going to be busy, but she had to get it all finished.

September was close and she had to get things squared away by then. She'd be starting her third year of nursing school at U of L when they returned from their honeymoon.

Nikki looked up from the screen, eyes tired and unfocused. Wade lay sleeping in an exhausted sprawl on the narrow couch. He didn't sleep here much, but when he did, it was always on the couch. In fact, he almost seemed to avoid the queen size bed they would share in a few weeks. He was only here tonight because she had decided to go ahead and move her word processor over and wanted to get some work done.

Nikki had thought he liked the little ranch house as much as she did, but maybe she was wrong. He ended up at her apartment every morning after work, and slept there on her narrow twin bed until she got home from work.

To top it off, his sleep was fitful. Often he'd wake the minute she got home and tumble her down onto the bed within, holding her tightly against his side as he drifted back into uneasy slumber. Wade insisted nothing was wrong, just that he was working too hard, busting his ass to save more money for the honeymoon.

Her mind drifted around in circles, trying to pinpoint if she had said or done something, to make him act this way. There had been that fight, two months ago but it wasn't the worst they had ever had.

Since then, they hadn't fought about anything. Wade, in fact, went out of his way keeping things quiet between them.

She didn't even realize he had woken until she heard him whisper, "C'mere, Nikki."

She smiled and rose, somewhat stiffly, from her chair. Stiffened muscles protested as Nikki stretched and forced them into action. She bent over from the waist to touch her toes briefly before she went to couch, perching on the edge.

Watching her with burning eyes, Wade waited for her with an outstretched hand. As she settled against him, his arms closed around, pulling her down next to him. With a turn of his body, Wade neatly tucked her under him. "I love you," he rasped, his voice intense. "I always will. If I ever lost you, I don't know what I'd do."

She opened her mouth, determined to find out what was going on with him, but then he settled his mouth over hers, and the question, like all thought, flew out of her head.

Later, wearing only her T-shirt, she mentioned that she had seen Jamie Sayer in the store earlier that day with her father. "She looked like hell," Nikki commented. "Sick or something."

"Stomach virus going around," he said, his voice curt. "It's been a hell of a week because of it. Everybody and their brother think death is just around the corner. Using the ambulance because their belly hurts, instead of going to the doctor."

"Does she still call you?" Nikki asked, her voice mild.

"No," Wade snapped, tossing aside a magazine he had been flipping through. "Look, I really don't want to talk about Jamie Sayer."

Eyes narrowed, she rose. "Oh, well, pardon me. You don't want to go eat. You don't want to see a movie. You don't want to talk to me about anything, much less Jamie. Today is the first time we've had sex in nearly a month. You're always too tired," she cooed, voice sugar sweet with mock sympathy, batting her eyes at him.

"What in the hell do you want, Nikki?" Wade growled, his own eyes narrowing. "I'm working five or six twelve hour shifts a week. Of course I'm tired. I don't feel like wasting money on going to a movie and God forbid you actually cook something for a change."

Her eyes narrowed as she glared at him, anger

streaking through her. *Enough.* Turning on her heel, she stalked out of the room, into the kitchen.

Behind her, she heard him mutter, "Aw, shit. Nikki, wait a minute."

Ignoring him, she stormed into the kitchen, her own temper raging.

Wade caught up with her as she was pulling food from the refrigerator. "Look, Nikki. I'm sorry. We can go eat, do whatever you want." His voice was cautious, conciliatory, as he said, "You know what an ass I am when I'm tired."

Nikki didn't even glance at him as she set about slamming pots and pans about. Fuming, she threw some sausage into a skillet to brown while she started water boiling for pasta. Finally, he retreated to the living room while she dressed in between draining the sausage and adding the sauce.

Within thirty minutes, she held a plate full of steaming pasta. She found him staring morosely out the picture window in the living room, clad in jeans, his unbuttoned shirt and rumpled hair. The despondent look on his face only added to the tragic romantic air about him.

Wade turned to find her standing behind him, hazel eyes glinting. "You didn't have to cook. I know you've been working hard and you've got to be just as tired as I am. We can go do whatever you want," Wade said, testing the waters carefully.

Not careful enough. Even the way he looked at her was enough to make her mad all over again. Like she was a ticking time bomb.

Tick, tick, tick.

Sauntering up to him, she moved the plate to the side and traced a hand up the golden muscled wall of his chest. Gently, she traced a path down his chest and abdomen and back up before hooking a hand around his neck. "What I want?" she whispered in his ear. "What I want is for you to stop acting like an ass. What I want is for whoever took my fiancée's place to get out. And I want my man to come back to me."

And with that, Nikki shoved the plate of hot food at him, not caring when he didn't catch it in time. He bobbled then lost control. His yelp was muffled by the sound of the plate striking wooden floors and breaking. She was out the door before Wade recovered and mounting her bike before he came raging out the door.

"Damn it, Nikki, get back here. You can't ride your bike home. It's going to be dark soon," Wade roared, lunging over the porch rail.

She paused to look at him, her eyes narrowed. "Go to hell. And stay the hell away from me until you start acting like yourself again. I'm tired of you not being *you.*"

Then Nikki was furiously pedaling toward home. It took less than thirty minutes what was normally a forty-five minute ride.

A dozen pale yellow roses appeared at her work the next day, along with a handwritten apology.

If she wasn't still so pissed, she would have cried. He hardly ever sent her flowers.

Three hours later, she left work to find Wade out in the parking lot, leaning against the hood of his car, looking more relaxed than he had in weeks.

"Aren't you supposed to be working tonight?" she asked, irritably, the roses tucked under her arm like they meant less than nothing.

He shrugged and said, "I called and said I was done with twelves. They didn't need me for it any more anyway. Got some new people trained and hired."

"Well, if your attitude isn't going to improve, I really would rather you be at work," Nikki snapped, moving around him.

Catching her arm, he tugged and turned until she was pinned between him and the car. The hood was cool, meaning he had been out here waiting for a while. "I'm sorry. And you're right"

*****

Things were good…for while.

Her wedding dress, something that seemed too beautiful to be real, hung in her closet, minute adjustments made in the waistline. Satin ballet slippers dyed to match resided in a box close by.

Everything was already set. Decorations were at the church. She had already mailed the *Thank You* cards for shower gifts and there wasn't anything left to be done, except the wedding itself.

The wedding was to be small and simple, since they had to pay for everything themselves.

Even the honeymoon was simple, a four-day weekend to Gatlinburg. A real honeymoon would have to wait.

It was a hot and humid Tuesday. The air was so

thick and muggy, even breathing seemed like work. Sometime after noon, the rain started, a steady downpour that didn't seem in any hurry to end. A trip to the mailbox had Nikki borrowing her dad's car, something she rarely did, because she hated driving a stick shift but she hardly noticed it as she drove over Wade's in a daze of excitement. Hands shaky, a smile a mile on wide on her face, she pulled into the driveway, danced up the porch.

The deafening silence when she threw open the door should have warned her.

How could silence sound so ominous?

Now, Nikki stood on one side of the room, staring out at the thunderstorm that had rolled in only minutes earlier. The excitement was gone, forgotten as misery, shock, and anger roiled in her belly. She'd completely forgotten about the letter in her pocket, even though it had seemed to burn a hole the entire drive over.

If asked why she had driven over, Nikki would have admitted she didn't have a clue.

Wade was across the room, on the floor, face buried in his hands, shoulders and hair wet with rain. When Nikki had gotten there, she had found him sitting outside on the deck in back, oblivious to the rain that was pounding down.

"Baby, I'm so sorry," he whispered. "Damn it, I'm sorry."

"Who is she?" Nikki asked numbly, her face gone stiff. She wasn't hurting yet. It hadn't really hit her but she knew the pain was lying in wait. It was like a man who had suddenly had his leg cut off and could feel nothing for the shock of it.

When he didn't answer, she whirled and snapped, "Who in the hell is she?"

Raising his head, Wade stared at her from black eyes. Those eyes, always so warm and full of life, looked cold and lifeless. Before he even said it, she knew.

"Jamie Sayer," he said, his voice almost soundless.

That was when the pain came, ripping through her like a forest fire, consuming everything in its path. Body vibrating and shuddering, pressure building in her throat, she stared at him. Her knees gave out then and she slid to the floor, a mirror of Wade's dejected slump. Drawing her knees up, she held them clutched to her chest as she started to shake.

Picture perfect, beautiful slender Jamie Sayer. Jamie who thought the sun rose and set on Wade. She'd started stalking him ever since she had returned from college three months earlier. Nikki hadn't worried about her after the first few weeks, because of how amused Wade had been by it. Amused and then irritated when it didn't stop and the girl wouldn't take a hint.

"Jamie," she repeated, her voice dull. "Tell me, did you enjoy making love to a woman who thinks of you as some sort of God? Was she a virgin? Of course, she was. She wouldn't have dirtied herself the way I did."

He looked away, his pale skin suffused with a dull red.

A harsh laugh tore from her throat. "Tell me, Wade, Was it better from a woman who's unblemished? Was it everything you'd hoped for?

"Nikki, don't," he whispered, his voice thick with tears. He rose, coming to kneel in front of her, taking her hands in his, holding tight when she tried to pull away.

"Don't what?" she demanded. "Don't ask for details? Considering you just destroyed me with this little bit of information, I think I have right to know some details." Her voice rose with each word until she was shouting.

Wade flinched as she became more graphic, disgusted with himself for doing to this to her.

"Nikki," he said, his voice pleading. "I was drunk, so damn drunk I don't even remember it. I didn't know what in the hell I was doing. Hell, I was probably too drunk to remember my own name."

"You'd obviously forgotten mine," she bit off, pulling away. Her eyes dropped briefly to the region of his fly and she bitterly added, "And you obviously weren't too drunk to get it up, were you?"

Blinded by tears, she stumbled into the living room. "All this for something that happened before I even met you. Are we even now?"

"Nikki, stop it. It's not about that," he insisted.

"It's always about that!" she shouted, whirling to face him. "That's what the fight with Jared was about. You thought I'd been leading him on. That's what the fight with Zach was about at the Derby party at Lori's. You insisted I'd been flirting with him, tossing myself at him, just to see if he would notice. I slept with Dion one time, one damn time, at a time when I so messed up inside I probably should have been institutionalized. One time! That doesn't make me a whore!"

"I've never thought of you like that," he rasped, jerking her against him and covering her mouth with his hand. "Never."

Nikki bit down on his hand and jerked away. "The hell you haven't. I saw the disgust in your eyes when you found out the rumors you had heard weren't rumors. Do you think I'm blind? Or stupid?"

She paused, trying to drag air into her lungs. She had to know. She hated herself for it, but she absolutely had to know. "Tell me something. Is she the first? Or just the most recent?" she asked.

"It only happened that one time, Nik. I swear to God. I wouldn't have hurt you like that," Wade insisted, moving cautiously to stand closer to her.

Looking in his bleak eyes, Nikki cursed herself for being a fool. If she had learned anything from her father, it was that things like this seldom happened 'just once'. But she believed him.

It didn't make the pain any easier to bear.

Edging away from him, Nikki turned, staring out the window, unable to see for the tears of pain and fury that blinded her "I slept with somebody for no reason other than I needed some attention. You did it because you were falling down drunk." Then she laughed. "But apparently not too drunk, or the equipment wouldn't have been functioning. We both acted like a couple of irresponsible fools. So I guess now we're even. And there's nothing left to say"

She bit back against the wave of agony that rolled through her, like a bout of nausea as she grabbed her purse from the table and headed out the door. Wade moved like a bolt of lightening, blocking her. "Nikki, you can't just walk out," he pleaded, reaching for her.

Her shoulders rose and fell in a helpless shrug "What else can I do, Wade? What am I supposed to do? Damn it, I don't even know how to feel."

"Damn it, Nikki," he rasped, pulling her against him, his forehead dropping to rest against hers. "Damn it all to hell."

Pulling away from him, Nikki looked at Wade and flatly said, "I am in hell."

With a vicious jerk, she tore away from him, moving backward until there were several feet between them. "And I can't even figure out what I did to bring this on," she told him.

"Nikki..." Wade reached for her once more, his hand stretching out.

Nikki stared at his hand, entranced, for a long moment. And then, she looked up, met his eyes, mutely shook her head. Turning on her heel, Nikki ran for the back door and dodged out into the rain. She didn't know where she was going, but she couldn't let him touch her. Couldn't let him get to close. She'd fall apart for certain then....

She dodged a mud puddle and headed for the trees, wishing for the first time that this place wasn't so isolated. A nosy neighbor right now would help. Wade caught up with her, snagged her elbow, and she slid, causing them both to end up on the wet grass. As rain fell around them, he stared down at her with anguished eyes. Removing her glasses, Wade covered her face with kisses, hot little nipping ones at her mouth, gentle soothing ones against her streaming eyes.

Don't let him do this to you. It's over. Just get out of here. The tiny voice whispered over and over in her mind while her heart pleaded with her to stay. *It's over. This will be the last time, the very last... Don't you deserve one more time?*

After an internal war, Nikki reached up and locked her arms around his neck. One more time. She had to have just one more time. Hot hands slid under her shirt, stroking rain-cooled skin. She gasped, arching up. A jerk of one of the hard hands popped the buttons on her worn cotton shirt, baring her breasts to him. Through the lace of her scanty bra, he nuzzled her nipple before taking it into his mouth, nipping and licking until she whimpered beneath him, clutching his head close to her.

Nikki's hands raced down his shirt, freeing buttons and streaking over smooth hard, muscled planes as Wade fought to free her from the wet denim of her shorts, shoving his own jeans down just far enough.

Positioning himself between her legs, Wade whispered, "I'm sorry, but I can't wait. God, I need you so bad." Then he arched her hips up and drove into her, burying himself to the hilt.

He moaned, deep in his chest while one hand lifted to knot in her hair while the other caught her knee, pulling it up and opening her body until he could slide even deeper. Her sheath closed tightly around him, wet and hot, muscles convulsing.

"Damnation," he whispered, pausing only long

enough to catch his breath before pulling out and slamming into her again, harder and harder until he was lifting her with each deep thrust.

Overhead, the storm continued, rain pounding down, thunder crashing through the sky. Nearby, lightning flashed. The smell of ozone mingled with the scent of sex and sweat.

Pleasure slammed through her like a runaway train, sending her flying before knocking her flat. Her breath caught and held in her throat and she squirmed against him, seeking more

Wade bit the side of her neck, and Nikki screamed, light exploding behind her eyes before everything dimmed. And he kept on moving. Drained and panting for breath, she lay passively in his grip, until he reared up and grabbed her behind her left knee, hooking his arms under her legs and opening her body wide, leaving her unable to move. She whimpered slightly in protest, then gasped in dazed pleasure as he fell forward again, driving deeper.

"Look at me," he whispered. "Damn it, you look at me."

She turned bleary eyes to his as he slowed his pace, until he was barely rocking against her, each tiny movement rushing through her like fire. Her eyes focused on his and he rewarded her with a twist of his hips that had her gasping for breath, then whimpering with gratitude.

Then Wade resumed his pace, holding himself back until she arched up weakly and screamed a muffled little half scream that echoed down his spine and seemed to explode through him. He stiffened above her, pinioned her hips with his and held her in place as the fire spread from her body into his, joining them.

Seconds later, Wade slowly collapsed against her.

It was over in moments, but left Nikki weak and shaking as though lightning had struck her, instead of just flashing in the sky overhead. Shuddering, she didn't protest when he turned onto his side, tucking her body snugly against his while they waited for their hearts to slow and their breath to return. The rain slowed to a gentle mist, cooling overheated bodies until goosebumps covered their flesh.

Sometime later, Wade roused enough to right his jeans, then he gathered her clothes and tucked them into her arms, before taking her in his and rising, carrying her out of the rain and into the house. He laid her on the bed, heedless of their filthy bodies, spooning up behind her, tucking her against him. His arms locked around her middle as though he never intended to let go.

It was after midnight when she finally freed herself. She hadn't slept. Her mind had chased itself in circles but she knew what she had to do. Wade was a throwback, an old-fashioned man in modern times. His honor would insist that he marry Jamie. Nikki's pride demanded that she leave.

Turning, Nikki paused to look at him, light from the hallway casting half his face into shadow. He looked exhausted. She had noticed the lines of strain forming around his mouth and eyes, but she had attributed them to work. She knew otherwise now.

It had been guilt. And it had probably been guilt

that dulled his appetite to the point of not eating. Weight he hadn't needed to lose had melted off, leaving him far more lean than normal. There was nothing on him any more but muscle and sinew

Gently, she brushed back a silky black lock of hair that had fallen into his eyes. Then, as a sob threatened to burst free, she turned away.

Silently Nikki gathered her filthy clothes, just as she silently laid her diamond engagement ring on the dresser, next to his keys and a mess of coins. Then she slid out of the bedroom. She dressed quickly, donning her ruined shorts, tying her shirt in a knot at her rib cage to keep it closed. She grabbed her purse and keys and was out the door without looking back.

If she looked back, she'd never be able to leave.

*****

Early the next morning, Nikki stood in front of her closet, staring at her fairy tale wedding dress. The rain from the past night hadn't ever stopped—it flowed down in heavy sheets from the leaden sky. Her belly hurt. The smell of the rain drifting through the open windows in the apartment might have chased away the cigarette smoke and the stink of beer, but it brought with it a memory she was already trying to bury.

Last night...the rain, his hands moving across her slick flesh while thunder clapped overhead.

In less than two weeks, she would have worn that dress as she walked down the aisle to marry the only person who had ever meant anything to her.

Dimly, through thin walls, she heard the low

sound of her father's voice as he spoke on the telephone. He had called on some of Nikki's friends to help relay the news of the canceled wedding. Earlier, Jack Kline had held her in his lap while she cried her heart out. The shower gifts had been removed from her room, her brothers roped into dealing with them.

Staring at the creamy ivory silk of the dress, Nikki wished she could feel bitter. If she could be bitter, angry, this hurt wouldn't be so bad, so complete.

Reaching out, she touched a shaky hand to the vinyl that protected the dress. Lightly, gently, her fingers skimmed over it, to the faux seed pearls at the sweetheart neckline, down the embroidered bodice to a skirt that was elegantly simple, with just a few touches of lace at the hem.

Nikki had known the moment she had seen it that this was the dress. Every single penny of the six hundred dollars she had plunked out for it had been worth it, even though it had involved sacrificing some of her hard-earned savings, even though she had put in double shifts to pay for it over the summer.

Suddenly, her hand closed around the vinyl casing and she jerked it from the rod. Mechanically, she turned on her heel and marched out of the bedroom. Jack called out her name, but Nikki didn't hear it as she continued down the stairs and out the door. Both of her brothers tossed each other a look, then bounded out of their chairs to come after her.

Within seconds, her hair was plastered to her skull. She crossed the street in muddy rainwater that covered her bare feet up to the ankles. Lightning lit up the sky in brief intervals, highlighting her stark face as she moved to the dumpster.

Holding the dress out in front her, she studied it as she had when she had selected it from the rack in the discount bridal store. Gently, almost lovingly, she ran her hand down the casing, now slick with rain. And then she hurled it into the dumpster, along with all of her dreams.

Now…

Nikki came back to herself slowly, sitting in front of the refrigerator, cold and aching inside as though the years hadn't passed. As though it had just happened. She wiped away her tears, and shakily pushed herself to her feet. Nikki rested briefly against the counter before moving woodenly into the living room. She had left Wade that night, thinking it was all over.

But it hadn't been.

On that final night, something had gone incredibly wrong. Or incredibly right. Onthat turbulent night, with their bodies soaked with rain and sweat, Wade had planted a child in her. And by doing so, he had saved her life.

Painful as it was, even Nikki couldn't deny the irony of it all. She was the one who ended up like the interloper, for by the time she knew about the baby, Wade and Jamie were married. And Nikki had stayed hidden away during the few months remaining that she would live in Louisville. By the time Halloween rolled around, she and her family had settled in Monticello in a rented house while they waited for their own house to be built.

She mechanically went through the motions as she flew to New York with her younger brother who had taken on the responsibility of parent since Jack had fallen into another drinking binge, signed contracts with the publishing company, then endorsed a check for more money than she had ever dreamed of having. It meant less than nothing to her.

Jamie had set up housekeeping while Nikki withered away to nothing, her interest in life all but gone. While Nikki couldn't even work up interest in finally having the money to get the hell out of Portland, Jamie had taken over the home that Nikki and Wade had selected together.

It should have been her living in that house, sharing all the new things with her husband. Nikki should have had him with her as she went to the doctor, listening to the baby's heartbeat, coaxing her to eat. Wade should have been there to help her when her body was too cumbersome to get out of bed easily, her stomach too big for her to see her own feet, much less tie her shoes. He should have been there to share with her all her fears and her hopes.

Instead, Nikki had sat, scared and shaking, through each doctor visit, each time awaiting to hear some bad news. Each time, she expected to hear the baby wasn't going to make it after all. Her dad sat with her the first time they had the baby's heartbeat. He had been the one to dry her terrified tears and calm her when the anxiety got too bad. Her brothers and father had been the ones to help haul her up out of chairs.

She had borne her baby with a nurse she didn't know serving as the coach while her father and brothers paced the halls.

She had left the line of 'father' on Jason's birth certificate blank.

Oh, yes. It was very ironic.

And very painful.

Chapter Four

Wade stood outside the bookstore, staring inside at the display. It was a salute to local writers, featuring none other than Nicole Kline. He tucked in his hands into his back pockets and rocked back on his heels as he counted the books featured. Three of them. Damnation, she had really done it.

He went into the bookstore, to the display stand. He took down one book, the one that had drawn his attention. The rendering on the front was what had caught as his eye as he wandered through the mall, waiting on his mother and Abby to finish up their 'girl stuff.'

The man looked just like him.

He was dressed in odd clothing; in one hand he held a sword, in the other, a ball of light. In large letters, it read: Times of Darkness. Below that, in smaller letters, were the words Chronicles of Dien No. I.

Opening it to the first few pages, he scanned them over. A knot was in his throat. It was hers, all right. One page was list of thank you's and acknowledgments. He hadn't read anything she had written, but he recognized names, turns of phrases that she would use. Damn it, she really did it.

The next page was blank save for these words: *This is for all the people who said I could do it. And all of those who said I couldn't.*

He flipped back to the front, looking for the copyright. When had her books started to sell? He knew she had sent them off sometime that last summer, but hadn't ever heard anything.

Then he saw the first printing date. The book fell from his numb hands. July 1995. It took a minimum of twelve months, if not longer, to get a sold book into print. He knew that because Nikki had often fretted about not being able to wait that long, should she ever sell one.

Finally, he had the answer to a burning question. He had wondered for years what had brought her to his house in the middle of such a bad storm.

Nikki had shown up at his house that last day, her eyes bright and shining with a secret. Rain had soaked her clear through, plastering her white cotton Oxford to her torso, her wet hair clinging to the shape of her skull. She had practically danced onto the deck, face glowing, shouting that she had unbelievable news.

Son of a bitch. Nikki had come to tell him the most important news of her life. He'd bet his next paycheck she had shown up to tell him something about the story she'd sent to New York.

And he had handed her news that could have destroyed somebody weaker.

Congratulations on the book, Nik. And by the way, have a cigar. I'm about to become a papa.

Damn it, could things have possibly turned out worse for her?

Hands shaking, Wade scooped up the fallen book before gathering up the books with her name on them and took them to the counter.

What was really ironic was that in the time she had been writing, he had never paid much attention to what she had been putting into words. Wade hadn't a clue as to what kind of stuff she liked to write. He really hadn't cared that much, didn't think it would ever come to anything. After all, how many aspiring writers ever really sold anything?

Wade hadn't been one of the ones who said she couldn't do it, but he had never really expected her to. And lo and behold, years later, Wade was nothing more than a paramedic. A burned out, disillusioned paramedic. Nikki was a published writer, with three books already published, and more on the way. What had she been doing in Monticello? Did she live around there?

Maybe have a cabin somewhere on the lake?

Was she married? Was she happy?

Damn it, if she lived there, and if she was married, would he be running into her and her husband all the time? Could he handle that?

Dropping down on the bench, Wade stared morosely into the fountain. All around him he heard the babble of too many people talking at once. Crowded malls on a Saturday afternoon weren't exactly his favorite way to spend his time. But he had promised his mother he would bring Abby back one weekend a month when he broke the news that they were moving

Abby wasn't happy with Monticello, away from all her old friends, her grandparents, and Uncle Joe. He had begun to question the wisdom of this move.

But if he hadn't moved, he wouldn't have seen Nikki again.

At this particular moment, he couldn't decide

whether that was good or bad.

*****

It was late Sunday when they returned home. Wade knew he'd be lucky to catch five hours sleep before he had to be up for his six a.m. shift. Working three twelve hour days a week was great for the most part, freeing up time to spend with Abby. But it was wearing, and would be doubly so, on so little sleep.

Fortunately, nothing much seemed to happen around here. His job mainly consisted of chauffeuring little old ladies to the doctor's from the area's lone nursing home. On occasion, it was a broken bone, and once, a little boy had eaten one of his grandmother's suppositories and his mother had screamed over and over that the old woman had poisoned him.

It was a relief in itself to be away from gunshots and stab wounds. He was off the night shift and far away from the violence of Louisville. Wade prayed never to see it again.

But Wade's dreams of late had turned bloody and his sleep restless. The last run he had made in Louisville before his vacation lived large in his mind. A four-year old boy shot by his older brother because the little boy had threatened to tell his parents that the older brother was smoking cigarettes.

That four-year old child had died beneath Wade's blood stained hands and nothing modern technology produced could change that. That was what had prompted the move to a smaller town, someplace a little further away from the violence seen all too often in the city.

Shoving the thought firmly to the back of his mind, Wade dressed a sleepy Abby in her pj's. With a soft sigh, she turned on her side, pulled her blanket up to her neck, and slipped right back into sleep.

Wearily, Wade dragged himself to his room, checked the alarm and fell down face first on the mattress, without bothering to undress.

This time his dreams weren't bloody, but they were far from pleasant…

"Aw, shit," Wade groaned, then instantly wished he hadn't. His head was ringing from too much booze the previous night. A thousand tiny soldiers were playing reveille with glee in his skull. Bright early morning sunlight streamed through shades he had forgotten to pull and the light was killing him. Or at least, he wished it would. The inside of his mouth tasted horrible, of stale whiskey and beer and felt as dry as cotton.

But all of it had been for nothing, because he vividly remembered what had driven him to Zack's, one of his oldest childhood friends. The beer had flowed endlessly and he had drunk a vast amount before his memory faded. But it was what happened after the drinking that was a blank. Not what happened before.

Why in the hell had he gone and picked that damn fight with Nikki? Damned if he knew. Wade's lower lip was swollen and throbbed like a son of bitch, but it was the very least he deserved.

Wade forced himself to roll over, knowing he had to get out of bed, make an attempt to look human, and go find Nikki and apologize. Eyes wide open, he stared at the ceiling above, wishing he could undo the past twenty-four hours.

Forcing himself to sit up, Wade cradled his aching head in his hands while he waited for the world, and his stomach, to stop spinning. He stifled the urge to whimper and almost crawled back under the covers in an attempt to escape the misery.

"G'mornin," am unfamiliar husky feminine voice drawled behind him.

Wade froze. His head came up and he briefly wondered if he was dying and this was an auditory hallucination.

Slowly, dread curdling low in his belly, he turned.

And stared

Damnation, what had he gone and done last night?

Jamie Sayer, her cornsilk blond hair tumbled and attractively disheveled, peered up at him with sleepy, sated cornflower blue eyes. And she was as naked as he. Shaking, he rose, trying to get his frozen vocal cords to work. "What are you doing here?" he finally croaked, his headache forgotten as shame and revulsion ate its way up his throat.

She frowned and sat up slowly, tucking the sheet around her as she did. "Don't you remember?" she asked softly, her eyes darkening.

"Remember what?" he growled "I might have been drunk, but it would take more than that to invite you here."

"I drove you home," she reminded him. "You were too drunk to do it, so I volunteered. Zack was pretty wasted, too."

"That doesn't explain what you are doing in my bed," Wade said through clenched teeth. "Or what you were doing at Zack's. I don't remember you showing up there, and I doubt he invited you." He spied his jeans laying tangled on the floor, next to something silky peach. As he jerked his jeans up, it fluttered down to the floor.

Staring at that soft silky bra, Wade swallowed against

the bile rising in his throat.

Damn it, what had he done?

Jamie seemed not to notice his discomfort as she stood and pressed her body against his, arms wrapped securely around his neck. "It was everything I had always dreamed it would be, Wade," she whispered in his ear. "It was perfect. I always knew that you loved me."

For a moment, he was frozen, arms held rigidly at his sides as he tried to make his brain function once more. What in the hell had happened?

Careful, not trusting his temper or his state of mind, Wade freed himself from her arms and moved away. "I don't love you," he said calmly, turning to face her once there was distance between them. "And I sure as hell can't believe that I would invite you into my bed. I don't remember a damn thing, and I sure don't remember you showing up at Zack's."

She smiled softly and shrugged. "You were upset," she said gently. "You finally broke things off with that... girl from Portland. It's normal for you to be upset. You wasted the past few years on her."

"None of the time I spent with Nikki was a waste. And I haven't broken up with her. But after this... Hell, I deserve to horsewhipped. I just might do it myself," he said grimly, the fog of shock starting to retreat. "Damn it, how could I do this?"

She paled in anger. "You don't have to sound so disgusted. You can't talk to me like that. I'm not your little Portland tramp."

Coldly, he eyed her up and down. "Tramps aren't confined to Portland, angel," he drawled "I may not remember last night, but I do remember other times when I clearly told you that I wasn't interested. In fact, I think I even told to just stay the hell away from me."

"You don't mean that," she whispered, her eyes filling with tears. "I know it was wrong for me to push it like I did last night, but I just love you so much!"

"I want to know what happened last night," he said, softly, not moved at all by her crocodile tears. After knowing her all his life, he was well aware of how manipulative she was. "I want to know it now and I want the truth."

"Well, you were just so upset, and crying over the terrible fight you two had..." Jamie said, forlornly, sitting on the edge of the bed. "She had been so mean to you and made you feel guilty over absolutely nothing. You were just so upset.

"I... I felt so bad for you, I was trying to comfort you and it just happened."

"Like hell," he snarled, grabbing her arm and jerking her to her feet. He put his face close to hers and said, "I know a lie when I hear it, Jamie. The truth."

"That's the truth," she whimpered.

"Bullshit," he said succinctly. "Part of the reason I wanted to get so drunk was so I'd forget that I made an ass of myself by picking a fight over nothing. I do remember being drunk on my ass and blubbering to Zack about what I could do to make it right.

"And I damn well wouldn't have come to you for comfort, Jamie," he finished. "That would be like asking a black widow for comfort."

Tears spilled over and vaguely, Wade felt some guilt. Damn it, this was just as much his fault as hers. But what was he going to tell Nikki?

He hadn't realized he had spoken that final thought aloud.

"What do you mean, what are you going to tell Nikki?"

Jamie shouted. "It's none of her damn business. You're mine now!"

"Screwing you didn't turn me into your lapdog, Jamie. Apparently, it wasn't memorable enough for me to even be interested in a repeat performance. I'm going to talk to Nikki and if I have to crawl and beg, I will. Because I am hers, and there's nothing else I want to be."

Damn, what had he done?

...What had he done?

Wade jerked awake just as the alarm went off, body tense, remembered shame eating at his stomach like acid. Damn it, why did he go from one nightmare to another? Wade scrubbed his eyes with the heels of his hands before shutting off the alarm. He felt as though he had been through an intense five-hour war, instead of five hours of restless sleep.

Dragging himself out of bed, Wade shed the wrinkled clothes on the way to the bathroom. His stiff back screamed at him and his eyes were gritty from lack of sleep, a tension headache was already throbbing behind his eyes.

Hot water was the only cure for this. Lots of it.

Turning his face into the hot spray, he let the water wash away the cobwebs and the oily feel that remembered guilt left on his skin. His stomach churned and burned, letting him know it would be another Rolaids breakfast. Hands braced against the tiled wall, he prayed that the day would get better than it had started.

*****

It got worse.

Wade came face to face with a young hazel-eyed man with brutally short ash blond hair. A man who looked ready to kill him. He topped Wade by a good four inches and was lean muscle from the neck down. Those shrewd cold hazel eyes studied him, hate burning in them.

Wade had been gassing up the ambulance when the Harley pulled into the gas station. Wade admired its clean lines, his gaze wistful and a bit envious. Obviously rebuilt and carefully done. He had lifted his eyes to comment on it only to find the rider shucking a helmet and moving to stand toe to toe with him, his dislike palpable.

It was difficult to place him at first. But something about the way he moved registered as familiar. As did the way his chin lifted insolently. But it was those shrewd hazel eyes that finally clued him in. Even back when he had been nothing more than a mouthy hoodlum from Portland, Wade had recognized that this boy was a force to be reckoned with. Those eyes could cut a man off at the knees from ten feet away.

Dylan Kline.

There was nothing left of the sullen boy he had known. He didn't resemble Nikki much, save for the spiky long lashes and sulky mouth. He had always been long and lean, but in the past few years he had filled out.

"Dylan," he greeted, removing the nozzle and replacing it before screwing on the tank lid. "You're looking well." *And strong enough and ready enough to rip my guts out.*

"What are you doing here?" he snapped, his words clear and precise, none of the 'gangsta' drawl left.

"I live here," he said calmly

"Since when?" Dylan demanded, those hazel eyes narrow.

"Since four weeks ago. I suppose your family is here now? Lived here long?" Hopefully, Dylan would see the sense in not mauling him in broad daylight. He was, relatively speaking, the calmer of the Kline brothers. If Shawn were here, blood would already be flowing.

Wade was honest enough to admit that very little blood would have been Kline blood.

"Stay away from Nikki, buddy. She's had enough grief in her life. She doesn't need you to add to it," Dylan warned, his eyes glinting with a promise. *Just give me one reason,* he was saying. *One good reason.* And then, he turned and stalked away.

Close call. It wasn't all that long ago that Dylan would have pounded into somebody he had taken such a dislike to, without even waiting for a reason.

Wade did wonder a bit of the reversal in loyalties. There had been a time when Dylan Kline hadn't even spared his older sister a second glance. Hell, he had let that bastard Dion mouth off for weeks on end, before he took exception to it.

Wade had never seen Dylan stand up for anybody but himself, much less bother getting into a fight over it. Shawn might have done it, but only because he was a natural born brawler. He would have done it for the fun of it, not out of any loyalty or love for his sister.

Time apparently did change things.

*****

Wade spent the next few days convincing himself that he shouldn't hunt Nikki down. There was no point in it. No point in rehashing old times, no point at all. So much time had passed and they hadn't parted fondly.

Better to just leave things as they are, he told himself as he went to bed Tuesday night.

Wednesday morning, he woke with the sole intention of finding her. He had to at least talk to her, if only this one time.

The thirty-minute drive gave him more than enough time to question his motives. He insisted that all he wanted to do was clear the air. They had been friends once upon a time, and it was only right that he try getting things on a friendly note between them.

And Wade didn't believe a word he told himself, either. The winding road led up a steep hill completely covered in trees. Gravel crunched beneath his tires and he began to wonder if he had misread the directions. Surely she wouldn't be living this far from…

The trees suddenly opened up to reveal a large cabin style house constructed of wooden beams and glass. A black Ford Explorer was parked in front of a large two-car garage. The front of the house seemed to consist of little more than windows. And damn, what a view. It was practically perched on the face of the hillside, overlooking a deep valley that was bisected by a wide lazy creek. Rolling waves of impossibly green grass surrounded him, marked here and there with the chaotic colors of wildflowers.

The glass shimmered under the sun, sparkling bright. The porch spanned the entire width of the house, a comfy porch swing in at end. The treated wood gleamed a soft mellow golden brown. Birds sang and called from tall graceful oaks. Toward the back, he caught a glimpse of sun reflecting off water. A pond.

This was very different from the cramped, dirty three-bedroom apartment she had grown up in.

Gravel crunched under his shoes as he headed for the front door. He mounted the steps slowly, studying the fine construction. This place must have cost a fortune. Intricately carved oak and beveled panes of glass made up the front door. That alone probably cost more than he made in a month

Who would want to live alone in a house like this? Surely it was too big for just one person. If ever there had been a place built for raising a family, this was it. He already knew her family lived in Monticello, so was she sharing this place with a boyfriend? Or worse, a family of her own?

Five years had passed, certainly long enough for her to have found somebody and fallen in love.

No, Wade thought, his gut wrenching. Damn it, he didn't know if he could stomach the idea of her belonging to somebody else, even though rightfully he had no hold over her. But what if some guy answered the door? Or worse, a child?

Gritting his teeth, he raised a clenched fist to pound on the door. Tucking his hands in his pockets, he half turned away to wait. And prayed that it would be Nicole answering the door.

*****

Nikki heard the motor long before she saw the vehicle. She stifled a groan as she saved and shut down her computer. Who in the hell could that be? Whoever it was, they weren't welcome. Her father only came up on weekends because of work, Shawn would be in school and Dylan was working.

From the large floor to ceiling window in the living room, she watched. From time to time, she caught a glimpse of shiny black paint and silver chrome. It rounded the bend as Nikki tried to remember if she knew anybody who drove a truck like that.

Glancing down at herself, she grimaced. After an attempt to smooth down her wrinkled t-shirt, she gave it up for lost. She looked like a waif, but this was her own home, so she guessed it didn't matter all that much.

She stopped by the bathroom and ran cold water, shivering as she splashed it on her face. The dark circles under her eyes were just hopeless, though, since she didn't feel like messing with makeup. Running her hand through her tousled hair, Nikki muttered, "That's good enough."

By that time, a knock sounded on the door. Through the beveled cut of the glass, Nikki could make out a dark shadow as she moved to answer the door. The polite smile she had fixed on her face wobbled, then collapsed when she opened the door.

Wade...

He was staring out over the verandah, hands tucked into his back pockets. He turned as she went still, his eyes sweeping over her from head to toe, much as she was gazing at him. Finally, their eyes met, but she still didn't have single word to say. Her heart was pounding fast and hard.

You still look the same, she thought helplessly as her eyes searched for changes. His face looked a little more solemn and he looked like he had filled out a little more through his chest, but other than that and the shorter hair, he looked just as he did when she had last seen him.

Maybe if I close my eyes and wish hard enough, the past few years will just fade away, she thought, leaning against the doorjamb, swallowing. *Just a bad dream...*

And then she kicked herself. No. She wouldn't undo them, even if she could. Not for anything would she have given up the brief time she had with Jason.

Wade looked so exactly the way he always had.

But she had changed. Nothing in her life was the same now, nothing at all. And as empty as her life was, she didn't think there was room in it for the likes of Wade Lightfoot.

Thank God he was alone. She couldn't take it if he had brought his daughter with him.

"Nikki."

"Wade."

He looked away, a sigh escaping his lips. He looked...flustered. Under her steady gaze, his hands left his pockets, thumbs hooking in his belt loops as he rocked back on his heels. She could still remember the pleasure those hands had been able to evoke. "I was surprised to see you here," he said, his voice sounding tight and rusty.

"Were you?" Nikki asked calmly, trying very hard to pretend she hadn't taken off running from him. She didn't quite succeed. That dark red flush, the very bane of a redhead's existence, spread up from her neck, heating her flesh, staining her cheeks but she determinedly ignored it.

Wade blew a sigh out, his eyes narrowing. With irritation written all over his face, he said, "I was even more surprised when you took off running like a jackrabbit, Nikki. I've never known you to run before."

"I'm hardly the same person you knew, Wade. There's a lot about me that you don't know."

"I wouldn't think that turning yellow would be something to be proud of." Then, a wide smiled flashed. "I've seen your books. Bought them, as a matter of fact. Congratulations, Nikki. You did exactly what you said you would do," he told her, his eyes gleaming. "I'm proud of you"

She blinked away the sting in her eyes. How could those words still mean so much to her? How could it make her heart swell inside her chest? In a flat voice that she hoped covered her chaotic emotions, she told him, "I couldn't care less if you're proud of me or not. I didn't do it for you"

With a careless shrug, Nikki added, "You never really cared all that much about it any way. It has nothing to do with you."

His mouth spasmed slightly and he said wearily, "No. I don't guess it doesn't." He studied her again, his eyes narrowed and intense. "Yeah," he finally said, quietly, as though to himself. "I guess you have changed."

"It's to be expected, I'd think. I'm not the person I used to be, anymore than you are the person I thought I knew," Nikki said, folding her arms across her middle. "I certainly never would have expected what you did to me. Or expect you to hide it the way you did. I wonder, if Jamie hadn't gotten pregnant, would you ever have told me?"

"No," Wade said, clearly and without hesitation. "I wanted to, hell, it was killing me inside. But I couldn't lose you. It was the wrong decision I know that now. Hell, I knew then. But if she hadn't been pregnant, you never would have known." His eyes met hers straight on, unblinking and steady.

Looking away, Nikki absently rubbed the back of her neck. Why did it still hurt so much? Hadn't enough time passed for her to be over this by now, over him? "Well, at least you can be honest about it now," she said quietly. "But it's a little late." Closing her eyes, she summoned up her strength. Then coolly, she looked back at him. "What are you doing here, Wade?"

"I guess I wanted to apologize," he told her, turning away. He walked to the edge of the verandah, bracing his elbows on the railing. A breeze lifted the edges of his hair, tugging at them, while the sun gleamed down on it. Broad shoulders strained at the seams of his shirt. His voice was lower as he spoke again. "I made a lot of mistakes with you, Nikki. I hurt you. And I'm sorrier than you will ever know."

Nikki's eyes closed briefly and she lowered her head. Pressing her fingers to her eyes, she thought...*Sorry...he is* sorry?

With a sigh, she looked back at him, her eyes searching for something she couldn't quite define. She had experienced too much grief in her life in the past few years to wish it on another, even somebody who had hurt her as much as he had.

He meant it. Wade looked... tired. As if the past few years hadn't been easy on him. Despite what had happened, she hadn't wished him ill. She had never wanted him to be unhappy.

He was though; there was unhappiness in those dark eyes, in every line of his body.

Nikki moved out of the doorway, shutting it behind her. With a sigh, she seated herself on the porch swing, one knee drawn up to her chest. "Apology accepted, Wade."

"Just like that?" he asked, turning to face her. With disbelief in his eyes, he stared at her, watching her closely. "Aren't you going to rant and rave or give me the cold shoulder?"

"It's in the past now, Wade. I've never wished you ill. It just wasn't meant to be with us, and I've accepted that," she said, not looking at him. "It wouldn't do any good to rant and rave now."

Damn, I'm good... Nikki could almost believe it herself, almost convinced herself that her heart wasn't bleeding inside. The past seemed like it was just yesterday, the pain still every bit as true as it had been then.

But convincing herself wasn't what mattered. All she had to do was convince him. Make sure he didn't know that she hadn't accepted or dealt with anything, at least, not very well. Make sure he didn't know she woke up crying at night, for him, and for their son.

Frowning, Wade stared at her. With a heavy sigh, he looked away. "How have you been doing the past few years? Did you finish college?"

"No." How could she tell him that she never went back, her interest in it gone, too depressed to care about a nursing career at the time. And later, when she had been interested, the doctor had strictly forbidden it. She hadn't needed that stress then. After that, when she had Jason, she had been too happy, too satisfied to need anything else.

And now... now she just didn't care. About anything.

"Why not?" Wade asked, another frown darkening his face. "It was always the most important thing to you, other than your writing."

"No," she corrected. "Both of those fell way below you."

Closing his eyes, Wade swore quietly under his breath. "Damn it, Nikki. You always did know how to twist the knife."

Nikki ignored him as she added, "Besides, nursing didn't seem quite so important once my writing got off the ground." Another lie. She had kept writing, once she found out about Jason, but it had been little more than a job.

It wasn't until Jason was suddenly gone that she

started to cling to her writing like it was a lifesaver. During her pregnancy and while Jason had been alive, she had written only because she had been determined to make certain her son had a good life, better than her own childhood had been.

Later, after she had come home to an empty house, and stared at Jason's empty room, the need for her stories had resurfaced. Like a drowning man clinging to a life preserver, she wrapped herself in her make believe worlds, and tried to forget. And while she wrote, for a little while, she could forget.

Without the stories, she would have lost her mind. It was all she had left now…

A feeling of despair was rising in her, her throat tightening, her eyes stinging. An empty house, a handful of books, and an empty nursery

Damn it, if you get right down to it, I don't really have much at all, she thought bleakly.

Determined to keep thoughts like that away, she said the one thing guaranteed to help her get back on track, to get refocused, and get him the hell off her mountain.

"Your daughter looks just like you, Wade. I imagine you and Jamie are very proud of her."

"Jamie's dead."

Just as she congratulated herself on the return of her composure, she felt her foundation crumple under her. Shaken to the core, she closed her eyes as his words echoed over in her mind.

Jamie's dead. So calmly, so flatly stated…*Jamie's dead.*

"What?" she whispered

"Jamie's dead. She died three years ago, Nikki."

It was then that she finally noticed he wore no wedding ring.

Jamie's dead…

Nikki felt as though the ground had opened up under her, leaving her standing on thin air. Scrabbling for purchase.

The woman she had spent years hating was suddenly no longer alive to hate. One hand went to rub at her stomach, which was churning with all the stress she was keeping bottled up.

Shakily, she said, "I'm sorry." Her eyes flew up to meet his, certain she would see total desolation there, but all she saw was a distant sort of regret before he turned away, staring out into the trees that lined the northwestern side of her property.

Wade was silent for so long, she wondered if he was going to speak at all. When he finally did, his voice was so quiet she could hardly hear him. "Don't be. She was miserable with me, Nicole. I did the best I could, but I couldn't give her what she wanted. She never could understand that I didn't love her, that I was only there because of the baby. She had my name and a ring, but nothing else."

Turning to her, Wade stared at her with intense eyes, mesmerizing eyes. Unable to look away, Nikki sat helplessly as he moved closer to her. He sank down on his knees in front of her, reaching out to trace the line of her jaw with a feathery touch. Softly, he said, "She could never understand that in my heart, I still belonged to you."

"Don't say that, Wade. We were finished the night

you told me she was pregnant." Jerking her face away from his touch, Nikki gave a harsh laugh and said, "Hell. We were over the night you spent with her. I just didn't know it."

"None of that changed the fact that I loved you. None of that changed the fact that I still do love you." Still staring at her with those dark eyes that held her pinned to her seat, he lifted her left hand, studying it intently. Gently, he pressed a kiss to the back of it. If he noticed the trembling, he didn't remark on it.

"No wedding ring, Nikki. But is there somebody in your heart now? Am I going to have to fight to get you back?" His voice dropped as he spoke, as he hooked one hand behind her head, drawing her closer.

His softly spoken words, dark hypnotic eyes had soothed her, lulled her into believing, into hoping, dreaming. If only, she thought wistfully.

The gentle touch of his lips on her broke her out of her spell. "No," Nikki said, her voice faint. "No," she repeated, her voice stronger this time as she shoved him away and shot to her feet, moving to the far railing. "I'm not interested in rekindling an old flame, Wade. I'm certainly not interested in reliving the past or rebuilding something between us."

"Why not?" Wade asked, moving on silent feet until he stood so close, she could feel his body heat warming her back.

"Because you turned out to be everything I hate in people. You betrayed me, you lied to me."

She watched as he flinched at her words, like she had slapped him. And then she turned her back on him, staring out in the trees.

*****

Nikki's words lashed at him, pouring salt into the still open wounds of his heart. His guilt over what had happened had never eased, but he had succeeded in burying it. Now, it returned in full force, making his gut clench and his throat constrict. Reaching for her, he started to speak "Nikki—" only to have her cringe away from his hands.

Nikki flinched away when he turned her around to face him. "I don't want you touching me, Wade," she said, her voice thick. "I don't want you here. So go away."

Well, that went rather well.

He cursed himself as he drove away, shaken. He hadn't meant it for to go quite like that. He certainly hadn't expected to see a cold, quiet woman in place of the feisty girl he had known.

Nikki had lost weight, so much that she looked lost in her baggy clothes. And her eyes...so sad and distant. He couldn't see any of the thoughts going on in her mind.

He had always been able to read those eyes, know what was going on in that quirky mind of hers. It was very disturbing to look into those eyes now and see nothing. Absolutely nothing.

Hell, Wade. What did you expect? Did you think she would throw her arms around you and tell you how much she had missed you?

While he hadn't been expecting it, he had been hoping for a warmer reception than what he had received. *Damn, optimistic fool.*

Anger, he expected, even if he did wish for something more. But anything, even her anger, would have been better than that ice edged disdain.

Wade looked up and blinked, his heavy thoughts retreating slightly. Damn. He was home. Looking up at the little ranch house, he didn't even remember driving there.

Later that night, Abby sat watching a tape of Sesame Street, while her father sat behind her on the sofa brooding.

Wade hadn't gone looking for Nikki after she had left his house that last day. He had been ready to, had even gone so far as to head for her dad's apartment. Then, half way across the bridge, reality had hit and he had realized she had done the only thing she could. He had instead gone to the riverfront, staring moodily into the muddy Ohio.

Nikki had done what she had to. And he didn't really have much choice either. There was only one thing left for him to do, after he told Nikki and killed their life together.

He'd married Jamie, fully intending to make the best of his marriage, telling himself he'd forget about Nikki. Wade had failed at that, but he kept her memory tucked away deep inside, rarely allowing himself to think of her.

He'd had hoped over the past few years that she had found somebody who made her happy. Even though the thought of her with another man made him want to howl, he knew Nikki just wasn't the sort of woman meant to go through life alone. She deserved somebody who would love her, whom she could love with all the fierceness and passion she had within her, somebody who could help her have the babies he knew she wanted, and bring laughter to her life.

Those hopes were gone now.

Today, her soft hazel eyes had looked at him like a beaten dog, cowering, frightened, just waiting for another blow. Physically, she looked no older than she was, but there had been an air of grief wrapped around her, of sadness that added decades to her. It didn't seem fair that he had been the one to screw up and she was the one who was so totally miserable.

Wade had not been happy with Jamie, but then Abby had come along and she had stolen his heart from the first. Jamie hadn't cared about being a mother, had retreated inside herself more and more each day. It was so different from what he had imagined his family life would be like, when the time for him to have a family finally came. Jamie had never once entered into the picture.

And the picture had certainly never had him winging it all on his own.

For the past four years, he had been caring for his and Jamie's little girl solely on his own. He had stood in the delivery room, completely awed by what was taking place. Completely deaf to the curses and insults hurled his way. The nurses had told him not to take it personally, that Jamie didn't mean anything she said. Wade knew otherwise…

"You sonovabitch! You did this me," Jamie screeched, her face red and sweaty, lips dry and chapped. Hospital gown rucked up about her waist, skinny legs propped in stirrups, Jamie stared down at her bloated stomach in disgust.

"I never should have told you," she whispered as her belly tightened in another contraction. As the contraction ended, she stared up at him with bitter eyes. "I should have gotten rid of the damn baby."

Jamie never once held Abby, falling into her own world, one of silence and anger. She refused all calls, all visitors as she retreated further and further inside herself.

She left Wade alone, as he fumbled through the first few weeks of sleeping only while his newborn daughter slept. He learned on his own how to prepare bottles of formula, had changed diaper after diaper, picked out clothes for the tiny little baby and awkwardly dressed her, his hands seeming huge and clumsy. Those clothes seemed to shrink overnight as Abby rapidly outgrew them almost faster than he could buy them.

Alone, Wade took her in for her first week's check-up, embarrassed and awkward as he tried to explain why the baby's mother wasn't there. He had fought to keep from cringing from the sympathy he saw in Dr. Norland's eyes.

"Is your wife still not feeling well?" Dr. Norland had asked, his pale blue eyes concerned.

"She, uh, well..." Wade's words trailed into nothing and he turned his head, staring out the window with unseeing eyes.

Recognizing his discomfort, the pediatrician had quickly changed the subject.

By himself, while Jamie slid further into

depression, he had sweated through Abby's first cold, had practically camped out at the doctor's when she was one, having caught the chicken pox from Daycare.

He had searched out that perfect Daycare, asking questions the pediatrician had sympathetically written down for him. Mistake after endless mistake, night after sleepless night, he had worried if was doing anything at all right.

While Abby sat on the floor, sounding out the 'cat' and 'dog' along with Elmo, Wade remembered how tense things had been when he had brought her home from the hospital. Jamie and he couldn't speak a civil word after that. Horrible fights had been conducted in whispered tones, as their daughter slept next door.

Wade had whispered because he didn't want to disturb Abby. Jamie had whispered because she couldn't stand the thought of seeing the baby. Hell, she had told him time after time that she couldn't stand the sight of her own daughter.

Even before Abby was born, things were bad. Wade had slept in the living room until he had been able to buy an extra bed for the third bedroom. The first few nights after they had gotten married, Jamie had finally figured out just how little he wanted her.

"Can't you even touch me, Wade?" she pleaded. "I'm your wife." But nothing stirred inside him at her touch. He couldn't make himself want her.

He had never been able to share a marriage bed with Jamie, and he knew that he carried as much blame for the failed marriage as Jamie had. But touching her only reminded him of what his mistake had cost him. Jamie had tried, night after night, and night after night, he had rejected her. His body went cold any time Jamie even came near. He had hurt her and he knew it, and despised himself for it, but he still was unable to bring himself to welcome her. And eventually she stopped trying, as her body grew large with their child, and her face became more and more lifeless.

She quit bathing, quit wearing make up and quit fixing her hair.

By the time Abby was born, Jamie looked nothing like the girl she had been. And as Abby got older Jamie became more bitter, wanting nothing more than to be alone with her TV and her own anger for companionship.

Then the day came when he arrived home to find her laying peacefully on the huge four-poster oak bed he had bought for Nikki.

The silence should have warned him. The radio wasn't blaring, the TV wasn't on, not even a fan stirred the air. As he crossed over the threshold, his gut clenched.

There she was laying on the bed, clad in a set of expensive silk pajamas she'd received as a bridal gift from a friend. Spilled on the floor was what remained of a bottle of prescription sleeping pills. A half-empty bottle of Jose Cuervo sat on the night table.

"Oh, Jamie," he whispered, lowering himself to the bed, sitting at her side. Her skin had already cooled and her features had taken on a waxy cast.

Wade waited for the grief to hit, the pain, the anger. But it never came. All he felt was regret, and guilt.

After burying Jamie, he had had his mother

repaint the master bedroom, sold all the furniture and bought new. And still, he hadn't been able to sleep in that bedroom. Jamie had slept in there, had died in there, the room that he was supposed to have shared with Nikki.

He hated himself because he hadn't seen it earlier, hadn't seen how desperately Jamie needed help, had needed him. He was just as much to blame for putting her in the coffin as if he had forced the sleeping pills down her throat himself.

How had everything gotten so messed up?

Because you, Wade Lightfoot, are a total screw up, he told himself. He pressed the heels of his hands against his eyes, forcing himself to look at the clock. He couldn't do this just yet. It was time to get Abby in bed and himself as well. He had to be up again before five in order to make his shift.

He nudged Abby's round belly with his foot as he shut off the VCR. She smiled up at him without griping as he told her, "Bedtime, brat." He softened the words with a loud kiss to the side of her neck as he scooped her off the floor. She giggled and kissed his cheek noisily while he drew in the scent of her baby powdered skin and Mickey Mouse bubble bath.

She was so beautiful, this child of his. From the top of her shiny black hair to the bottom of her sneakered feet, she was perfect. She rarely fussed or cried, hadn't even when she was a tiny baby; instead, she was unfailingly patient with her fumbling father. She was the only good thing he had in his life, but she was enough.

She was also the scariest thing.

Wade had never guessed that fatherhood would be so tough, but maybe if he had somebody there to help him, it would have been easier. And Wade knew he had himself to blame for that. If he had been able to be a husband to Jamie, maybe Jamie would have been able to be a mom to her daughter.

By now, the bedtime ritual was easy for him, established over many nights over the past few years. Once Abby was snug in her bed, the tried and true Tigger tucked into the crook of her arm, they read a story. As he perched precariously on the edge of the bed, he glanced at her often, smiling inside as her lids drooped heavier and heavier.

He wasn't even on page six and Abby was sound asleep.

After kissing her cheek, Wade left the room, leaving the door wide open. The hallway light was left on and his own door ajar. Wade had grown accustomed to sleeping with the lights on in the past few years, accustomed to awaken and find Abby snuggled in bed with him.

Briefly, he prayed for a dreamless night, knowing he was probably wasting his time. The dreams that chased him through the nights were his penance for all the mistakes he had made

But what he wouldn't give for a one night that wasn't plagued by blood and innocent lives lost. Or worse, him reliving his own mistakes.

*****

Nikki's own dreams were far from pleasant. She

hadn't slept in nearly three days. The last time she had slept, she had woken screaming, fighting. She had been in her Blazer, Jason strapped securely in the back seat. It had tumbled down the embankment and once again, she had fought her way free to get to the baby seat. In the passenger seat next to her, Shawn lay dead, the simple gash now a gaping wound that had laid his head open to the skull.

And the baby seat didn't have the still body of her baby boy, but rather, the larger sturdier body of Abigail Lightfoot, Wade and Jamie's little girl.

Now Nikki sat in a half daze, staring at the monitor before her. Her hands rested beside the keyboard, for she was too tired to even try to work on her book. Involuntarily, one of those hands crept to her flat belly, her fingers searching.

And she wondered, unable to stop herself, if Jamie had felt that wonder when that tiny little baby had moved inside her for the first time. Had she cried when the ultrasound showed a healthy baby? Had she cried when she had learned she was pregnant, carrying the baby of the man she loved more than life itself?

Nikki hadn't cried. She had been too stunned, too shocked.

Then…

"Nikki, I don't think you understand the gravity of the situation here," Dr. Graves said, his eyes kind. "You almost waited too long to come in here. You're in bad shape. We can help you, but the baby…"

Logically, Nikki knew he was only telling her

what was best for her.

"No," she repeated for the third time, her voice shaky, practically soundless. She sat motionless on the exam table, clad once again in a shirt that reeked from being worn day after day against an unwashed body. Her limp, greasy hair hung in her eyes, eyes that she couldn't seem to take off the floor. Her father had literally carried her into this office against her will, bound and determined to do something about her.

"Nikki, listen to me. You have developed an irregular heartbeat, something that's due to your malnourished state. If you hadn't come here, you would be dead in a matter of weeks. Your heart would fail. The human heart cannot function if it's not given the nutrients it needs.

"Now, you are well over three months pregnant by my estimation. You are severely underweight, and badly malnourished. I imagine the blood work will show that you have all sorts of electrolyte imbalances and vitamin and mineral deficiencies.

"If this was just you we were talking about, the problem would be fixed easily enough. We can get you healthy again, but it's too late for that little baby. The first three months are critical. I seriously doubt you could even carry it to full term, but if you did, it could have numerous problems, mental and physical handicaps. The first trimester is the most important time for a fetus, development-wise. That is when the foundation for a healthy baby takes place. Your baby's groundwork is...precarious. It probably wouldn't live very long if it even made it to full term."

Her father stood staring out the window, hands

buried deep in his pockets while they listened to the doctor. And as he reached up, patting his pocket, she knew he was craving a cigarette, that he could practically feel the smoke burning its way down his throat, soothing his shaking hands.

And he probably wanted a drink. She wanted to feel angry about that, but she couldn't. She just couldn't.

Nikki stared at her stomach, one thin frail hand resting against it. Wade's baby was in there, struggling to live, despite her not taking better care.

She couldn't get rid of it.

"But, more serious than that is the fact that this pregnancy could very easily kill you. You are not healthy. Your body has probably forgotten what it's supposed to do." He paused, looking at her, wondering if he was getting through to her. "Do you understand what I'm trying to tell you?"

"Yes." And she did understand. She had completed two years of nursing school, had taken advanced courses of anatomy and physiology in high school. She had studied up on obstetrics quite a bit; she'd intended to go into that area after graduating.

Oh, yeah. Nikki understood very well what he was telling her. This would very likely kill her baby, and quite possibly her. "But I won't kill my baby," she said, her voice hoarse from disuse.

"Mr. Kline," he said, trying a different tactic, turning beseeching eyes to the man who seemed to have aged ten years since stepping into the office. Jack turned around and met the doctor's eyes, but the look he saw in those eyes was no different. "She's made her choice, Dr. Graves. I'll support her, regardless of the outcome," he said quietly, his voice gravelly and rough from the years of abuse he had heaped on it.

Sighing, the doctor rubbed the back of his neck before saying, "Very well. It's your choice. I'm going to refer you to Dr. Gray. He's new in Somerset, and has practiced in Louisville for quite some time..."

*****

"...I completely agree with Dr. Graves," Dr. Gray was saying as he sat, poring over the blood work and ultrasounds he had been sent. Wire rimmed glasses perched on a thin blade of a nose, wide, intelligent blue eyes poring over the records and lab results.

"This is going to be extremely risky. Nikki, he wasn't lying when he said this pregnancy could kill you. You have some serious electrolyte imbalances, which have caused you to develop an arrhythmia in your heart.

"Do you understand what that means?" he asked, studying her with intense eyes.

Nikki sat on the table, her chin tucked against her chest. Dull stringy brown hair framed a face so thin and pale, her own father barely recognized her. Weak and tired, all she wanted to do was find some place quiet and just sleep. But that was what had led her here. What would probably kill Wade's baby.

"I have to try," Nikki said softly. "I can't just go and kill this baby. It's not his fault I wasn't taking care of myself. I was taking the pill and I never even thought...I didn't know" Tears welled in her eyes, remorse and grief filling her chest. "I didn't know..."

Gently, the doctor took her hand. "Nikki, I understand. And I believe you. You've obviously had a rough time lately and I'm not blaming you. Nobody is. I'm just trying to make certain you understand what we are up against. I can't guarantee anything. I can't even guarantee your own safety, should you continue with this pregnancy."

"Dr. Gray, we have to try," Jack said. "We will do whatever it takes."

He sat in the seat next to Nikki, holding his daughter's hand tightly. He had let her down so many times. She had already lost so much, her mother to depression, her father to the bottle, and Wade to another woman. And now possibly the baby.

But they couldn't change the past. This baby was Nikki's best hope for a future. Maybe her only chance. The air of desolation that hung around her was palpable. She didn't really want to keep on living. He had seen such a look before, on his wife's face, in the months before she had taken her own life. He hadn't saved her, hadn't even tried.

Jack vowed that Nikki would not end up that way.

"Whatever it takes," he repeated.

And the doctor smiled. "I certainly hope so. The first thing we have to do is get her to the hospital. I'm going to put her on an IV to get fluids into her. We need to put her on a heart monitor to see how severe this arrhythmia is."

It was worse than Nikki had thought, but the doctor didn't seem surprised. Her blood pressure was dangerously low. The heart arrhythmia was critical, but he said medication would help that.

"But won't that hurt the baby?" she asked, her hand on her belly, wondering about the little life inside.

Dr. Gray had smiled and gently said, "Nikki, if that heart of yours stops beating that will be bad for the baby."

On top of all of that, her stomach had started to atrophy and she had to learn to eat all over again. Small meals, mainly broth and Jello® the first week. Five times a day, she had the pleasure of eating the typical sick person's menu and for the first few days, she hadn't been able to eat more than two or three bites.

By the end of the first week, she was starving.

But Nikki remained in the hospital another week, until her heart rate had regulated and her blood pressure wasn't so low. She had gained two pounds in that time, but still wasn't anywhere close to what she should be.

Nikki was well into her sixth month before the obstetrician was able to detect a heartbeat. The size of the baby then was what it should have been at three months.

At the end of her sixth month, Nikki felt him kick .

When she was seven months along, she awoke in a pool of blood. There was no pain, but there was a lot of panic. While she sat there, shaking with fear, her father had gathered her up and put her in the truck, drove her to the hospital, all the while crooning quietly to her.

After a week in the hospital, she was allowed to go

home, but Nikki was now on partial bed rest. On top of her numerous other problems, she had a condition called *placenta previa.* The placenta had settled in the lower part of her uterus—that was what caused the bleeding. Scary as hell, but nothing that would harm the baby.

And when he was born nearly a month overdue more than three months later, Nikki realized that God had given her another chance. Another miracle.

In a hospital room bright with sunlight, she sat on the bed, head elevated while her tiny son nursed awkwardly. He felt fragile in her arms, so tiny, so little. He didn't even weigh six pounds. But bright curious eyes stared at her out of Wade's face and beneath her questing fingers, she felt his little heart thumping strongly against his chest.

Jason was alive and he was healthy.

His head fell away from her breast, his Cupid's bow mouth wet with milk, slack from exhaustion. Lowering her head, she pressed a kiss to that tiny little damp mouth, then pressed her lips to his brow, rocking him back and forth as she absently patted his narrow little back. She could feel the tiny bumps of his spine as she soothed and stroked him into sleep.

She settled back, stiff, unbelievably sore.

Incredibly happy. As she cuddled him closer to her chest, she stroked a finger down his soft satiny cheek. His head was perfect, not the least bit marred from the easy birth. He was so little he had practically slid into the world all on his own. Staring down at his sleeping face, she wondered out loud, "How did we do that?" The love she already felt for this tiny little being was so great, she feared her heart would burst from it.

"Wade, how did we do that?" she asked again, wishing he was there to answer.

Her only answer was silence. Conceived in a fit of fury and desperation, that last time in the woods, conceived while pleasure racked her body and agony tore its way through her broken heart, this child was an absolute miracle. Her lifesaver.

Even more amazing was how he had survived inside her neglected body all those months before she had learned he existed. How he had defied all medical laws and knowledge and pulled through even though she deprived him of everything he needed those first few months of life. By all logic, he shouldn't be here in her arms.

But he was.

Salty tears streaked down her cheeks. Tipping her head back, she stared blindly up at the ceiling. "Thank You," she whispered, her voice soundless.

Now...

Nikki came back to herself slowly, unwilling to relinquish those memories. Her throat was tight and aching. Her eyes were dry and burning, the pain she felt too deep for tears. Crying brought her no release. Beneath her questing hand, her belly was smooth, flat and hollow. She felt horribly empty.

The room down the hall stood with the door closed tight, the toys untouched, the crib unslept in, and the laughter forever silenced.

Chapter Five

"Why don't you like my dad?"

Nikki jumped, startled. She looked away from the parade going down Main Street to find Wade's little girl standing next to her.

Abby. Her name was Abby, Nikki thought, unable to think of anything else.

"Well?" the little girl demanded, impatiently, her hands going to her hips in a gesture that mimicked her father's.

"Ah," Nikki said, uncertain what to say. "Ah, who said I didn't like him?"

"Anytime he tries to talk to you, you take off. That's not very nice," Abby informed her, her face prim. Polite.

Reaching up to scratch her nose, Nikki hid her grin. She could see the hand of Wade's mother in this child. "Just where is your dad? I don't see him and I don't think he wants you running around by yourself," Nikki said, kneeling down and looking the little girl in the face. The girl smelled of baby lotion, candy, and innocence and she looked like a mirror of the brother she had never known.

"This is important," Abby said, sounding very adult. "Dad will understand. Why don't you like him?"

"Are you sure you're only four years old?" Nikki asked, buying time while she struggled to come up with an answer that wouldn't be a lie but also wouldn't make this precocious little girl upset.

"I'll be five in April"

"Ah. That explains it," Nikki said, sagely, nodding her head. Never mind that April was more than half a year away.

Unable to resist the urge to touch, she reached out and stroked her hand down Abby's raven black hair, knowing she would find it soft and thick. "Honey, it's not that I don't like your dad. But we've had some problems in the past and it kind of hurts for me to be around him." Would she understand that? Nikki wondered.

Solemnly, the little girl nodded. "That's what he said. But you know, when somebody hurts you, if you let them say that they are sorry, it helps. Did he hurt you?"

"A little," Nikki said, her smile weak and shaky. That was the understatement of the century.

Abby smiled brightly and said, "Then just let him say that he's sorry and things will be better. I know he's sorry, otherwise he wouldn't look so sad when he sees you."

Nikki wasn't able to answer her just then. Wade swooped down out of the crowd, snagging his daughter and catching her in a tight hug. "Abby Lightfoot, what were thinking, running off like that?" he demanded, his eyes closed tight.

"I'm sorry, Daddy. But I saw Miss Kline standing over here and I had to talk to her. Girl stuff," Abby said, twisting until her father released his death grip and saw Nikki standing there.

"Thanks for watching her, Nikki," he said gruffly, transferring her to his left arm.

Nikki shrugged and said, "She sort of found me, Wade." As quickly as she could, she averted her eyes, ready to escape into the crowd.

Sternly, Wade said to Abby, "Don't you ever take off like that, little girl. That's just asking for all sorts of bad things."

"I'm sorry, Daddy. Please don't be mad. It was real important," Abby said softly, her eyes sober, her mouth pursed in a pout.

Nikki watched as Wade fought not to melt under those sweetly spoken words. Abby's face was properly solemn and chastised, utterly repentant. And Nikki knew without a doubt, that should something else 'important' come up, the little girl would do just as she had. Would Jason have been like this? Sweet and stubborn, determined to get his way?

Turning away, Nikki started to find someplace else to watch the parade, only to have Wade snag her arm. She looked up and met his eyes without speaking.

"Why don't you watch the parade with us?" he asked, his dark eyes caressing her face. On her arm, his hand was warm and despite the heat of the day, she felt goosebumps rising, felt her pulse kicking up a notch or two.

"I don't—"

"Dad, I think you need to say you're sorry first," Abby interrupted before Nikki was able to make good her escape. "After you say you're sorry, you can be friends again, then she can watch the parade with us."

"Is that right?" Wade asked, studying his daughter's face. "Are you sure that is how it works?"

All the while, as he talked with his daughter, he drew Nikki closer, his hand cupped around her elbow.

"Of course it is. Now say you're sorry. That's all she's waiting for," Abby stated, a very adult look on her little face. For all the world, she looked like a kindergarten teacher correcting two unruly students.

Wade turned his eyes back to Nikki, smiling slightly. "I am sorry, Nikki. I thought you already knew that," he said quietly.

"See, now wasn't that easy?" Abby asked, squirming until her father set her down. Then she grabbed Wade's hand in one hand and Nikki's in the other, pulling them closer to the front of the crowd. "I knew that would help."

Nikki stood next to the little girl, a frozen smile on her face.

Just walk away, she told herself. *Just take your hand back and walk away.*

But she couldn't find it in her heart to wipe that happy smile off Abby's face.

The hot summer sun beat down her bare shoulders and arms but did nothing to warm her. Her scoop neck tank top and cut-off denims had been comfortable earlier, but now she wished for sackcloth, a sweater, turtleneck and jeans, anything to warm her chilled flesh. What was she doing here? She was watching a Fourth of July parade with the man who cheated on her and his daughter, the result of that union.

She was insane, absolutely insane, just begging for punishment.

With one eye on the clock, the other on the parade, she prayed for it to end quickly.

*****

Wade wasn't certain what had prompted Abby to go seek out Nikki, but he was damn glad of it. She was standing less than two feet away, and though Nikki had yet to say a damn thing without being prompted, she hadn't taken off in the other direction. Yet.

Something told him she was just biding time. His instincts proved right when he caught her eyes dart to the clock in the square for the second time in only minutes.

He shifted until he was standing more behind Abby and Nikki than beside them. One hand rested on his daughter's shoulder as she leaned against Nikki's side, laughing at the clowns and squealing at the floats that went past. His other hand he kept fisted in his pocket to keep from wrapping it around Nikki's waist.

A gentle breeze fluttered her hair around her face. She'd cut her hair, those gleaming chestnut strands cropped to chin length, and even curlier than before. Again, her glasses were missing. She wore no jewelry, no make up, and her nails were ruthlessly short. Her soft mouth set in a firm line, her solemn eyes were fastened on the parade and she looked neither up nor down the street.

She could have been standing before a firing squad, with all the pleasure she showed.

Nikki didn't want to be here. Wade knew that as well as he knew his own name. She was here, though. That was something, right? Closing his eyes, he inhaled, dragging the scent of her skin into his lungs, heating up blood that was already pumping hot. His eyes fastened on the soft skin of her neck and shoulders, bared by the tank top she wore. If he put his mouth on her there, where her neck and shoulders joined, would it still make her gasp?

If he rubbed gently, would it still make her sigh with pleasure?

"—fireworks with us?"

Wade snapped his head around, looking down at his daughter. Abby was tugging on his pants leg with one hand, the other holding tightly to Nikki's, as though she, too, feared that Nikki would disappear into the crowd the moment she had the chance. "Sorry, baby. I didn't hear you."

"I want to know if Nikki can watch the fireworks with us," she repeated patiently.

He looked up to find Nikki staring straight ahead, her eyes blank. "She's welcome to, if she wants," he said quietly, already knowing what her answer would be.

"I can't. I promised my family I would come by after the parade," Nikki said, giving Abby a half-hearted smile. "Let's just finish watching the parade together, okay?"

Wade sighed as Abby looked away, her face crestfallen. He picked her up and settled her on his hip. "Maybe next time, brat," he whispered in her ear, nuzzled her neck. "Okay?"

Nikki said nothing, her eyes fastened on the marching band as though she had never seen such a sight.

For the next thirty minutes, she ignored him.

Except for her brief answers to Abby, Nikki might as well have not even stood there. She kept her eyes straight ahead, not once looking over at him. Wade knew, for he didn't take his eyes off her.

Frustrated, he wondered how much longer she would persist in ignoring him, or running away. How could she ignore him, when the very thought of her was enough to set his blood afire? His hands itched with the need to reach out and draw her against him. He wanted to sit down with her snuggled up next to him, for her to tell him what she had been doing the past few years. And he wanted to tell her about Jamie, about raising Abby on his own. She had been his best friend and he hadn't realized it until she was no longer there. Without her, there was nobody to talk to, nobody who understood him inside and out. Damnation, he had missed her.

He wanted her back.

Wade hadn't expected her to continue to ignore him for as long as she had. She wasn't even willing for them to just be on friendly terms. She had made that abundantly clear.

How long would she keep this up?

*****

Nikki jumped involuntarily when a hand settled on the curve of her hip. Stiffening, she tried to move away, but the crowd had gotten a little too close.

She aimed a quelling glare up at Wade, only to find him talking to Abby. All around the crowd talked, music played, children laughed. The noise buzzed in her ears but she heard none of it

A tiny shudder raced up her spine as his thumb moved up and down. On bare skin. The bottom of her top barely touched the waistband of her shorts and now his hand was kneading her naked flesh. Long clever fingers played over her waist while she tried hard to ignore it.

She wasn't succeeding. Her stomach felt warm and jittery, her heart pounded harder, her skin felt far too tight, hot and prickly.

Damn it, how much longer until this thing's over? she thought wildly as her insides continued to do a slow meltdown

Her shoulders ached with the effort to keep tension in her body, to keep from relaxing against him. It would be so easy, just to let her head fall back against his shoulder, let him wrap her in his arms.

Why was he doing this? Hadn't she made it clear she wanted nothing to do with him? Why was she still standing here? Abby no longer held her hand in a death grip, wasn't looking at her every few seconds as if to say 'isn't this fun?' Nikki could have left several minutes ago, so why she was torturing herself?

She stood frozen as Wade shifted until he was standing just behind her and slightly to her right. That hand slid around her middle and exerted enough pressure to pull her flush against him. The heat from him felt as though it was branding her flesh.

Her eyes closed as Wade leaned down and whispered in her ear, "You don't want to stay away from me any more than I want you to. Don't keep running away, baby."

"Stop it," she bit off, her own whisper harsh.

"Stop what? Stop dreaming about you? Loving you? Can you stop thinking about me? Is it really that easy for you?" he asked in a low voice, nuzzling her ear gently.

Her eyes flew open as Wade's hand slid under her shirt again, now caressing her midriff with agile, knowing fingers. She grabbed his hand, stilled it with her own, and slipped away from him.

"The parade's over," she said, her voice hoarse, heart pounding. Her palms were damp and her hands were shaking. And he had hardly touched her.

She shot a strained smile to Abby and disappeared into the crowd.

*****

Nikki sat silently on the deck while her father cooked steaks on the grill. A lukewarm can of soda sat untouched next to her while she tried to figure out exactly what she was going to do about Wade

He wasn't taking the hint very well, but that was simply because he didn't want to. He had decided that he was going to get back in her life and that was what exactly he intended to do. Wade Lightfoot was a man who could turn the answer "No," into a clear resounding "Yes."

I could go to New York, she thought, chewing her lip. Kirsten had been nagging her to come up for a visit. But she hated New York. Hell, she could hardly stand to go to Louisville anymore.

Besides, the thought of running away galled her.

So what did she do?

What she had to do was make him understand that she wanted nothing to do with him.

But how was she going to do that?

He knew, in that way of his, that she wasn't dating. He figured that left the field wide open for him. He was going to keep coming around until he wore her down.

So how do I keep him from coming around?

Make him mad. Narrow that field a little bit.

His temper didn't appear to flare as easy as it used to, but Nikki figured if she got him mad enough, kept him at a distance, she could handle him. She couldn't handle him coming around, coaxing and wooing.

So she just had to figure out a way to piss him off.

*****

Wade froze in action, his hand hanging limply at his side, instead of reaching for his wallet. The teller at the window repeated, "That will be nine dollars, sir."

Automatically, he paid her, accepted the tickets and moved away. Abby chattered away about the upcoming movie, but for the life of him, he couldn't process anything she said.

Nikki was here, with a tall, lanky man he recognized dimly. It was the guy who owned one of the two repair shops in town. That bastard had one tanned muscular arm wrapped securely around Nikki's waist as he led her into the theater, head bent low, murmuring into her ear.

Son of a bitch, he fumed silently as he let Abby tug

him through the double glass doors and into the line at the snack bar. What in the hell is she doing with that guy?

Searching the lobby, Wade's eyes narrowed as he spotted them in the line next to theirs. He saw red as the guy stroked his hand down Nikki's cheek…and she *smiled* at the guy, a real smile, one Wade hadn't seen in years. A smile that had that lone dimple flashing and her eyes crinkling up at the corners.

His gut churned with jealousy as the two purchased one large popcorn and one large drink. She was going to be sitting next to that guy in the dark, sharing a buttery tub of popcorn and a drink, and she wouldn't give Wade the time of day. How in the hell could she do this? Why in the hell would she do this?

Not only that, she was dressed up in a killer little dress that left a lot of arm and leg bare, and left very little to the imagination. It was a deep apricot color and it displayed a lithe toned body and made her skin glow. Her full mouth was painted the same shade and her eyes were made up to look huge and slumberous. She'd pulled her hair up into a loose knot and long sparkling earrings danced and gleamed as she cocked her head to look up at him.

Impotent fury swelled in him as he watched them leave the lobby, but it paled next to the rage he felt as they walked side by side into a theater that was showing a sexy new thriller. Just three days ago he had asked her to go see it with him and she had said she wasn't interested.

Movies don't do much for me any more, Wade, she'd said, voice cool and disinterested.

Through an hour and a half of Disney cartoon antics, Wade sat rigidly, his hands clenching and unclenching as he thought of the two in the theater next door. How long had she been seeing him? Why hadn't she said anything? Why hadn't he seen them together before now?

Why was he sitting there when he could be one theater over, murdering the bastard with his bare hands? As an animated shark insisted he was a vegetarian, and all the kids in the theatre laughed in delight, all Wade could think about was making the man next door into a girl.

Drumming his fingers on the armrest, staring blindly at the screen, he simmered and stewed. Wade calmed himself down again, and then an image of Nikki linking hands with the slack-jawed hick had him gritting his teeth all over again.

She wasn't serious about this guy. She couldn't be. Wade remembered how she had melted against him, unwillingly as she may have been. And the hot need that had burned in her eyes. Needs she didn't want to have, but couldn't stop.

She wasn't immune to him.

He calmed himself on the drive home. This was the first time he'd seen them together. In fact, Nikki was always alone. So maybe this was just a one-time thing. After all, she wasn't completely indifferent to him and as honest as she was, if she was serious about this guy, she would have told him.

Hell, Nikki would rejoice in telling him she was unavailable, not that it would have stopped him. She would have rubbed in it his face time and time again, just like a sadistic slave master would rub salt in the wounds of his slaves.

No… there was nothing going on. Right?

He'd calmly go talk to her the next day while Abby went on a picnic with the twins next door. And if he didn't like the answers he heard, he would simply lock her in a room somewhere until she came to her senses.

Only the next day, she wasn't home. Nor was she at home that night.

*****

Dale grinned down at Nikki as he led her to his restored Thunderbird convertible, away from the Italian restaurant. "He looks like he's ready to rip my head off. Maybe I ought to start collecting hazard pay."

Nikki settled into the leather seat before replying, "He's generally not the violent type, Dale. I think you're safe." Wheedling and pleading, she had coaxed Dale Stoner into going along with her for a few weeks as she attempted to discourage Wade.

"Y'know," Dale had drawled, watching her with deep lazy blue eyes. "Y'could always tell him that you just aren't interested."

Those lazy blue eyes saw too much and rather than try to lie and say she wasn't interested, she had given a noncommittal shrug. Jerking her mind back to the present, she listened as Dale continued to warn her she was playing with fire.

"Under normal circumstances, he isn't violent,"

Dale said, slowly, thoughtfully. Reaching up, he scratched his head, ruffling the sun streaked blonde hair with long agile fingers. "Now let me see. You've gone out of your way to go out with me every weekend. You even went to the church picnic, figuring you'd see him there. And you're dragging me into this mess. He's seeing you with some jackass and you won't hardly speak to him. You're driving him insane with jealousy. Are these normal circumstances?"

"You're not a jackass," Nikki replied, ignoring the rest of his speech.

"That's not what he thinks. Hell, he probably wakes up every morning, fantasizing about sending me to the glue factory."

Nikki patted him on the arm. "Don't worry. I'll protect you."

He chuckled and asked, "Who's going to protect you? He looks like he's ready to haul down your drawers and spank you silly." Then he shot her a sideways look and said, "Of course, if I was him, and I got your drawers down, spanking you would be the last thing on my mind. Well, maybe not the last thing, but definitely not the first thing."

Her face heated and she muttered, "Shut up, you idiot."

"Your wish is my command, milady," he swore, starting the car and rolling down the window. "But just in case, I want to be buried wearing my Grateful Dead T-shirt."

Nearly a month later, Wade watched grimly as Stoner once again led Nikki away from him. She had deigned to smile politely at him and Abby that time, but only after the little girl had squealed out her name in the middle of the restaurant.

This time, she wore a dusky rose colored dress, with a skirt that swirled around her hips as she walked. Wade's jaw ached from clenching as he noticed how many other males had noticed that short flirty skirt and her long legs. The straps, less than an inch wide, went over strong smooth shoulders, to crisscross in back over a long sexy back.

How in the hell had she ended up looking like that? How could a woman who was only five foot four have legs that went on endlessly and a long slim back that just cried out to stroked?

Worst of all, that full, made for sex mouth was painted a dark glossy rose that curved up often in a smile for that bastard. More than once, the bastard had covered that mouth with his own, for the briefest of moments.

She had let that bastard pour her wine and had giggled over things he whispered in her ear. Wade couldn't even get her to smile at him.

A month had gone by. A month of seeing them together at least once a week, if not twice. The jealousy that ate at him was like acid and he could taste it in the back of his throat as he mechanically smiled and talked with the twins' parents. He shouldn't have come. They had invited him and Abby to join them for the little girls' birthday dinner and he should have just sent Abby.

That way he could have sat at home and just brooded about thoughts of those two together. Instead he had been forced, yet again, to watch them together.

Wade closed his eyes as the doors slid shut behind them and cursed silently as images rose to taunt him. She hadn't even looked back in his direction, even though he stared a hole in her naked back.

Nikki had said she wasn't interested in starting a relationship with him. Was it because she was more interested in starting a relationship with somebody else?

Wade sat in the shadows of the porch, staring into the darkness. She wasn't home yet and it was nearly midnight. He knew because he had been sitting here waiting for her.

Nikki was out with him again. No big surprise, he knew. She had been out with Dale Stoner nearly every weekend for the past two months.

He would give it an hour more then he was going looking for her. And God help them both if they were at the mechanic's house.

A tiny little voice in his head berated him while he sat brooding.

You're being an idiot. She doesn't want you. Haven't you figured that out by now?

Shut up, he thought, grinding the heels of his hands into his eye sockets. *Just shut up.*

"He can't have her," Wade said aloud

But she wants him. Not you.

"Too damn bad," he snarled, rising to his feet and pacing. He'd wear a damn hole in this wood if she wasn't home soon.

Wade was right there waiting for her to settle down and let the past go, and she was running around with Stoner.

And God help that guy if he tried to go inside with her.

God help them both if—

Down the hill gravel crunched. And he could see headlights. He retreated back to his shadowed corner, waiting.

*****

Nikki sat quietly in the seat. Dale was acting... odd. Even for him. In fact, the past few nights they'd been out, he had been acting different. And she couldn't figure out what could be wrong. He didn't seem mad, but he wasn't exactly happy either.

Out of the silence, he said, "I want to come inside. I need to talk to you."

She turned her head, but could hardly see anything in the darkness of the car. "Okay," she said, her voice cautious. "Is something wrong, Dale? Are you having trouble finishing up the faerie tales you've been working on?"

"No," he said, his voice rough. "Not a damn thing wrong with the stories. Unless you consider a hillbilly mechanic who fancied himself a storyteller a little strange."

"You're not a hillbilly, and there's nothing wrong with being a mechanic. Hell, I was a high school kid who that fancied herself a storyteller," she said, her brows lowering over her eyes at the cynicism she heard in his voice.

"You're different," he murmured, a soft sigh

escaping him.

"No, I'm not. I want to tell stories. You want to tell stories. We both do it...that's what we are. No difference, at all."

The silence stretched out until Nikki just couldn't take it any more. "Dale, something's up," she said flatly as he pulled into her drive. "Anything I can help with?" she asked.

Dale laughed, the sound totally without humor. "Yeah, there's something wrong. And you could help, if you wanted."

As she waited for him to come around the car, she ran her tongue over her lips. Her gut was feeling tight and raw and it didn't help any as she saw the look in his eyes as he helped from the car. Ever the gentleman, Dale was. But this time, after helping her alight from the car, he didn't release her hand. In fact, he tugged her closer, grasped her chin and lifted her face. "Yeah, there's something wrong," he repeated. "This."

And then he fit his mouth over hers while Nikki stood there motionless. Shocked. Stunned.

Oh, hell.

Gentle strong hands cupped her face and Dale rained loving kisses over her face while she stood passively, unsure of what to do. "I can't keep doing this, Nicole," he groaned, burying his face in her neck, his strong arms locked around her back. "I can't. You're all I've thought about for years and it's killing me to be this close to you, knowing you don't want me for anything more than a friend."

Hard, hot hands trailed over her shoulders and arms, caressed her back as he whispered, "From the moment I saw you, I wanted you. Every moment since."

Nikki had to strain to hear him as he whispered into her hair. As he sought her mouth again, hot little darts of pleasure raced through her. He was so warm, felt so good against her. And he was safe. Dale wouldn't ever hurt her. She had felt enough love in her life to know what it was like to receive it and there was love and heat twined together in his embrace.

"Just give me half a chance, Nikki. I swear, I'll make you happy," he promised.

It was tempting.

So tempting.

She was so lonely…

She couldn't. Tempting or not, lonely or not, she couldn't do it. It wouldn't be fair to him, and he deserved so much more than a woman with only half a heart.

"Dale, I can't," she whispered, freeing her mouth, and turning her head aside. "I just can't. I'm sorry, but…"

"Nikki, please—"

Reaching between them, she rested her fingers against his mouth, shaking her head. "Dale, I can't. I'm sorry. This wasn't fair to you," she said quietly, putting distance between them as they spoke. "And as much as I would like to, as flattering as it is, it's no good. I'm not whole. I can't give you everything

"Which means I can't give you anything, because you deserve so much better," she finished softly, sadly. *If it had been my choice, it would have been you,* she thought. Her eyes showed her deep regret and her hand, gentle and strong, dropped to grip his once before backing away.

Staring at his almost poetically beautiful face, she shook her head and repeated once more, "I can't."

"But I want you," Dale said, his voice whisper rough, his hands gentle and caring as he eased her back against him. "I'll take whatever you can give me. I just want you"

With a sad faraway look in her eyes, Nikki smiled at him. "If I've learned one thing in my life, it's that we can't always have what we want. I'm sorry, Dale." She reached up, cupped his cheek in her hand. "If I could have chosen, Dale, I would have chosen you. You mean so much to me. You got me through some very rough times, and I'll never forget that.

"But I can't be what you want. Or what you think you want."

"I know how I feel. I know what I want and don't want."

"Yes, I guess you do. And I know what I can't give. I am sorry, Dale."

Dale stroked her cheek, his own eyes sad and wistful. "So am I. Does he have any idea how big a fool he was to let you go?" he murmured, shaking his head.

*****

Wade stood in the shadows, unable to breathe, unable to see, his anger was so great, so deep. He was touching her, kissing her, and she was letting him. His gut roiled and churned and blood pounded thickly in his head. Hands clenched and unclenched spasmodically. He had one hand on the railing, ready to leap, when Nikki pulled back, shaking her head.

What were they saying? They spoke too quietly for him to hear. Heads bent close together, the mechanic's large hands were holding her as if she were made of the finest porcelain, they spoke quietly in low whispers.

Nikki touched her hand to Stoner's face and shook her head. She was telling him no, Wade realized as Stoner pulled away, his hand lingering on her cheek for a moment before he got in his car, drove away.

Wade moved quietly, until he was standing at the head of the steps, and waited for her to turn around. He didn't know what he was going to say now, but only one thing mattered.

She had sent him away.

Moments passed, and still, she stood there, hugging herself tightly, shoulders slumped, head hanging low. A picture of total desolation.

"Have a good time?" he finally asked when Nikki continued to stare in the darkness. His voice was silky, his eyes bland. Only he could tell that he was quivering inside with both rage and relief.

Nikki jumped, startled. Her hair swung around her face as she spun to face him, her eyes wide. Hands went up, clenched and ready, until she recognized the voice, the vague shadow standing there.

"Wade!" she gasped, her voice slightly shaky.

He continued to stare at her, at her slightly swollen soft mouth, at her sleepy eyes. Another man had touched her, had made her looked lazy and satisfied. How many times had the bastard put that look her face? How many nights had she spent in his arms while Wade suffered and sweated them out alone, aching and miserable?

"What are you doing here?" she asked, flatly, her arms falling to her sides, hands still clenched, ready for battle.

"Waiting for you to come home." He moved down the stairs and closer until he stood only two feet away. "Out awful late, aren't you, Nik?"

"What business is it of yours?" Nikki demanded, her voice cool, her chin going up in the air.

Catching that stubborn chin in his hand, he ignored her remark as he studied her face. "Tell me, Nikki. Are you going to make him wait a year to get you in bed? Or is that on the schedule for the next date?"

"I don't answer to you," she said, her voice low and angry. "Now why don't you get the hell off my property?"

"Why? Is lover boy heading back up here?"

"If he is, it's no business of yours," Nikki replied, icicles dripping from her voice as she rooted through her purse for her keys

"I see him here again, I'm gonna tear him apart," Wade drawled, his voice friendly, his smile bright, and vicious. "And then I'll lock you up and throw away the key."

Locating the keys, she snorted and moved around him. "Get over it, buddy. I'm not yours. That's over with. In the past"

"It's our past, present and future, doll," Wade

promised, following her up the stairs. He trapped her by the door as she fumbled with the lock. "And I've learned from past mistakes so the future is bound to be better."

"Wade, I don't see how my future could be worse than my past," she said calmly, finally unlocking the double locks on her door. "However, I don't see how my future has anything to do with you."

Temper suddenly gone, Wade lowered his head to nuzzle at her neck as she spoke. Gently, he nipped at her earlobe and smiled to himself when she shuddered.

"Everything you ever do in life is going to have something to do with me," he said quietly, catching hold of the doorknob and holding it firmly shut. He lowered his head enough to speak quietly against her ear, not touching her, but standing close enough that the scent of her swam in his head.

"Just as everything I do will somehow include you. We're part of each other, Nik, the same way my heart is a part of me, the way your brain is part of you. It's been that way for years, even when we were miles apart and I was married to someone else"

Nikki said nothing, just stood there, her back to him, her head lowered. Gently, Wade made her turn, lifted her chin in his hand and stared into carefully blank eyes.

"I love you," he whispered. "I never expected to see you again. But I've always known that I'd go to my grave loving you. Can you tell me that you don't feel the same?"

*****

*To the grave...*his words echoed over in her head. Hell, yes, she'd die loving him. She had already been to the edge once, though, because of his love. She wouldn't ever let herself get that way again.

Nikki's eyes slid shut and she turned her head, the smooth sweep of hair hiding her face from him. "What I feel for you is not what I felt eight years ago. Or even five years ago," she murmured, her throat burning. Gathering her courage, she turned her head and met his eyes and said, "Things change, Wade. Feelings can change. Especially when somebody rips your heart out of your chest and smashes it. It makes it much easier for feelings to change. Or disappear altogether."

Damn you, Wade, she thought, half hysterically. *Just leave.* Nikki knew damn well there was no way she was going to be able to keep her distance if he kept this up.

Cupping her cheek in his hand, he asked softly, "Do you really expect me to believe that you feel nothing for me?"

"It really doesn't matter what you believe, Wade. It only matters what I believe," Nikki stated simply. She forced a sympathetic smile when sympathy for him was the last thing she felt.

"Poor Wade," she clucked, shaking her head. "You lose a silly little girl who adored you and gained a wife who only wanted to own you. Once she had you, she probably didn't even know what to do with you."

Ducking out of his arms, she moved a few feet away, sliding him a sly glance from under her lashes.

"How was your little virgin bride, Wade? Did she keep you happy?"

The porch light illuminated his face enough for Nikki to watch his jaw clench and his eyes narrow. But he continued to stand there, like he had no intention of ever leaving. "Now the wife's gone and you think you can get that silly girl back." Nikki moved closer to him and gently patted his cheek like he was a five-year-old child.

"It's a pity that you just can't accept the fact that little girl doesn't exist any more. Even more pitiful is the fact that I would have been anything you wanted me to be, given up anything, become anything," she whispered passionately. "Life's not very fair, is it?"

"Nice try, Nikki," he said, his voice hollow. "I'm very impressed. You can be quite the bitch when you want."

"I've developed a number of talents over the years," she said calmly, even though her heart was pounding away within her chest.

"Obviously. You never used to lie so well." He caught her chin in his hand and arched her face up to his, lowering his mouth until not even air separated her lips from his. And he hung there, waiting, for a long moment.

"Fortunately," Wade whispered, his breath fanning across her face. "I don't give up that easily. I'll be around, Nikki"

And then he was gone.

*****

Dylan's long legs trailed out from under Nikiki's Bronco. He cursed loud and long as he attempted to finish doing something or other with her oil. Nikki sprawled on the grass nearby, listening with amusement. For a guy who pretended not to understand simple English, he was very... fluent in certain aspects of the language.

After one particularly inventive phrase, Dylan muttered, "Eureka,' and emerged from beneath her car, liberally covered with grease and grime and God only knew what else. She would never understand the love-hate relationship both of her younger brothers had with motor vehicles. "I suppose you're going to want to come in and clean up," she said, arching a brow at him.

"Considering I saved you a trip into town and some money changing that oil for you, it's the least you can do. And I wouldn't mind supper."

"Don't you have a date or something going on? I thought you and um, Lauren- is it? were going to see a movie," she said, shoving herself to her feet and stretching

"Cairey. And we broke up"

Cairey... how could I have forgotten that name? she wondered as she lowered her arms carefully to her sides, her muscles still aching. Studying him, she repeated, "Broke up?"

"Yeah."

Waiting silently, Nikki stood there watching him

With his back to her, Dylan finished gathering up his tools, his shoulders lifting and falling as he sighed. Finally, he looked over her shoulder at her and shrugged. "It wasn't working out, Nik. That's all."

Nikki continued to stare at him, her head cocked. A lazy summer breeze drifted by, tugging at her hair as she rocked back on her heels, tucking her hand into her pockets. "It took you eight months to figure that out? You used to be a lot quicker than that."

He sighed, wiping his forehead with his arm before aiming an aggravated glance in her direction. "She was messing around with some guy she met in Frankfort. I didn't know."

"I'm sorry."

Turning his head, Dylan gave her a small smile. "Why? You never liked her. Too shallow, I think you said. Among other things."

"You did like her, or you wouldn't have spent all that time with her," Nikki said, shrugging her shoulders.

"I don't know if I liked her or not. She was really just a way to pass the time. Just interested in having some fun. That was all I wanted. But I'd just as soon not have fun with her on Friday," he finished cynically, his eyes cold, "And on Saturday, she has fun with some college kid in Frankfort."

Nikki followed him into the house, wondering if she sounded as bitter and world-weary as he did. Probably worse.

Nearly an hour later, Dylan mentioned Wade's name.

Nikki froze momentarily, then she went about adding milk to the potatoes as she listened to him. She watched her hands, making sure they stayed steady. Dylan didn't miss much these days, she knew.

"I saw him and his little girl in the store. Looks like he's settled in, Sis," Dylan said, leaning back so that his chair was propped on the two rear legs.

"It would appear that way, especially since they've been here all summer," Nikki said dryly. "Feeling guilty you didn't throw him a housewarming?"

"Naw. But I thought you might be," Dylan said, shrugging his shoulders. "Seeing as how you two were so close. Pretty little girl."

"Yes. I know." Without even closing her eyes, Nikki could picture that little girl. So much like Jason. Her eyes started to sting with tears that she quickly blinked away.

"Are you going to tell him?" Dylan asked, his voice close.

Nikki went still as he rested a hand on her shoulder. Her head fell forward and she sighed. "No. It doesn't concern him."

"He was Jason's father. How can it not concern him?"

"Because he wasn't there. He had his own little girl to raise. Jason was mine," she whispered savagely.

Mine. He wasn't there, Dylan. I had to do it alone. I am not going to share it with him now, so he can try to put together the pieces when there's really nothing left," Nikki said, her voice harsh. She shrugged away his hand, moving aside.

"He ought to know."

"No. I'm not going to dredge it up back up merely to satisfy a father's rights. It would hurt me too much and I'm just now healing," Nikki snapped, her eyes flashing at him her younger brother. "If Jason had lived, maybe it would be different. I could handle it if Wade found out and wanted to be involved in his life. But Jason is gone; my memories are all I have of him. And I shouldn't have to share those with somebody who didn't even know he existed. And it doesn't concern you, so I suggest you stay out of it."

Dylan held his hands up and backed away, silently saying, *'your call'*. But I don't agree with you.

He didn't have to agree. He just had to keep his mouth shut.

*****

Sweat poured down the back over her neck, over her shoulders, to pool into her bra as she pedaled the bike up and over the crest of the hill. As the road leveled out, Nikki wiped a gloved hand over her forehead and tried to steady her breathing. Sports bra, tank top and bike shorts were all soaked with sweat. The muscles in her legs were quivering so badly she could barely keep her feet on the pedals.

Three hours on twisting hilly roads did more to improve her state of mind than anything else could. It had the added benefit of making her so damn tired, she'd probably collapse on her bed and sleep like the dead.

After two sleepless nights and restless days, she'd have given almost anything for one peaceful night of rest.

She rounded the final curve and stifled a groan as the trees gave way to reveal her home and the shiny black Ford Ranger. So much for falling into bed right after a quick shower and meal.

Nikki gritted her teeth as she swung off the bike by the porch. She paused only long enough to make sure her shaky legs would hold her before she pushed the bike onto the wooden deck.

Wade and little Abby were perched on the porch swing, moving idly back and forth. She was suddenly the focus of two pair of dark eyes, one shy hesitant smile from the little girl, and a bright easy smile from Wade.

"I don't recall inviting you up here, Wade," she said coolly and she opened the front door. Cool air rushed out to meet her and she sighed in relief as she moved inside. Behind her back, she didn't see the two of them look at each other, or Wade as he sighed and shrugged before scooping Abby into his arms and following her.

"I didn't know you still rode," he said after catching up with her in the kitchen.

After draining a glass of water, she turned her head, leveled out the hostility in her eyes before saying, "I was riding before I ever met you. I like it. I didn't do it simply because you did."

Then she forced a deep calming breath into her lungs before giving Abby a tired smile. "How are you doing, Miss Abby?"

"Okay," Abby whispered, looking all around. "You have a pretty house."

"Thank you," Nikki responded, her smile a bit more relaxed. It hurt so bad just to look at the child, but at the same time, it somehow soothed her battered heart. "I like it myself. There a TV through there, if you'd like to watch some cartoons." She pointed in the direction of the living room, wishing she were callous enough to dislike the child simply because of who her mother was.

Moments later, the child was safely stowed away in the living room, watching talking mice, Nikki returned to the kitchen. She splashed cool water on her overheated face and dried it before turning her eyes to the man sitting negligently at her table. His legs sprawled out before him and in one hand, he had a can of soda.

"Why don't you make yourself at home?" she drawled, her voice sugar sweet. She soaked a rag with cool water and lifted it to her nape, swiping her neck and chest and arms with it, taking perverse pleasure as his eyes heated.

"Don't mind if I do," he returned, sipping at the drink and winking at her over the rim. His eyes, however, lacked the lightheartedness that was in his words.

As she pressed the cloth to back of her neck, Nikki closed her eyes, trying hard to ignore him, but it was hard. She could feel his eyes on her as she swiped the cool rag over her hot flesh.

The pounding of her heart had nothing to do with him, she insisted. It was from the exercise, only the exercise.

"Need some help?" Wade offered, his voice going low and rough as her eyes opened and she studied him, her face flushed and damp, body gleaming slightly from her exertions.

Recognizing the look in his eyes, Nikki stopped playing with fire and threw the cloth into the sink. "What are you doing here, Wade?" she asked flatly, crossing her arms over her chest and leaning against the counter.

"I came to see you, of course."

"Why?" she asked, her eyes narrowed. Hostility all but radiated from her.

"Must be the charming company," he said, dryly, her anger rolling off his back. He had been in high spirits for several weeks now. Nikki hadn't been seen around town with Stoner since that last weekend.

Little rumors were floating around, that the guy was packing up and leaving town. A For Sale sign posted at the garage confirmed said rumors and he had grinned for an hour after he had seen that. "You being such a gracious hostess and all."

"You really can't take a hint, can't you?"

"You shouldn't be surprised to see me here, Nikki. I told you I wasn't giving up," he reminded her.

"I didn't say I was surprised. Disappointed is more like it." Running a fingertip over the rim of her discarded glass, she studied him quietly from under the shield of her lashes. And then she softly asked, "Don't you think you've done enough?"

His cheeks flushed a dull red and he looked away, sighing. "I guess I deserve that."

"And worse," Nikki added quietly.

"You're making this as hard as you can, aren't you?" Wade demanded, resisting the urge to slam his own glass down on the table. Carefully, he sat it down and stood, his hands going into his back pockets.

"Nik, I'm not going away. You might as well get used to that."

"Oh, you'll go away. Sooner or later, you'll figure out that I'm not who I used to be and I'm not somebody you want to be around." Somber hazel eyes drifted to the sound of childish laughter coming from the living room and she said, "Certainly not somebody you want your daughter around."

"You've always loved kids. And I've never seen a kid you couldn't enchant. Why wouldn't I want you around her?" he asked, watching her.

Nikki turned away, gazing out the window. Finally, she turned her head to him and her hazel eyes were sad. "I'm too morose, Wade. I never think about anybody but myself. I'm grouchy and depressing. I could talk an optimist in his grave within ten minutes. I bury myself in my writing for weeks and could happily ignore the rest of the world, if they'd just ignore me"

He had risen as she spoke and now was moving up beside her, cornering her between his body and the counter. As he moved closer, he saw the alarm in her eyes, and braced himself. She always struck out when she was feeling threatened.

Never one to disappoint, she tossed her head back. In a voice as cold as winter, she said, "And I can't look at you or your child without seeing her and remembering what you did."

Cupping her cheek in his hand, Wade sighed and softly said, "I'm not here to remind you of what I did. I just want to be with you."

I just want to be with you…

Those words tore at her heart. He made it sound so easy…

"Being with you does remind me," she snarled, slapping a hand against his chest as he leaned closer. The heat of his body rushed out and filled hers, making her feel more overheated than three hours of trail riding ever could. His eyes, so full of love and promises, seemed to mock her.

Wade was so full of life.

And she was so empty.

"You are making my life a living hell. Don't you think I've had enough of that?" she demanded, her voice shaking with the rage and pain she lived with.

His eyes glittered, the only proof that her words had any effect. Slowly, Wade leaned down and brushed a light kiss across her flushed cheek. "I don't want to hurt you. I never wanted to. I'll never do it again."

"Then stay the hell away from me!" Nikki cried, jerking her head back away from his. Shoving both hands against his chest, Nikki tried move him away, but he wouldn't budge. "You hurt me just by being around me. Stop coming around. Why in the hell are you still coming around?" she demanded helplessly.

"I keep coming around because I love you. And you love me," he whispered, covering her hands with his and leaning down to kiss her averted mouth. One hand caught and held her chin as he rained kisses over her cheeks and closed eyes. "I messed it up the first time, doll. But can't I have a second chance? I'll never hurt you again."

As he covered her damp mouth with his, Nikki

quaked. And prayed, first for him to stop. Then for him not to

Wade wrapped his arms around her waist and dragged her closer, dark delight spiraling through him as her arms clamped around his neck and shoulders. He tasted salty sweat and soft skin on his tongue as he trailed a line of kisses down her neck. Helplessly, Nikki rocked against him and he shuddered before gripping her waist and boosting her onto the counter top.

Moving between her legs, Wade rocked against the vee of her thighs as he covered her mouth for another kiss.

His teeth nipped at her lower lip then his tongue darted into her mouth while one hand pulled her hips to the edge of the counter until only cloth separated him from her. Nikki stiffened slightly as he moved against her but he paid it no heed. She wanted him. There was no denying that...and he wanted her, she could taste it in his kiss, feel in the hungry moan that vibrated up from his chest.

Her belly jumped as he ran his hands down her thighs and unwittingly, she wrapped her legs tightly around his hips, never wanting to let go. For a little while...she could forget.

Cupping her breasts in his hands, Wade dragged his thumbs over the nipples, and she mewled as they tightened and throbbed under the sturdy cotton of her sports bra. Her hand went back to balance her weight as he grasped the bottom of her tank top in his hands and pulled.

Blood pounded in his temples as she arched

against him, a weak moan falling from her lips. Mine, was all he could think. After all the time that had passed, she was still his, in every way that counted. Her words might be saying no but her body, her clinging hands, were saying something totally different

One lean hand cupped her, feeling the damp heat through the thin material of spandex. Nikki vibrated under his hand and whimpered as he massaged the heel of his hand against her damp cleft. He lifted his head and watched as her eyes darkened and her breath caught.

Feeling t=Triumphant Wade smiled as she started to convulse under the pressure of his palm. Quickly, he seized her mouth with his just as a rush of liquid warmth soaked both the spandex and his hand.

Mine. And all that mattered was marking her, making certain she knew just how strong his hold on her was.

Intent on peeling that spandex from her, Wade delved his hands inside her clinging shorts, wanting her naked and open; distantly, the sound of laughter and kid's music penetrated the fog in his brain.

Abby.

"Damn it," he muttered, his head dropping forward to rest on her shoulder. Nikki was shuddering against him, her hands clenching at his shoulders and back. Sweet heaven, Abby. He had totally forgotten his daughter was in the other room, just twenty feet away.

He raised his head looked at Nikki. Her face was flushed, her lips swollen and red from his. Her large dark eyes were soft and unfocused, full of need. Damn it, what timing.

Nikki dropped her head, taking several shaky deep breaths before she released his shoulders and pushed at him. "Let me down," she whispered, her voice faint.

Wade did so, knowing if he didn't move, he would take the chance, regardless of where Abby was. Clumsy, she clambered down, stumbling away from the counter. Quickly, she jerked her tank top back on before moving around until the table separated them and then she turned those dark eyes on him, her lips parted as she drew in deep draughts of air.

"Damn you, Wade," Nikki whispered, her voice rough and unsteady.

Grimacing, Wade agreed silently as he leaned back, adjusting his jeans. He sure as hell wouldn't be doing much sleeping tonight. "Nothing like a little trip down memory lane," he drawled, crossing his arms over his chest and waiting.

"That isn't going to happen again."

"Ever?"

"Absolutely never," she swore, her eyes slowly clearing of the fog.

Nikki kept her hands pressed flat to the table, hoping to hide their trembling. Her knees were weak, watery, and she was having trouble staying upright. Hot molten need still flowed through her veins and her loins throbbed.

Idiot. Fool. Why did you let that happen? She asked herself, staring at him from the relative safety of ten feet away, across the solid oak of the dining table. "Never," she repeated, her voice certain.

Too damn bad she didn't feel as certain as she sounded. Her knees still felt like water and her brains like mush. Even the thought of what just happened was enough to make her want to whimper with need. All he had done was touch her and she had exploded

"That's an awfully long time," Wade mused, drawing one knee up and looping his thumbs through the loops of his belt. His erection strained against the worn denim that cupped him, his stance was cocky and arrogant, his smile full of promise, eyes glinting with need and humor.

Just looking at him made her mouth go dry.

And he wasn't helping, as he cocked his head and studied her with hot eyes. Eyes that studied her flushed face and trailed down her neck to focus on her tank where her nipples thrust against the sturdy cotton. The corner of his mouth quirked up in a slight smile as Wade added, "Especially considering your body would like nothing more than for me to come over there and finish what we started."

"What you started."

"I wasn't alone in that, Nikki. I wasn't kissing myself," he drawled, scratching his chin. "One of us just climaxed and it certainly wasn't me."

"It won't happen again," she said, clenching her jaw.

"Why not?"

"Because I won't let it," she answered, her chin rising.

"Why won't you let it?"

"Because it isn't going to change anything. I'm happy with my life the way it is and I don't want you in it"

"You know something, Nik? I look at you and get the feeling that you've forgotten what it's like to be happy. We were happy together once, Nikki," Wade reminded her. His heavy lidded eyes and long smoldering look reminded her of things long past, but hardly forgotten. "Do you remember that? There was a time when we all we needed was each other to be perfectly satisfied with life."

"That was before I figured out what real life is, Wade," she said coldly, dredging the memory of long nights spent alone. Of a stormy day when she had lost everything. Of rainy days in which she prayed to forget. And of a tiny little grave twenty miles away.

The backlash of pain that welled up inside her nearly knocked her to her knees. She had lost everything that had mattered. She couldn't let anything matter again. She'd never survive if she lost it all again.

Speaking of it, thinking of it, was like opening a floodgate. Nikki had refused to let herself think of it, bottling it all up inside, and, now, it was ready to be set free. If she couldn't control the pain, then she would use it.

Harshly, Nikki said, "You don't know what you did to me. You destroyed me. You tore out my heart and soul and I still haven't recovered from it." The pain spread throughout her entire body, leaving her weak and trembling, throat tight, hands shaking from the raging emotions.

"Nikki—"

"Don't say anything, not a single thing, to me,

Wade. There is nothing you can say that could make up for what I lost. You can't even begin to comprehend what I lost. But even if you could," she whispered, dashing away tears that leaked over, "it would change nothing. Nothing would ever make up for it."

"I want the chance to try."

She started. She hadn't even realized that he had come closer until she felt his hand resting on her shoulder.

"Talk to me," he whispered, cajoled. "Tell me."

Tell him?

Tell him?

She shouldn't have to tell him, he should already know, because he should have been there with her when it happened. *I shouldn't have had to go through that alone.* But she couldn't tell him that. He would have no clue as to what she was talking about.

Closing her eyes, Nikki shook her head. "There's nothing to tell, Wade. You told me everything in glorious detail five years ago. If you can't figure out what's wrong, then you have something seriously wrong with you."

"Don't give me that," he rasped, shaking her gently. "I know you. I know you inside and out, remember?" His voice dropped, intensified. "I know you love me. I know that you want me."

"Wrong. I don't want this! My body might, but I don't. I will never want it." Shrugging his hands away, wrapping her arms around herself, Nikki turned and stared out over her land. Then she closed her eyes. "I don't ever want to care about anybody like I cared for you. I don't ever want to love again. Those kind of emotions give others power over you. The power to destroy. Like you destroyed me."

Wade's hands froze in the act of reaching for her, to draw her back against him, but the honestl and the pain in her words pierced his heart and left him bleeding inside. His hands clenched impotently into fists as they fell to his sides, empty still.

Looking at him over her shoulder, her eyes so empty and so lifeless, Nikki swallowed and spoke around the knot in her throat. "Get out of my house, Wade. Get off my property and don't come back."

She heard him sigh. Heard him leave the room. As the door shut gently, Nikki closed her eyes against a fresh onslaught of tears.

It took every last bit of strength she had left in her not to reach out to him.

Chapter Six

Wade sat on the couch, a can of lukewarm beer forgotten in his grasp.

Haunted eyes, so full of pain, were tearing at him. Nikki had looked at him as though he had cut her heart out. And he knew he had. But it had been so long ago. He hadn't imagined the pain would still be so fresh. He hadn't bargained on seeing that agony in her eyes.

The girl Wade had known had been tough, smart, and so full of pride, almost arrogant; she would never have let him do this to her. Nothing Wade or anybody else had done could have put that look of hopelessness and despair in her eyes.

Nikki had always been so strong, so self-assured. He had figured after a little time had passed, she would have decided, Screw him. He wasn't worth it, and she would have gotten on with her life.

Wade hadn't expected to find her closed up in her extravagant house on the hill, shut away from everybody but her father and brothers.

And he couldn't get over the feeling that she wasn't sharing it all with him.

There was a time when she had told him everything, when they had tried to solve their problems together.

Nikki didn't want that any more.

But Wade had a feeling that was what she needed.

She had to let the past go, because it was destroying her. Even if in the end, nothing else came of it, Wade had to try to get her to let it go. He owed her that much.

The darkened room hid the misery in his eyes as he replayed her words over in his mind.

Haven't you done enough?

You destroyed me.

I still haven't recovered.

You have no idea what you did to me.

Yeah, he did. He had ruined her life. Raising his beer in silent salute, Wade toasted himself and his ability to destroy the lives of women he cared for.

Jamie lay cold in the ground for nearly three years now.

Nikki had given up on her dreams. She might be the writer she had always dreamed of being, but it hadn't made her happy. Nothing seemed to really make her happy. And he was the cause of it.

Even more guilt to pile on his conscience.

No wonder he couldn't sleep at night.

However, he sure as hell wasn't giving up.

*****

Nikki now understood what it felt like to be stalked. Every place she went, he was there. Church. The bookstore. The library. The gas station. Wade and his beautiful sweet little girl that made her heart ache every time Nikki saw her. She pulled into the grocery store lot and prayed she would get in and out before he tracked her down there. Again.

Of course, five minutes later, she would have been happy even with Wade's company.

"Dinner, Miss Kline?" David Ellis repeated,

walking far too close for her comfort. His overpowering cologne was making her feel slightly queasy. Her head already ached, and the feel of his cold dry hand on her elbow made her skin crawl.

Elbowing him in the gut, she sidestepped him and went around as she snapped, "How many times can I possibly tell you that I'm not interested?"

He smoothed a hand down his tie and gave her a look that clearly said, 'how could you not be interested?' His smile was big, white, almost blinding in its intensity. It was also the most phony thing she had seen since the 'diamond' necklace Shawn had once given her as a gag gift.

"Nicole, all I want to is to take you out to dinner. Just a few hours of your time, some conversation. Nothing much. Just a nice quiet evening.'

"And top it off with a night of rowdy sex?" she asked dryly, rolling her eyes.

Before he could respond, she walked away. "I've more interest in dating a toad than you. Get the point?"

His answer was lost when he stumbled into a display of ice cream cones, sending them crashing to the floor. Nikki left him smooth talking the irate stock girl and headed down the frozen food aisle.

From the frying pan into the fire, she thought morosely as she ran headlong in Wade. Her voice was flat, expressing her irritation as she asked, "Are you following me?"

Before he could answer, Abby announced, "He saw your truck. And then he remembered he needed some food to fix tonight."

Wade clapped a hand over his daughter's mouth and had the decency to look sheepish.

Nikki took a deep breath, counted to ten and pushed past him. She offered Abby a small smile and asked, "How are you doing, Miss Abby?"

"Okay," Abby answered, smiling brightly. Then her brow furrowed and she cocked her head. "Do you know Daddy talks about you when he sleeps?"

Amused, Nikki turned her eyes to find Wade blushing a deep shade of red. "Oh, does he now?" she asked, chuckling as she added a gallon of milk to her basket.

"Honey, do you know how to be quiet?" Wade asked, shifting from one foot to the other.

Abby looked up at him and shrugged. "It's true. I came into your room last night after I had the bad dream." Flashing Nikki a sweet smile, she added, "Daddy is real good at keeping the bad dreams away. I climbed up into bed and you were tossing and turning all over. Then you made a funny sound and said 'Nikki' real funny like." Her face puckered in a frown as she asked, "Were you having a nightmare, Daddy? You sounded awful funny."

The painful red blush staining his lean cheeks left no doubt in her mind what kind of dream he had been having.

"Talking in your sleep can be real enlightening, Wade," Nikki said. Her eyes danced in amusement as his obvious discomfort. "All sorts of interesting secrets slip out."

His lids lowered and the discomfort was suddenly Nikki's as he whispered, "Hardly a secret." Abby had spotted a friend from Daycare and was waving at her from across the aisle. While she was distracted, his eyes burned into hers, telling her exactly what kind of dreams he had been having.

Mouth dry, heart pounding, Nikki looked away. She knew what kind of dreams he was having, the same kind she had been having off and on for weeks now and lately, dreams that left her so empty and aching that even taking a shower or laying down nude on the bed intensified the need until she felt ready to shatter.

Giving up the pretense of shopping now that he had her attention, Wade abandoned the empty cart and scooped his daughter up into his arms. She waved goodbye to her friend before smiling over at Nikki. "We're having 'sagna tonight. Wanna eat with us?"

"Ah..."

"Why don't you, Nik?" Wade asked, grinning at her. "I can tell you about my dreams. You can tell me all about yours."

Nikki's face flushed as she headed for the checkout line. And she stifled the urge to laugh when Abby offered, "I dream about being an 'astr'naut and flying in space. And having a dog," Stroking the stuffed dog she carried everywhere, she added, "A real dog, not a stuffed one."

Abby's eyes were gleaming with a hopeful light as she said, "We had to leave my dog back at my old home. He was my grandma's dog really."

"What do you say, Nikki? Dinner?" As he spoke, Wade moved to help unload the groceries, and he took the opportunity to whisper in her ear, "We could see about making those dreams a reality." His hand reached out and traced the line of her throat and he smiled slowly as goosebumps raced down her arms, followed by a rush of heat through her middle.

To her horror, her nipples tightened and pressed against the silk of her camp shirt. And he noticed. His eyes locked briefly with her before traveling to the evidence that she was hardly immune to him. They darkened and she heard a deep intake of breath, but she didn't know if it was his or hers.

Shaken, Nikki backed away. Right into David Ellis. Now the goosebumps returned for a totally different reason. "Nicole, you forgot all about me back there," David drawled as she moved to extricate herself from his hands. "Did you run into a friend of your brothers?"

"Actually, I'm a friend of Nikki's," Wade corrected, straightening and meeting the taller man's eyes without blinking. "I was trying to talk her into joining us for supper."

"Well, I'm sorry to ruin your plans, but she's made arrangements for dinner with me," Ellis lied smoothly, dismissing the darker skinned, causally dressed man.

Nikki took a deep breath and moved up to the cash register to pay for her groceries. She smiled distractedly down at Abby as the little girl asked, "Who's he?"

"Nobody, honey," Nikki said.

"If he's nobody, why are you eating with him instead of us?"

With gritted teeth, she handed over money and accepted the receipt before she moved to push her cart away. Behind her, the two men were glaring at each other, blocking the aisle as others tried to pay for their food.

Nikki closed her eyes and reached for patience as the two men moved out of the aisle, practically circling each other like a couple of dogs. "I'm not having dinner with him, Abby," she said, loudly, drawing attention her way. "Apparently, the man has lost his mind because I never did, and never would, agree to dinner with him. I'd rather eat with a cannibal than with that man."

Large blue tinted eyes narrowed on her as she nudged Abby toward her father. "And I can't eat with you tonight, Wade. I've got things to do tonight." Flashing a brilliant smile at him, she added, "Like wash my hair. File my nails. Wax the floors. But you two enjoy." She waggled her fingers at them cheerfully.

And then she stormed out of the store, leaving Ellis red faced and trying to gather his dignity.

Behind her, Abby stared up at her dad forlornly as she asked, "Daddy, doesn't she like us?"

"I think maybe she likes us more than she wants to, baby. She just doesn't know it yet," Wade said, dropping a kiss on her head. "Let's go home."

*****

The screen was starting to blur before her eyes. Daire hadn't had an adventure in weeks. Each time Nikki got a page written, which wasn't very often, she would barely glance at it before trashing it.

"Concentrate," she ordered, pressing her fingers to her temple. But the ideas weren't there. They had been few and far between ever since a certain charming dark haired bastard had strolled into her life with his pretty little girl in tow.

Wade had shown up alone at her door the past night. Had nearly charmed her into watching a movie with him. Hell, he had charmed her into it right until he dimmed the lights and an old western came on the screen.

They hated westerns, not that it had stopped them from paying money for them…they had rented them several times a month while they dated. Putting the movie in, dimming the lights, and then making out on the couch for hours.

It had taken her no time to figure out his plans for the evening. It had taken nearly half the evening to get him out of the house. He had been in her mind all night, even after she kicked him out.

Forcing her mind back to the problem at hand, Nikki stared at the distressingly blank screen with its annoying little cursor. With a frustrated groan, she got to her feet and started to pace. "Okay, kid. Let's work this through," she muttered. "Writer's block. You've had it before. No big deal."

Daire just needed something new, she mused. What hadn't he done before? She grinned swiftly. Not much. In the past five years since he had come to life, he had killed dragons, slain evil sorcerers, he had faced death many a time and escaped it laughingly. He had escaped a slave ship and freed the slaves in the process. He had fought wars, fought friends, fought himself, and fought his destiny. He rescued damsels in distress and then loved 'em and left 'em.

Nikki's steps faltered, then slowed to a stop. Cocking her head, she studied the screen, not seeing it, as she thought that last thought through. Loved 'em and left 'em.

That was it. It was simple. So simple.

Daire had yet to meet his match. It was time for the hero to meet the heroine.

The early morning sun shone on her back as she seated herself in the chair. Without a moment's hesitation, she deleted the last three chapters and then settled back to think. Her heroine needed a name.

It was hours and pages later when she settled back in the chair, stiff and sore, but satisfied. Propping her feet on the desk, she spoke into the phone mouthpiece. "That's right, Kris. I changed the whole story line." She stared distractedly at the screen and added an 'h' to change the 'te' to 'the' before replying, "No. Kris. It's not a bowl of mush. In fact, I think it's going to be the best yet."

On the other end of the line, Kirsten demanded, "So what started the fire, sugar? You've been in a major slump for months, now."

"Dunno." Nikki frowned at the screen. Need to rewrite the line there. Then she turned away from the screen to concentrate on the phone. Thunderheads were piling the horizon. A storm was coming.

"So. Was it this boyfriend, Wade that stirred things up?"

"Wade is not a boy, nor is he a friend," Nikki corrected, pinching the bridge of her nose with her fingers. "And it has nothing to do with him."

"He's more than that, isn't he?" Kris asked, softly, "Want to tell me about it?"

"Nothing to tell," Nikki said. "He's determined to pick things up and I want to let them lie." And then she changed the subject by saying, "I think I can have a rough draft in six to eight weeks. I'll have it finished by Christmas. Want to see what I've got before that or just wait until then?"

Nikki heard Kris sigh and she braced herself.

But her friend let it slide, drolly commenting, "You certainly know how to change the subject. So subtle. So tactful. You'll have to face it sooner or later. Changing history or stopping time only works in your books. That doesn't work in real life."

"No. It doesn't. I have to go," Nikki said softly, her eyes burning. She ached to talk about it. To cry about it. But she was afraid if she started, she wouldn't stop.

And then she settled back in her own chair as a heavy torrent of rain started to fall. No, she couldn't change the past. But she sure as hell could keep from repeating it.

*****

Later that day, Nikki stood in front of the floor- to-ceiling windows in her living room, watching the wind whip through the trees. The rain had stopped and hadn't started back up, but it would soon. The watery, eerie green gray light coming through the windows disturbed her. Tornado light.

The knock at the door startled her and she silently prayed, *don't be Wade.*

Nikki nearly threw her arms around Dylan's neck as she opened the door to reveal her younger brothers standing there, arms laden with Chinese take out and movies. "Is this the best you two can do on a Saturday night?" she asked, trying to keep from laughing with relief. "Come and see your sister?"

Without responding, Dylan pushed past her to set the food down, while Shawn displayed his movies. "We have *Tango and Cash, Terminator One* and *Two,* and *Judge Dredd.*" He tossed them on top of the TV before dropping on the sofa and propping booted feet on the coffee table.

Dylan was emptying the bag as he announced, "I've got sweet and sour chicken, chicken curry, and chicken broccoli. Plus a whole mess of fortune cookies."

The brainless entertainment they had brought was welcome, the company even more so. If she was lucky, the storm might pass before she had chance to think about it. But at least she wouldn't have to wait it out alone. "Shawn, get your feet off my table. And Dylan, you call Dad and tell him you two are staying the night."

Shawn opened his mouth to object even as Dylan reached for the phone. But before he could even speak, Nikki silenced him with a look. "It'll be after midnight before these storms pass. You two aren't driving that late at night."

As she helped herself to the chicken curry, thunder rumbled outside the window. It was going to be a bad one. Outside the windows, lightening flickered across the sky. And it was far too dark for five o'clock in the middle of August. Nikki suppressed a shudder as thunder shook the mountain. "Pop in a movie, little brother," she ordered as Dylan hung up the phone, sulking.

Half past three in the morning, the credits rolled after Stallone had roared off into the sunset on his futuristic motorcycle. Nikki thumbed the remote and rubbed at tired eyes. Then she climbed off the couch, leaving Dylan to sprawl over the length of it. Stepping over Shawn's prone form, she paused just long enough to pocket his keys.

On the landing, Nikki paused, unable to see three feet outside the window. The first storm had passed after eight, but before ten, a second had moved in, followed by a third. Each had been more intense than the last. It was supposed to calm by dawn. Because she was so tired, her mind numb, she was able to leave the window without tears welling up in her eyes.

In concession to her brothers, she donned a pair of boxer shorts styled pajamas before crawling into the king size bed. The sand-washed silk felt cool against her already chilled flesh and she quickly burrowed beneath covers. The big bed felt so empty. Hugging a pillow to her chest, she turned her back on the light show going on outside her window. Rain beat against the windows and roof as she huddled in the middle of the big bed, shaking. Whether it was from cold or loneliness, she didn't know.

Closing her eyes, Nikki gave into the weakness inside her and wished for Wade. She wanted him there so badly that had he appeared, she would have forgiven him anything. She just wanted him there, holding her, keeping the painful memories at bay.

A cynical voice reminded her that if it hadn't been for Wade, the memories probably wouldn't be so painful.

Her aching heart told her that she really didn't give a damn.

*****

Thirty miles away, Wade was suffering as well. Rain brought back memories of the last time in the woods, something he hadn't been able to put of his mind. Had it been because it was the last time? Was that what made it so damn unforgettable, what etched it into his mind?

In the past few months, he had tried every viable way to get her to open up, to let him in. Everything from pleading to demanding.

Nikki remained firm. Polite, distant, and, if he could believe her, uninterested. But he didn't believe it, it was just the facade she put in place. From time to time, it slipped, letting him see the raw hunger in her eyes, her need. Nikki still loved him, still wanted him, but she held back, unwilling to trust him.

But Wade was being patient.

Hell, I'm being a damn saint, he thought derisively.

Vivid pictures of laying her down on his huge oak bed had driven him to the couch for the night. But sleep was nowhere to be found. Rain beat against the house as he lay there, unable to sleep, his body tormented by the images his mind wouldn't let go.

What is she doing? Is she awake, like I am? Hungry? Too damn hungry to sleep? He wondered what she slept in. Once he had known the answer to that. Nothing. Nothing at all. The few nights they had spent together, she had slept in his arms, her warm body pressed to his without a single barrier between them.

Groaning, Wade flipped to his back and kicked the sheet off the couch. He was hot, his body aching. Every muscle in his body was rigid with tension, and his aching erection pressed painfully against the fly of the old cut-offs he wore. Damn it, his cock was so damned hard, he hurt with it. And nothing would relieve it, except sinking his length into the hot, wet warmth he knew he'd find between Nikki's thighs.

He had half a mind to leave the house, drive the half an hour to Nikki's and wake her up. Abby was spending the weekend with her grandparents and he wouldn't have to worry about her. He could simply get in his truck and drive, be there before dawn.

"Stop it," he snarled, pressing the heels of his hand to his eyes.

But the image continued to flicker through his mind, taunting, teasing.

Would she welcome him? Half asleep, Nikki would be less likely to remember that she wanted to hate him. He could simply cover her mouth with his and then her body, pulling her beneath him and burying himself inside her before she even had a chance to catch her breath. Before she could wake up enough to remember that she wanted to hate him.

And then he would keep on loving her, keeping her from thinking. Could he do it long enough for her to forget that she wanted him out of her life?

Maybe. For a little while. Would it be long enough to bind her to him and keep her from slipping away like she wanted?

"Sonovabitch," he whispered through clenched teeth. Why did he torture himself like this?

Why keep remembering how sweet she smelled, how soft she was? How perfect she fit against him? If he just thought of it, he could feel her smooth skin under his mouth, and he could remember how she felt under him, over him...the snug glove of her sex gripping his cock as he sank deep inside her.

Damnation, why did he do this?

Because he couldn't stop himself. Everything reminded him of her. The rain reminded him of that last time. Rising with the sun made him remember all the sunsets and sunrises they had watched together. Tucking his little girl in at night made him wish his woman was there with him.

My woman...Nikki was his. She had been from the beginning and nothing had changed that.

Fuck. I need her...

And if he was in this shape, maybe Nikki wasn't much better off.

It was that thought that had Wade rising with the sun yet again, driving into the horizon.

*****

Nicole stood on the porch, leaning against the

column, her silk clad arms wrapped around herself to ward off the slight chill of the early morning. Her eyes stared sightlessly into the sunrise, her mind troubled.

The stormy weather had passed, leaving a breathtakingly beautiful morning, one that made her feel even emptier inside. A cold chill had settled over her body, one that ran gut deep.

Wade…

He haunted her thoughts, her dreams, her every waking moment seemed to revolve around him. She was going out of her mind.

And she was tired of fighting him, fighting herself. Maybe…

"Have you slept?"

She looked over her shoulder to see Shawn padding onto the porch, running a hand though tangled hair. His slid an arm around her shoulder, offering body heat and silent comfort. Too cold and lonely to deny either, she only smiled and said, "A little. Not much."

"Bad dreams?" he asked.

Ducking her chin, she mumbled an answer that was half fiction, half reality.

Teasingly, Shawn asked, "Or were they a different kind of bad dream?"

Scowling, a blush rising up her cheeks, she punched him in the gut and moved away. Quietly, she said, "It stormed nearly all night."

"Sis, it's been three years," he whispered, tucking her again against his side, resting his chin on her crown. "You can't spend the rest of your life hiding in your room with the curtains pulled every time it rains.

You need to let go."

He was right. She knew that. A grown woman just couldn't run to her room and hide every time it stormed. And she had spent most of her night, tossing and turning and thinking about Wade, not Jason. But she hated the rain.

"Letting go isn't the same as forgetting, Shawn. And it's not that easy to do either." She would have said more, but the sound of a motor silenced her. Her shoulders tensed and her gut clenched violently. She knew exactly who it was driving up her mountain when the sun was stilling hugging the eastern horizon.

Damn it. Not now. "I can't deal with him right now," she whispered harshly.

*****

If Wade was startled by the shiny black classic Mustang in the drive, he was absolutely shell shocked at the sight of Nikki standing half naked in the arms of a blond man who held her all too closely, his shirt hanging open. Both were mussed and sleepy eyed. What in the hell was she doing in the arms of another man when it wasn't even seven in the morning?

Bad enough she spent months with that jerk-off. Stoner. But now she was with somebody else?

This is the fucking last draw, baby. Get ready for a show down, he thought furiously as he climbed out of his truck, murder on his mind. If she thought she could go running to another man, she had another thought coming. *Gonna kill that bastard. Who in the hell does he think he is, touching her like that, holding her like he as a right to,* he thought viciously as he took the steps in a single bound.

Nikki stood there sleepy eyed, hair tumbled, face slightly flushed, as if she had just climbed out of bed after a night of loving. Ready to tumble right back into bed for some more.

Over my dead body.

First Dale Stoner, and now this. Cuddling up to the chest of another blond bastard, and it didn't look like she was in a hurry to leave either.

And here he had been imagining her aching to see him. He closed the distance between himself and the bastard he intended to kill with his bare hands.

The soon-to-be corpse ran a hand down a silk covered back and ducked his head to whisper in Nikki's ear. Probably suggesting they go back inside once their visitor was gone. His body practically vibrating with rage, Wade stood motionless as Nicole stepped forward, leaving the blond's arms and staring at Wade with blank eyes.

She stood quietly, her eyes calm, without a trace of guilt or remorse.

Wade could feel it as his heart tore apart, spilling over with bitterness and anger. It didn't even matter to her, that he had found her in the arms of somebody else.

Damn you, he thought, clenching his jaw. *Don't you know you belong with me? In* my *arms?*

She should have spent the night with Wade, and he damned well oughta be the one who was holding her as the sun rose into the clear blue sky. Instead she had been with another man who even now was laughing at him.

And then Wade's black eyes met the greenish hazel eyes of the stranger and the rage drained out of him. Hazel eyes, exactly like Nikki's. And a squared, tougher version of Nicole's soft rounded features. A face so similar to Nicole, they could have identical, except where she had curves, he had only angles.

The youngest Kline. The only one he hadn't come across in the months he had been in Monticello.

"Shawn," he said, his voice slightly hoarse from the residual emotion that had almost eaten him alive. The young punk had grown into a man Wade barely recognized. Formerly long hair was cropped close to his nape, and long sinewy, almost bony arms had thickened with muscle

Okay, so maybe this isn't the smartest thing I've ever done. He should have stayed home where it was nice and safe. And lonely.

Now Shawn looked absolutely delighted at Wade, a wicked gleam lighting his eyes, an unholy smile curving his mouth. Gently, Shawn moved his sister to the side and stepped closer, until he was toe to toe with Wade, all but snarling at the shorter man.

Pride kept him from moving back, even though he knew in a fistfight with Shawn, he was sure to lose. Wade may be able to hold his own in a fight- but Shawn had damn near written a handbook on street fighting. Wade had seen the results of his handiwork, and they hadn't been pretty.

The only one who had ever held his own against Shawn was his older brother, Dylan.

Before Shawn could even open his mouth, Nikki

had planted herself between them, shoving them apart with strong, slender hands. "Don't even think about it, little brother," she admonished. "I've never needed anybody to fight my battles for me and I'm not starting now"

Shawn replied, "All I want to do is make good on a promise I made to myself." And he sidestepped to face Wade once more.

"No."

Flashing a cocky grin, Shawn promised, "I won't kill him, Sis. Just maim him a little. Make him remember not to mess with a Kline again."

Without blinking, she stepped hard on Shawn's instep, reminding Wade that she, too, had grown up in those west Louisville slums.

"You mean little bitch," Shawn yelped, hopping up and down on his uninjured foot.

"You watch your mouth," Wade snarled, brushing past Nikki in an attempt to bust the arrogant brat in the mouth. He had almost succeeded when Nikki moved again, this time planting her entire five foot four inches in front of him, and snapped, "Don't even think about it. What in the hell are you doing here?"

Gingerly setting his foot on the ground, well aware that it would be bruised within a few hours, Shawn snapped, "He's here so I can kick his ass, of course."

"Watch your mouth," Wade repeated. "You still haven't learned how to show your sister any respect."

"And you did?" Hazel eyes flashing, Shawn asked, "Who are you to lecture me on how to treat anybody? At least I had the decency to not go making a woman any promises I wouldn't keep."

Nikki didn't even hear Wade's snarled reply. She was turning to go inside. Let them beat the hell out of each other. She didn't want to hear about it or think about it.

But apparently, other things were planned. Dylan had come outside without being noticed. With an ease that came from years of rough housing with Shawn, he deflected the first punch and before anybody could blink, he had Shawn trapped in a headlock he had little hope of breaking, unless he wanted his neck broken as well.

"What's up?" he asked calmly, as though every morning he stepped in the middle of a soon-to-be blood bath.

"Lemme go, you sonovabitch," Shawn panted. His face was red with anger and effort as he twisted uselessly to try and free himself. "All I'm gonna do is rearrange his pretty face a little."

"Did she ask you to?"

"No, but so what?" Shawn grunted, swiveling his hips, trying to jerk free. "You can't… tell me…that you never wanted to…do it yourself."

Casting a wistful glance at Wade, Dylan said, "If she wanted it done, she'd do it herself. She doesn't need us to do it." His wistful gaze clearly made Wade aware that all Nikki needed to do was say the word.

Nikki stood silently, her eyes empty and flat. Her silence told Dylan all too much. It had been months since the grim-eyed man from Nikki's past had shown up, and he had yet to leave. Which only told him that Nikki really didn't want him gone. But God help him if he hurt her again.

God would be the only left who could help him.

"Damn it, lemme go," Shawn demanded

"Sure," Dylan drawled, letting go suddenly and with a shove that had Shawn sprawling in the grass in front of the porch.

Young pride bruised, he leaped to his feet, ready to battle with both of them only to come up against the heel of Dylan's hand, and go sliding on his butt again. "Damn it, why in the hell are you knocking me around?" Body smeared with mud, eyes flashing. "I ain't the bastard who went and knocked—"

"Shawn!"

The strident demand stopped Shawn in his tracks and he dropped his head. "Aw, hell," he muttered, climbing to his feet. "Can't even beat the shit of a guy any more. Nobody used to look twice when I got into a fight." Gingerly, he moved up the steps, tossing Wade a look that said, *Just wait.* And then he was gone.

Dylan lingered a moment longer, silently asking if he should stay or go. Wade began to wonder if he wasn't going to have to do battle with one of them after all. But, finally, after long moments of silent communication, Nikki just shook her head at him and told him, "Make sure he cleans up the mud he tracks in. I'll be in soon."

Dylan shrugged and turned on a bare heel to go inside, casting one long unreadable glance in Wade's direction before shutting the door quietly behind him.

As he watched her, Nikki wrapped her arms around her middle, a tiny shiver wracking her body.

She met his eyes and just gave him a flat, blank stare. "What are you doing here, Wade? It's barely seven."

"I've been up for hours," he said softly, smiling as her face started to flush. "I meant it literally. I didn't sleep more than an hour or two."

"So you decided to come up here at the crack of dawn?"

He shrugged and tucked his hands in his back pockets. "You know, if looks could kill, you two would have been dead the minute I rounded the bend. I didn't recognize Shawn. He's grown up."

"He looks pretty much the same way he did five years ago."

"Not really. He looks like a whole other person. I hear he's training with a contractor, going into construction"

"That's right. Dylan leaves in a few months for Army boot camp. He might even have a shot at Military Intelligence. Neither one of them have been in trouble with the law in years. Shawn just broke up with the girl he swore he was going to marry, but he's not too upset about it. Dylan isn't really dating anybody in particular, but he says now isn't the time to start a relationship. Did you come up here to discuss my brothers' plans for the future?" she asked, arching an eyebrow at him.

He ran his eyes over her sweetly curved body, appreciating every exposed inch, and there were a lot of inches exposed, her legs poking out from under the hem of the green silk top and boxer shorts she wore, her nipples hard under the fragile cloth.

Hell, discussing anything was the last thing on his

mind.

"No." He moved closer, backing her up against the wall, forgetting about the eyes that were even now boring into his back.

"Back off, Wade," Nikki snapped, her brows drawing together. Her soft, full mouth firmed into a flat line as she leaned back into the wood, trying to stay as far from him as she could. Her eyes were dark, turbulent with emotions Wade couldn't even begin to understand. "I can't deal with this right now."

"Deal with what?" he asked absently as he lowered his head, eyes focused on her mouth. Her answer went unheard as he groaned and locked his mouth on hers, intent on making every vivid dream, every little fantasy of the past night a reality here and now.

Wade closed his eyes, nearly dying from the pleasure of feeling her moving against him. She felt like an angel, tasted like heaven. Sanity fell to pieces around him as his hands traveled under the silky top to find her bare beneath it. Nothing but soft smooth skin that trembled under his hands. Wedging himself between her thighs, he ground his erection against her and shuddered.

He clamped his hands over her silk covered hips, hiking her up, pressing heat against heat. Tearing his mouth from hers, he dragged air into his starving lungs. Her head fell limply back, coming in contact with the exterior of the house, but she didn't even flinch. Throat exposed, eyes closed, she was the very picture of surrender. Wade lowered his head and feasted on the smooth expanse of bare skin between neck and shoulder.

A soft whimper escaped her lips as the taste of him flooded her senses, Nikki felt her already weak resolve begin to crumple. This had always felt so right, she thought in despair. How could she fight off something that felt as natural as life itself? It might be easier to will her own heart to stop beating. She shuddered when he plunged his tongue into her mouth, his strong hands molding her against him, cupping the curve of her rump, lifting her up against him.

Nikki gasped, feeling the heat shimmer through her from head to toe, then center at her neck and groin. The blood in her head pounded in time to the thick heavy waves of pleasure that washed over her.

Have I lost my mind? she wondered frantically as those waves washed down to pool between her thighs. Her brothers were waiting inside, probably watching their every move. And here they were, ready to go at it like a couple of teenagers. Audience or no audience. And she really didn't care.

Fisting her hands in his hair, Nikki dragged his head back to hers, met his mouth again. Sharp teeth nipped gently at her lower lip before his tongue sought out the tiny hurt and soothed it. One hand left her hip to race up and close over her bare breast, dragging the pajama top up in the process. His thumb scraped over her nipple, drawing it tighter as he kneaded, massaged, stroked her breast.

Wade tore his mouth hers and lowered his head to nip at her neck, forcing his hands back, letting the silk fall until she was decently covered, then closed over her waist as sanity made itself known. Not here.

Damn it. What timing. "Come home with me," he whispered, frustrated need and lust making his voice harsh.

Her voice practically gone, Nikki shook her head, and said, "No."

"Yes," he demanded, biting her earlobe with none too gentle teeth. "You want this as much as I do." Pulling away, he stared down at her face, flushed with hunger. Desire had darkened her eyes until they were nearly black. That wide mobile mouth was red, lips swollen. "Damn it, I could unbutton my jeans and spread your legs right here and you'd love every second of it. I don't think you could stop me right now. I don't think you'd want to."

She closed her eyes and refused to reply. She wouldn't lie about it, but damn it, she didn't have to admit it either.

"If you won't come home with me, then get dressed and come walking with me," he coaxed, his thumbs caressing her ribcage and the sensitive underside of each breast. "I'll take you into the woods and lay down on the leaves and make love to you there." His voice was low, smoky, full of promises and need. "And I'll make you forget every second you ever spent without me."

The hot words and hot promises in his eyes wound themselves around her like a silken rope, pulling her flesh tight, making breathing nearly impossible. She was tempted. Sweet heaven, she was tempted.

"Wade, I can't," she whispered, the words coming hoarse. The lump in her throat was making breathing difficult.

"Sure you can. Just go throw on some jeans and come with me," he said, nudging the wet silver-covered cleft between her legs with his erection. His blue-jeaned legs rubbed against her inner thighs, the sensation almost painful to her sensitized nerves.

"That's not what I meant, Wade," she whispered brokenly. "This isn't going to solve anything." Understand. Please. I can't keep fighting you, not now. I'm too weak already.

She saw it in his eyes, the heated fog of lust clearing, as he started to actually hear her. She continued to stare at him, knowing he could see that hunger there, as well as her fear, and something that bordered on desperation.

In his eyes, anger started to flash and she braced herself.

"What's there to solve?" he demanded. "You still love me. I love you. We need each other.'

"I can't do this," she said, closing her eyes against the pain.

"You don't have to do anything at all. Just spread your legs for me and I'll do the rest," he snapped. "If you can't give me anything else, I'll settle for your body for now."

"I can't do it like that," she said sadly. "It's all or nothing"

"And if I need an answer now?"

Wade could see it in her eyes, on her face. Her throat worked as she swallowed and her eyes glistened with the wet sheen of tears. But her voice was firm when she answered, "It would have to be nothing."

"It's always been all or nothing with you!" he raged. Damn her, he couldn't wait forever! And in the way of all men, he decided to place the blame solely on her shoulders. "If you would just learn to bend a little, maybe we never would have had these problems."

She threw his hands off, her eyes going wide. "Me?" she asked, her voice low and shaking. "Me?" she repeated, her voice rising with shock and anger. "Learn to bend? Damn you to hell and back, I bent over backwards trying to please you. You wanted the one thing I couldn't give. I can't change the past, Wade."

"This has nothing to do with the past," he growled, slashing at the empty air with his hand. "Nothing to do with Jamie or with that sorry bastard. It has to do with us, you and me."

Snagging her neck with his hand, he dragged her forward and leaned down. "I don't give a damn about the past," he snarled. "It's over with. You need to let it go and stop letting it tear you apart." Frustrated beyond belief, he shook her slightly. "Damn it, what in the hell happened to you? You've turned into a damned hermit. You're barely a shadow of what you were. You think I can't see the pain in you? It's tearing you apart and I can't help but think it's more than just me. You never would have let me ruin your life, not after what I did. I wasn't worth it!

"Let it go," he finished, her voice ragged, his brow pressed to hers. "It can't affect us any more."

"The past made us what we are, Wade. It's not that easy."

Watching her from hooded eyes, Wade came to

slow realization. She wasn't going to give in. Not now or ever. "If that's the way it is, then I don't think I like what it's made you into. I don't think you like yourself much either."

His words cut at her, as her own frustrated desire turned into misplaced anger and hurt pride as quickly as his had. Her eyes narrowed, the hurt she was feeling showing in her face, she hissed, "If you don't like what I am, then you only have yourself to thank. It was you who did this to me. You and that damned slut—"

Before another word had left her mouth, Wade had her pinned against the wall, his hand clamped over her mouth. "Don't ever speak of my child's mother that way, Nik. Don't ever do it," he repeated, his voice low and hard, his eyes glinting like shards of broken black glass.

With a furious toss of her head, Nikki dislodged his hand, glaring. "Ah, yes. I mustn't say anything against the sainted Jamie. Never mind that she took you from me," she snarled, throwing his hands from her.

"That poor little rich girl, she grew up with anything and everything she ever wanted. She had everything. I had nothing. Until you. You were mine; you were the only thing in my life that really mattered and she took you away."

How can you defend her? Her heart breaking inside her, Nikki clenched her fists. She had bitten her tongue, had held back for years. And what had it gotten her? Nothing. Damn it, if she had done something *then* maybe this mess wouldn't have happened.

But she had ignored her, like she knew Wade wanted, and not done or said a damn thing to the woman who spent months chasing after an engaged man.

"Well, I say whatever I want against the bitch," she coldly said, whipping past him to stand her ground in the middle of the porch. She didn't back away as he advanced, just took out the one weapon she had left. "Like a dog in heat, she went chasing after you, no matter how many times you told her you weren't interested. She did everything to catch your eye except strip naked and plant herself in front of you."

Her lip curled up, her voice full of hate and derision, she said, "And to think that your hands touched her; how can you possibly think that I would want you after knowing you were with her? That your hands touched her? I don't want them on me. They're dirty"

Wade stopped in his tracks, anger suddenly replaced by pain, deep biting pain. He had never, in all the time he had known her, heard her speak to any one in that tone. And the look on her face, as though she had found something distasteful on the soles of her shoes. Dumbfounded, he stared at her. She couldn't mean that.

But one look at her furious face told him otherwise. She didn't want him there. She had told him time after time, but like a fool, he had kept coming back.

He needed her so badly, like a dying man needed

water, but she didn't even want him touching her. Had he imagined the way she lit up when he touched her? Had he imagined the need in her eyes simply because he so badly needed to see it there?

"You can't expect me to believe that you don't want me," Wade said, his voice sounding tight and rusty. "You can't expect me to believe that you feel nothing when I touch you." He only wished he was as certain as he sounded.

He watched as she flipped her hair back and shrugged her shoulders, carelessly, casually. "It's been a while for me, Wade." She smoothed her hands down her sides, ran her fingers through her tousled hair. "Been a busy few months. Haven't had time to get out much. After Dale left, well... I'm picky. And there's not too many guys around here who've caught my eye."

Wade looked into her eyes, looked for some sign that she was lying, playing out a role. But he saw nothing that could convince him that she spoke anything less than the truth.

I don't want them on me

The words replayed themselves over and over as he stood there, feeling vaguely lost, and very confused. The hurt and anger were waging a war within him, ripping at him until he was so damn torn apart, he could barely see. Nausea roiled sickly in his gut as her implication that any man would suffice sank in.

Had it come down this? Would fate be cruel enough to place her back in his life, to tempt with glimpses of what could be paradise, only to have his hopes and dreams smashed because she just didn't want him any more? Had Nikki been imagining somebody else in his place every time he touched her?

"Are you so damn perfect that you never made a mistake, never hurt anybody?" he rasped, growing aware of a desire to hurt her as badly as she had hurt him. Anything, even pain, would be better than that damned disdain that sat so haughtily on her face, surrounding her like an invisible cloak. "Never done anything that you would give anything to have undone? Never done anything that made you feel like the lowest life form on the planet?"

He couldn't see the guilt and the sorrow that started to form in her eyes and he didn't hear the soft apology in her voice as she quietly said, "I make mistakes. I've felt even lower than that, and I think you are aware of what I'm talking about"

Her voice sounded oddly, distant, flat. But it rolled off his shoulders like water as he tried to reconcile to the words… *I don't want them on me.* "Wade, I need time. I'm only human."

The unspoken apology went unheeded by him, as he heard in his head, over and over, *I don't want them on me.* The unspoken words he was hearing were *almost any man would do. You might be handy, but you're not good enough.*

He kept coming back, time after time, needing her so badly, and she kept kicking him in his face. That mental image of him crawling at her feet only to receive a boot in his face for his efforts had his pride kicking in, temporarily masking the pain he felt. He drew himself up, reined in the anger and pain that must have shown on his face.

"Yeah?" he asked, derisive. "I'm not so sure of that. A human would show some forgiveness, a little compassion. That's what happens when you have a heart. And from what I can see, you lost yours sometime ago. I'm beginning to wonder if you ever had one."

Damn it all, he was done begging. He was done crawling. No more.

Making his own face as cruel as hers had been, he continued, "Hell, I'm starting to wonder about a lot of things. But one thing is certain." Moving closer until he was nose to nose with her, he whispered harshly, "You ain't worth it."

"Wade—"

Her face was pale, the pain in her eyes registered dimly in some part of his mind, but he didn't acknowledge it. He had his pride, he wouldn't keep crawling after her. He had been patient, understanding, hell he had all but begged her to take him back.

And this was what he got for giving up his pride in the name of love.

Eyes as cold as the North Star, Wade inclined his head, his face expressionless, regal as he gazed down at her with all the arrogance his ancestors had possessed. He was the descendant of Indian chieftains and braves. He was done with crawling after a woman.

Coldly, he offered, "And as for time, well, take all the time you need, Nicole. What you do matters nothing to me." And then, without looking back, he walked away from her.

*****

Nikki walked woodenly into the house. It was over. She had won. She had driven him away and he would stay away.

What had she done?

Over the guilt, a soft voice whispered inside her, *exactly what you had to do. You had to be sure. Otherwise, it wouldn't have been fair to either of you. Or to Abby.*

But why had she been so hateful?

Sinking down on the steps, Nikki buried her face in her hands. Anger. Hurt. Self defense. Any one of those would have been right. Or at least, partly right. But the real reason was fear. She was so damned afraid of being hurt again, of losing it all.

"Nikki?"

She looked up, startled. Dylan stood before her, concern in his eyes. He knelt down in front of her, took her cold hands in his. Her eyes stared back into his, eyes so like her own. "Want to talk about it?" he asked quietly.

"No," she whispered, her voice soundless. With a gentle tug, she freed her hands and rose on none too steady legs.

"What are you going to do?"

She stared at him, her eyes lost. "I don't know," she said faintly. She badly wanted to run away and hide and lick her wounds.

So why don't you? She blinked, as the soft little voice repeated itself. *Why don't I?* she asked herself. Hell, it wasn't like she had any reason to stay here, not after what he had told her. Damn it, how could he like her any more? She didn't even like herself.

And he was done waiting. Just when she had started to think, maybe…just maybe…

Too late now. And the wishes and dreams didn't matter if he didn't want her any more.

A slight shudder wracked her body, like an echo of the pain she was holding trapping inside. Closing her eyes, she focused, grounded herself. Why in the hell shouldn't she take some time?

"I'm going to New York." And then she ascended the stairs to go pack.

*****

Wade drove around aimlessly until early afternoon. He restaged the fight time after time in his mind, and, in the way of men and women since the dawn of time, he came up with sharper retorts and an even more crippling parting shot.

How could she call him dirty? He hadn't gone and lost his virginity at the age of fourteen to a piece of trash. No, his conscience whispered softly. You were lucky enough to have family at home that loved you, cared about you. You didn't have to go looking for love; it was always right there.

But he didn't want to think about that. Even now in the midst of his rage, he realized he had let it go, some time in the past. Dion simply didn't matter any more. He never really had. He hadn't been worth it then, and he certainly wasn't worth it now. The only reason he let it bother him so much was sheer jealousy…and anger, for her. Because look how that bastard had treated her afterward. Some anger, directed at himself…if he had known her sooner, could he have protected her from that?

Hell, it didn't matter now. Didn't matter that the bastard had spread rumors, spread lies, pulled a million and one cruel jokes on her, or that he'd run her off the road…a snarl twisted his mouth and he wondered why in the hell he'd never kicked Dion's ass for that.

His thoughts jumped around, leaving that and returning to the porch, where she had told him, *I don't want them on me*

Didn't want him touching her, didn't want his love…didn't want him.

Nikki's words replayed over in his mind, like a broken record he couldn't turn off. She had finally said what was on her mind, and in her heart. If she had done so from the beginning, maybe he wouldn't have wasted all this time trying to get her back.

Wade conveniently forgot that she had been telling him, time after time, just that; he just decided not to listen.

"Hell, Wade. It's better this way. You know where you stand with the woman, now you can get over her," he told himself, drumming his fingers on the steering wheel.

Like hell.

Somewhere around three that afternoon, he entered Jefferson County and stopped at the first red neck bar he saw. Ready to get drunk and rowdy and pick a fight. Under the midday sun, the cinder block structure looked about as tacky and cheap as they come. The parking lot was littered with cigarette butts and broken glass.

Only a few vehicles were there, a couple of beat up pick up trucks and a Cadillac that looked to have been pieced together from other various colored Cadillacs.

All in all, it was a classic red neck dive.

It suited his mood to a tee.

Stomping in, he ordered a shot of whiskey. Tawdry neon lights glowed above a mirror that had more cracks than not. There were only a few customers, the bartender and a bored looking waitress who popped her gum as she tossed Wade a disinterested stare before turning her attention back to the TV.

Two grubby men in overalls shot pool while another sat listlessly at the bar, drinking beer and staring into space.

The bartender, an old man with more hair under his nose that on his head, eyed Wade knowingly. "A woman?" he asked, his voice raspy from years of whiskey and smoke as he poured cheap whiskey into a glass only the most careless of dishwashers could call clean.

What in the hell is it with people? Wanting to talk about things you'd rather let die.

Tossing the shot down, Wade grimaced as it burned a path to his stomach, deliberating whether he wanted to ignore the bartender or not.

"I guess you could say that," he finally muttered. Tapping the glass again, he waited until it was full and then he held it up in a salute. "I'm bidding her a fond farewell."

"Leave her, did you? Or did you get kicked out?" he asked.

"Left her. The way she's wanted all along. Better off without her anyway. Contrary mouthy little bitch," he muttered. The shot glass, once again, was full. Lifting it, he stared morosely into it as though it held the answers to all his problems.

The bartender spoke, disturbing him. "You know, looking the way you do, you may be better off with her. You're shit-faced in love with her, whoever she is," he said, watching Wade with knowing eyes.

"Me, I'd just as soon live without one. But some guys just ain't fashioned that way. They got somebody special that they just can't get outta their heads. I'd reckon she's well and firmly planted in yours. Mebbe you oughta go back, see if you can smooth things out."

"She don't want me." Already, the cheap liquor had shot to his head, worsened by too little sleep and no food. Pressing the cool glass to his forehead, he sighed with relief as sharp edged emotions started to dull. "She don't want me, or my little girl. Don't want anything to do with us."

"Ya sure 'bout that?"

"Been asking her for months. She finally gave me an answer." One he wasn't sure he could live with. One he wished to God he hadn't heard.

Wished he had never seen her in the store that day. Wished he had never met her.

His heart felt as though it had been ripping out of his chest, and thrown, still beating, on the floor.

He sure as hell wasn't going to ask again.

*****

Nikki sat in the passenger seat, her eyes dry and itching. She knew without looking that she was pale and wan looking. Shawn kept sending her worried little glances and she knew he didn't want to drive her to the airport. He wasn't happy about her traipsing off, away from home, and alone, in her current mood.

"How long are you planning to stay?" he asked, his eyes flicking from the road to her. Accordingly, the black Bronco drifted right.

"Watch the road, Shawn," she snapped, one hand instinctively bracing against the dash. As he corrected the vehicle, she answered, "I don't know. I guess I'll stay until I feel like coming home."

"What is so important in New York?" he asked, frowning, keeping his eyes on the road.

"A better question would be what isn't there, Shawn. Now just let it go, okay?" she answered wearily, reaching up to rub at her temple. Damn but her head hurt.

"Y'know running away ain't going to solve anything. It's not going to keep you from still loving him. It's not going to change that you want him." Shawn kept his eyes fixed on the road this time, a certain sign of how uncomfortable he was with discussing emotions. "Being in New York isn't going to change any of that. It's still going to be here when you get home."

Nikki remained silent. How could she explain that she needed someplace safe, someplace where she wouldn't see him, as she licked her wounds and tried to start all over again. She needed time to let her heart heal a little, as well as her pride. She knew she wasn't going to get over Wade, not now. Not ever. But she needed some distance from him, time to rebuild her shattered defenses.

Nikki needed the bliss of not thinking about the wreck her life had become. Kirsten lived in a social whirlwind and would pull Nikki inside it.

It wouldn't solve her problems, but maybe if she kept busy enough, she could forget, for just a little while. Right now, she was too raw to think about it, to try to put things into perspective.

In a while, after time had dulled the edges a bit, Nikki would think about it, and how stupid she had been.

*****

"Ms. Evress said to go on in, Miss Kline," Grace said quietly.

Nikki started, looking up. She rubbed her eyes and blinked before scooping up her purse and striding into the office. Bright sunlight poured in through the windows, momentarily blinding her.

The room was done in colors of rose, green and ivory, making Nikki think of cool English gardens. The carpet was plush, a deep forest green hue, ivory colored walls decorated with lovely watercolors. The furniture was all varying shades of rose from palest blush pink to the darkest shade imaginable.

The office was delicate, feminine, soothing. It was

also as unlike Kirsten as anything Nikki could imagine. Nikki knew the decorating had been Kris' mom's idea, and only out of love for her mother had Kris left it alone. With the exception of the fact that room was obviously designed for a female, and Kris was female, it so didn't suit Kris.

Nikki had met both of Kris's parents and often wondered how such an exotic take charge woman had sprouted from the laid back, soft spoken Mr. and Mrs. James Evress, III. Neither of the elder Evress' stood taller than five foot seven. Her mother, in fact, was shorter than Nikki. Both had plain brown hair, plain brown eyes, pleasantly bland features. While her father was a shark in the business world, he was, socially, very soft spoken and mild. She doubted Kirsten's mother could make a decision on her own.

Kirsten stood a strapping five foot ten and had the hourglass figure of a 1940's actress. Long thick naturally red hair was generally worn in a French twist, leaving her face unframed. High arched brows, a nose that was just the right length, a full mouth that could smile or snarl with equal effectiveness. By far, her exotic cat green eyes were her most beautiful, and most intimidating feature. Those eyes could turn from the warmth of springtime to the coldness of winter in less than a second.

All in all, she was a very impressive figure. Nikki sometimes couldn't quite understand exactly why they were the best of friends.

Just now, she was settled behind her massive oak desk, speaking into the phone. She saw Nikki, smiled and held up a slim hand to indicate she'd only be a few minutes. Nikki took advantage of that to dart into the bathroom.

A few moments later, she was staring at her pale reflection. It wasn't the creamy paleness of Kirsten's, but the chalk white of exhaustion. Her eyes had huge dark circles under them and lines of strain radiating out. She had slept exactly three hours the previous night. The hotel bed in Louisville had been comfortable enough but she had spent the night watching pay-per-view movies, unable to let her body relax enough to sleep.

If she slept, she'd start dreaming.

And she badly needed to *not* dream. Her dreams mocked her now, taunting her with what she might have been able to have again, if she could have just stopped being so arrogantly cold.

As she splashed cold water on her face, Nikki wondered if Shawn had gotten her Bronco home in one piece. She sincerely hoped so. He had a habit of driving too fast. There wasn't a cop in the county who hadn't cited him at least once.

After drying her face, she dug out the makeup kit she had brought in hopes of fooling Kirsten she didn't look as bad as she felt. It would be a total waste of time, but at least she tried. As she put it back in, her fingers brushed a small bottle and she tugged the prescription medicine out with a scowl. She'd forgotten to take that damned pill again.

Running a small cup of tap water, she swallowed the pill, with a silent reminder for *why* she had to take them.

Not only was her heart broken, it was damaged

too. Those pills were a necessity now.

Taking a deep breath, Nikki left the safe haven of the bathroom to face Kirsten. The only bad thing about running up here to hide was that she would have to explain it to her friend. She wasn't looking forward to that.

*****

Kirsten sat patiently at her desk, waiting. The older woman had missed nothing about Nikki's appearance when she had entered the room. She was pale, subdued and drained. Make up, rarely worn, but expertly applied almost hid the circles under her eyes. If one didn't look closely, she might appear fine.

But to Kris's experienced eyes, her friend was just barely hanging on. Her eyes looked vaguely wild and wounded. Her mouth was set in a thin straight line, but Kris could see the unhappiness there. The woman before her bore too much resemblance to the woman she had found closed up in her house on the hill after she'd awoken from a coma to find out her child was dead.

Kris had been certain she'd lose her then. Nikki simply hadn't cared about life at that point. She wasn't taking her medicine, she wasn't eating–nothing mattered to her anymore.

"Well, sugar, you don't look at all happy to see me," Kirsten said softly, cocking her head and studying her friend.

Settling in a cushy leather chair, crossing one silk clad leg over the other, she raised her eyes and met the cat green gaze that saw far too deeply. She smoothed down the pale green skirt with one hand and plucked imaginary lint from the coordinating jacket before she sighed. "Wade and I had a fight."

"I didn't realize you had gotten back together."

"We hadn't," Nikki said softly, her voice husky. "And it's not likely to ever happen now. I really blew it, Kris."

"I thought you weren't interested in getting back with him," Kirsten said, frowning.

"I didn't realize I was until it was too late," Nikki murmured. Kirsten watched as Nikki stared down at her hands, closing them into tight fists, anger and misery rolling off her in. "Or maybe I did, and I just wanted to punish him for what happened. Maybe I let things go on longer than they should have. Maybe I just needed a little more time." With a deep sigh, she added, "I guess maybe I should have told him that before things got so out of hand."

In short terse sentences, she explained the fight, leaving out nothing. "So now he's decided he doesn't want me after all. He kept pushing and pushing for an answer. I wasn't ready. I'm still not," she said, sighing. After moments of silence, she added, "Not that it matters now."

Her slanted eyes flashing with anger, Kirsten hissed, "After what he did, he owes you all the time in the world. Who in the hell does he think he is?"

"Kris, don't. I made things harder than I should have, said things I shouldn't have. I bungled it as badly as he did. I was too damn stubborn to give him a chance, too afraid of getting hurt. He made mistakes.

I made mistakes." Reaching up, she rubbed the heel of her hand across her chest, faintly surprised to find her heart still beating. "I just couldn't forgive him."

Moving around her desk, Kirsten went and settled on the arm of the chair, wrapping a maternal arm around the younger woman's shoulders. Clucking sympathetically, she stroked her hair back from her face. "Not everybody could, sweetie. He hurt you bad," Kirsten said softly.

"And I hurt him just as bad. Maybe now we're even. And that's all I'm going to say about it."

Kristen opened her mouth one more time, only to close it, leaving her words unsaid. She studied Nikki's wan face, knowing it would be useless to argue with her or try to get her to tell her any more than she already had. Rising to her feet, she studied Nicole with her slanted cat green eyes. Settling on a safer subject, she said, "Maybe I can finally talk you into going shopping. Check into a spa for the full treatment and go buy out Saks. I told you that when I got you up here next that was what I was going to do."

Nikki flashed a bright, fake smile and said, "Here I am. Ready and willing."

Arching a slim perfect brow, Kirsten asked, "Willing?"

"Well. I'm here, isn't that enough?"

Chapter Seven

I don't want them on me.

"Idiot. Fool," Wade muttered under his breath after his partner lost the toss and trudged into the little diner to get their lunches. Over a week had passed and the words that had tormented him into walking way still haunted him both day and night.

But now they only served to remind him of what a jackass he was. As rain splattered down on the windshield, he listened with half an ear to the radio as he muttered more accusations at himself.

If only he hadn't been pushing so hard. She would have come around sooner or later. Nikki had all but admitted that. If Wade was totally honest, he could admit he had been waiting for years, ever since Jamie had died, hoping against hope that would have another chance; what harm would a few more weeks, a few months, had done?

With a ragged sigh, Wade closed his eyes and let his head fall against the back of the seat. His eyes were reddened and bloodshot, dark circles beneath his eyes emphasizing his haggard look. He couldn't keep going on snatches of sleep. His job wouldn't allow it.

His heart wouldn't let him just let go, even though his pride insisted that he not go crawling. And that was probably what it would take. He had been a total ass. About all of it.

His mouth compressed as he remembered Nikki's harsh words against Jamie, the first she had given voice to. It made him angry, hell, yes; she was Abby's mother, his friend from childhood.

But how could he not expect Nikki to harbor resentment? Throughout the entire time that Jamie had pursued Wade, Nikki had kept her cool, kept her mouth closed, and her wits about her. God knew, if Nikki had been of a mind to, she could have ripped Jamie into so many pieces, there wouldn't be enough left to bury.

The blow up he had expected the night he told her about Jamie hadn't happened.

How long had Wade expected her to keep the lid on her temper? With a grimace, he remembered how blind with fury he had been when Nikki had been dating the blond mechanic, how murderous he had felt before he had recognized Shawn. He was lucky Nikki had kept it to words and had held her tongue this long.

The door swung open, letting in the rain-drenched air as J.D. swung into the cab of the ambulance, two bagged lunches in hand. "Here you go, one gourmet hamburger, complete with grease, saturated fat, and sodium. A walking heart attack. And to top that off, there's fries to go with it."

"Thanks," Wade mumbled, taking the bag with a noted lack of enthusiasm. He wasn't hungry. Everything tasted pretty much the same, like sawdust. Things weren't going to get any better, he knew, until he resolved this with Nicole.

"—so here I was, in bed stark naked with this girl, and the Pope is pounding on the door," J.D. said, around a mouth full of food. "I ended up jumping out of the fifth floor window, wearing her pink robe and a pair of bedroom slippers. Elvis caught me when I landed and we took a trip out to Vegas."

Glancing up, Wade frowned. Had J.D. been talking long? He couldn't remember a damn word that had been said. "Pardon?"

"I had a feeling you weren't hearing me," J.D. said, shaking his head. "You wanna tell me about it?"

"Nope," Wade replied, taking a bite of the rapidly cooling burger.

As if Wade hadn't spoken, J.D. said, "You know, I'd guess it was a woman problem, but you haven't ever once mentioned a woman, not in the three months we been together. If it wasn't for the fact that you got a daughter, I'd wonder if you knew what women were for. But you must know what women are for because at least once, you put one to good use." He wagged bushy black eyebrows before taking a sip of his soft drink.

Wade scowled over at his partner before taking another bite of the burger.

"Course, I seen you with that girl, Nikki Kline, once or twice. She don't talk to many guys, so I guess you must be doing something right. I'm surprised her brothers ain't scared you off. I tried to get her to go out with me a couple of times, but any time I talked to her, those two showed up and they got trouble written all over their faces. I heard they were both gang members up in Louisville a few years back," the other medic said, chewing up his fries as he spoke. He paused only long enough to wash the food down with a soft drink before continuing. "Is she who you're moping about?"

"I am not moping," Wade said, slowly, spacing each word out. "Now why don't you mind your own business?"

"Because my partner can hardly keep his head out of his ass and this ain't the kind of job you can do if you aren't focused on it," J.D. snapped, his blue eyes narrowing. "If this was a big town, you'd already been waist deep in hot water. But sooner or later, something more serious than a broken bone or an upset stomach is going to pop up and you'd better be able to handle it."

Having made his point, the older man turned his attention to his half-eaten lunch, dismissing Wade and his dilemma with the words, "You'd better get things worked out quick. Otherwise you're going to get your ass thrown into the street."

Hell.

*****

Wade turned his truck up the drive, grimly refusing to think about how much he might have to crawl. Damn it, she'd probably call the cops and have him thrown off her property, and wouldn't that cap things off nicely?

But he had to try. Wade had to try to make her understand how sorry he was. And with a whole lot of wishful thinking on his part, he was hoping she would let the sorry incident at her house go. He had to try to smooth things out, apologize and get her to understand.

His life wasn't worth a whole hell of a lot without her in it.

The man who had sworn to himself that he wasn't

going to beg was ironically aware that begging was exactly what he intended to do, in front of God and everybody if that was what it took.

Gravel crunched under his tires as he pulled the truck to a stop. The overcast sky promised more rain before the day was out and as he climbed out of the truck, he caught the cool scent of the coming fall on the air. He helped Abby out of the booster seat in the back of the extended cab before turning toward the silent house.

Her jacket buttoned up against the faint chill in the night air, Abby snuggled against his chest as they both looked at the empty house before them. Curtains drawn and secured, windows dark. "Daddy, Nikki's not here, is she?" Abby asked, her face puckering in a slight pout.

"No, baby. It doesn't look like she is," he answered gruffly. And from the looks of the things, he had a feeling she wouldn't be back any time soon. The house had the vacant air to it of one that was going to be empty for some time.

"She'll be home soon, right? We could wait," Abby said, her eyes hopeful. "We could sit on the swing again and wait like we did last time."

"Angel, I don't think she's coming home any time soon." He turned away, then, helping Abby back into the car, strapping her into her child seat. He paused by the driver's door, looking back at the house. Where in the hell had she gone?

As the days turned into weeks, and weeks into a month, the house on the hill outside of town remained empty. The questions he started asking of her family went unanswered. Her dad was cool and polite, Shawn taunting and insulting. Dylan was simply silent, staring at Wade with flat hazel eyes that saw too much.

Wade finally heard a rumor that Nikki had moved to New York.

No. He told himself she wouldn't just up and leave. Not for good. But all too soon Halloween was over and the holidays were looming on the horizon; he had yet to hear anything more about her.

As his regret died, it gave way to anger, the apologies he had been rehearsing turned to ashes on his tongue. So he had meant that much. After one fight, she had just given up and turned away, walking out of his life, not giving him a chance to try to heal the wounds before they festered.

Wade spent several weeks in that mind set, stewing and steaming over it. The anger certainly felt better than the guilt and he was able to function a little better.

After Thanksgiving dinner with his parents, Wade returned to Monticello, wondering if he ought to return to Indiana. At least Abby would have her grandparents close by and be back with her old friends. And he wouldn't have to live day by day, wondering when Nikki would come back.

If she would come back.

Abby was lonely. The twins had started kindergarten and in the careless manner of children, decided that Abby was too young for them play with any more. And she was unhappy, probably sensing her father's state of mind. It was wearing on both of them.

At least twice a week, Wade made the long drive to her house outside of town, up that winding road to see if she had returned. He would prowl the woods behind her home and slowly go out of his mind while he wondered.

Pacing the floors at night, the four walls of his house threatening to close in on him, Wade worried and wondered. The anger was giving way to desperation and dismay. Something wasn't right. The woman who had fled from him wasn't the girl he had known.

Nikki would have stood her ground, dug in her heels, and lifted that arrogant chin. Damn it, she would have laid into him, teeth bared. Where had that girl disappeared to? How had she changed so much?

And why had Wade done that? Acted that way? Handed out ultimatums he had no right to hand out?

Why had she let him? Why hadn't she fought back the way she would have before? She had stood there, letting him pile it on her and rage away before she could dive into him with claws bared.

It was like there wasn't much fight left in her.

And so December dawned, cold and gray, an echo of the grief he carried inside.

*****

Nikki stared at the sumptuous food piled high on the table. She was having Thanksgiving with Kirsten's reserved but loving parents. It was clear that they thought the sun rose and set on their only child. And they were more than happy to welcome Nikki into their home for the holidays.

With a polite smile, she answered questions softly, nodding and forcing herself to smile. Finally, they seemed to understand she was really not in the mood for conversation and they steered the conversation away from her. By then, the smile had frozen on her lips, and her muscles ached from the strain of keeping her expression free of the distress she felt inside. Nikki had once glimpsed Kirsten whispering something in her mother's ear and she looked away as Alice turned a sympathetic understanding smile in her direction

She took a bite of the exquisitely prepared turkey that tasted like sawdust. Her appetite had turned to nothing but still, she forced herself to eat a little of everything on her plate. She washed it down with wine and water, and prayed the day would end quickly. All she wanted to do was curl up in her guest room at Kristen's with a book and forget all about the rest of the world.

She wondered if Wade was spending his holiday with his family. Or was he with another woman? Nikki had been in New York for six weeks now, plenty long enough for him to have met somebody else. Maybe some prospective young mother for Abby had whipped up their Thanksgiving feast and they were sitting down now to enjoy it.

Nikki winced inwardly with self-disgust as her mind started down that trail. Just what she needed, to start feeling sorry for herself, and getting angry at some faceless woman who may not even exist.

Homesick, she ached for her family and the

comfort of her own home. She wanted to curl up in her own bed, and wake up in the morning to the sight of the sun rising over the hills. She wanted to ride her bike over those hills, feel the cold winter wind biting at her face. She wanted to go visit her son's grave.

But Nikki wasn't ready to go home. She was deeply afraid that she would find that some other woman had taken her place in Wade's life again, and until she could handle the heartbreak of that, she wasn't going to face him

Until Nikki felt she was strong enough to handle facing Wade once more, knowing he no longer wanted her, Nikki wasn't going home. She'd be damned before she fell apart in front of him. Damned if she would beg.

She couldn't forget how coldly he had spoken to her, how cruel his eyes had been when he informed he didn't give a damn what she did or didn't do.

He had meant it. Wade had never really been able to lie worth a damn. He was well and truly fed up with her pushing him away with one hand while pulling him to her with another.

Disgusted, Nikki knew that was exactly what she had been doing.

Coward, she told herself as she trailed after the family into the drawing room for brandy and small talk. Nikki settled herself in an overstuffed chair that sat beside a huge picture window, overlooking the lavish family estate.

Kirsten came from old money, and it showed. The house was over a hundred years old, grandly built and lovingly cared for. At one time, Nikki might have shown interest in it and would have wanted to wander the grounds and home, but now she sat idly in the chair, staring outside while conversation hummed around her in muted tones.

She knew she was being rude, but she couldn't bring herself to join the conversation. Nikki wasn't feeling overly thankful about much of anything; she was too damn angry with herself. For not fighting back while Wade had lashed out at her. For fighting with him about the wrong things. For lying and deluding herself and him.

For being a weak witted fool.

Disgusted with herself, she recalled the words she had spoken about Jamie. Though the woman had hated Nikki and had stolen Wade from her, she was a pitiable creature, one who had died lonely, and alone, despite a husband and a baby daughter.

Nikki couldn't abide those who spoke ill of the dead. That was something she had always refused to do then when it was most important, she had gone and slandered the mother of the child Wade adored. While Wade might not have loved Jamie, he had cared about her, had made her his wife, had buried her and raised her little girl on his own.

Sipping at the brandy, letting its artificial heat warm her insides, Nikki closed her eyes and let her head fall back against the seat. She wanted to go home.

She dreaded doing so.

She hated herself for being an indecisive idiot of a female.

But hadn't she been doing that for the past six

weeks?

*****

Kirsten paused outside the bedroom door, her hand resting on the smooth wood. In the other hand, she held a cup of rum-laced eggnog, her plans had been to convince Nikki to nip a few drinks, and open up. The misery inside her was eating at her, and it wasn't letting up any.

But at the sound of the deep muffled sobs, she halted. Kirsten, like Nikki, was a private person.

So she quietly retreated back the way she had come, cursing Wade Lightfoot in three different languages as she did so.

*****

Wade glanced up as his partner dropped down on the chair across from him. His face was grim, his eyes shadowed and dark. "The boy didn't make it," J.D. rasped, his voice raw and strained.

"Damn," Wade whispered, useless anger curling within him. "Damn it."

"Massive head trauma. If he'd lived, he would have been a damned vegetable. The mother is still in surgery, but they think she'll pull through. Hell of a piece of news for her to have to hear while she's fighting for her life." J.D. slouched in his chair and rubbed his eyes.

Their shift had ended well over two hours earlier, but neither had been able to leave until they heard the news. Wade was now wishing he had left. He wanted to rip something apart with his bare hands. Knowing he didn't want to know, but unable to keep from asking, he gave in. "The driver?"

"Mild concussion. Mild lacerations. A few bruised ribs from his impact against the safety harness," J.D. said, his voice flat while his eyes burned. "Ain't that justice?"

"You boys need to head home."

Wade looked up as one of the ER nurses came into the lounge. A soft comforting smile on her familiar face, Leanne Winslow settled into a chair next to Wade and took his hand. "You've had a rough night. You need to get some rest. This isn't even your normal shift."

"Saving money for Christmas," he muttered, folding his cold hand around hers. "Any more news about the mother?"

"Some. And it could be good news. She's about four and half months pregnant and the fetus is hanging in there. She hasn't spontaneously aborted yet, so that is definitely a good sign. If all goes well..."

Wade grimaced and shook his head. "Too many things can go wrong, especially that early in the pregnancy."

"If she'd had been much farther along, much bigger, the baby's chances wouldn't be as good. As it is, the little girl is small enough that her mother's body sustained much of the damage. She pulled through surgery but... well, the pain meds and antibiotics, those are what's worrying her OB right now. At least she's past the first trimester. We've located her husband."

A soft hand stroked over his brow and he fought off the urge to shrug it away. Wade never should have accepted her offer to dinner that night. But now, any time he decided to call things off, he was struck with a bout of loneliness so strong, he lost his resolve.

Leanne was sweet, gentle, and unassuming. She looked at Wade as though she thought he was some type of god and made him feel like he wasn't a walking disaster.

And Abby liked her. She hardly even mentioned Nikki any more. The past three weeks had been easier, but he didn't know if that was because Leanne was there or because he was adjusting to the fact that Nikki was gone.

"Wade, you need to go home," Leanne ordered softly, gazing up at him with concerned blue eyes. "Get some rest before that little girl of yours comes home from Daycare. With Christmas coming, you're going to need that rest."

Rest. That had become a precious commodity in his world. On the rare nights that Wade slept for more than four or five hours, he always dreamed of Nicole.

The tasks of working two extra shifts of a week, trying to get Christmas shopping done and dealing with a rambunctious four year old were an exhausting combination enough, but when the father couldn't sleep, it made it even worse.

Rest? he thought cynically. Yeah, right. Not in this century. But Wade forced a smile and nodded. "You'll let me know about the mother?" he asked as he stretched his arms over his head and forced his stiff body out of the chair.

"Yes. But she's going to pull though. She's stable and she's young. I just hope her baby makes it. Losing one child is hard enough," Leanne murmured, rising gracefully to her feet. The baggy blue uniform rustled softly as she leaned close enough to peck him on the cheek. "I'll call tonight, once you've had a chance to get some rest. You, too, J.D. Get some sleep"

She smiled sweetly at him and left the lounge on silent feet. Her ebony hair, wound in an intricate braid, swayed as she walked away. That girl moved like dancer. She was beautiful, sweet and intelligent, a perfect dream. She was happiest when she was fussing over people.

And, more often than not, two hours after leaving her, Wade could hardly remember what she looked like. Certainly couldn't pull up her image in his mind, couldn't remember how she felt against him, or smelled, or tasted.

"That is a fine piece of work," J.D. murmured as he rose, sliding his rumpled jacket on as they headed out the lounge. "You two serious?"

Wade shrugged. "We've gone out a few times."

"About time. That girl's been practically begging you ever since you moved here. Nice to know you finally developed a brain."

Wade shot his partner a dour look and said, "That's not a brain you're thinking of, buddy." His steps slowed as he passed by a man being wheeled outside, with an armed escort. He was sobbing theatrically and waving his arms in the air as he begged and pleaded with the officers.

"Damned murdering son of a bitch," J.D. whispered under his breath as the two men slowed to a halt. "Listen to him, saying he wasn't drunk at all. That bastard had empty beer cans all over the back seat."

The bastard in reference had kept trying to grab his treating paramedic the entire time she was with him. He had been singing loudly and begging for 'a special performance' while Wade and J.D had been laboring over a tiny three-year-old boy, trying to pump life back into him. Bastard was so damned drunk, he hadn't really realized he had been in a wreck.

As he sang merrily, unaware of what was really happening, Wade and J.D. struggled to make that boy live.

They had succeeded only to have the boy die in the ER

"What's likely to happen to him? In Louisville, some fancy ass lawyer would get him off with a suspended sentence and community time."

J.D. grunted and raised his shoulders. "He'll be tried for manslaughter. And unless his family is rich, he won't get a lawyer fancy enough to even try to talk down a thing like this. And, even then, folks around here don't take too kindly to bastards like that. This isn't his first offense, either. Multiple DUI's. He'll do time.

"But that won't bring that little boy back," J.D. finished savagely, glaring in the direction of the cruiser.

"But maybe it will save another one," Wade said, holding onto that thought. That helped. Not a whole hell of a lot, but it did help. "You have to remember that. If he got away with a slap on the wrist, this would be a hell of a lot harder to handle." He cast a glance up at the cold winter sky as they resumed walking to the ambulance. "Hell of a Christmas that family is going to have."

Once home, Wade shed his clothes on the way to the bathroom and turned the water to as hot as he could stand it. He felt his skin was as saturated with blood as his uniform. So much blood for such a small child. Sharp needles of water pounded his face and chest as he scrubbed as his flesh.

How was that poor boy's family going to make it? If he lost Abby…

His little girl was all he had. Losing her would kill him.

No parent should ever have to bury a child.

Exhaustion kept him from dwelling too long on that thought. Stepping out of the shower, water sluicing off his body, Wade forced his mind not to go down that road.

He fell face first down on the bed without even drying off. Wrapping up in the comforter, he prayed for oblivion.

Waking shortly before Abby was due home, Wade's stiff muscles protested as he climbed out of bed and stretched. The dull ache of grief resided in his chest but he pushed it aside. His little girl was on her way. And with Christmas only four days away, she was becoming more and more hyper and required every bit of his energy.

Every other word out of her mouth was

'Christmas'. 'Have I been good?' ran a close second. Even without the extra hours he was putting in, she would have worn him down. And in two days, his parents were coming to spend the holidays with him and Abby. Which meant he had to clean the damn house.

To top that all of, he couldn't get Nikki out of his mind.

Was she home yet? He hadn't gone up the mountain in two weeks and he finally stopped hounding her family

How much longer was she going to stay away?

Not that it mattered. Wade had finally given up waiting. He had accepted that this was her way of making a clean break. It was over for her.

But not for him. And that was the most pathetic part of it. Because he was the reason she had decided to make that break. Him and his damned pride. If he had been a little more patient, he would have had her back.

And then he had gone and screwed it up.

Again.

Later that night, Abby sat scrubbed clean and dressed in pink and blue flannel pajamas, her eyes focused on the Christmas special on the television. 'Small One,' Wade thought. It was a sweet cartoon, and Abby was enamored with the donkey.

He reached blindly for the phone when it rang,

knowing automatically who it was. Leanne's slow southern drawl sounded in his ear and he tuned out the television as he listened. The mother was fine. The baby was hanging in there. He sent a silent prayer heavenward and thanked Leanne for letting him know.

"Are we still on for Christmas Eve?" she asked softly.

"Yeah. And don't forget you're welcome to come by Christmas night when you get done working your shift."

She chuckled. "I may not be in the mood for celebrating by the time my shift is over. You know how holidays are in the hospital. Even here in the country, we get our share of folks drowning their holiday blues with Jack Daniels and sleeping pills."

"Cheerful thought," he muttered, pressing his fingers to tired eyes hoping to push out memories of a dead woman clad in blue silk, her face peaceful. Jose Cuervo had been her drink of choice.

"You sound tired. Didn't you get any sleep?"

"Yeah, but it doesn't feel like it now," he replied, closing his eyes against the glare of the television. The six hours of unconsciousness might as well not have happened. "The extra work is catching up."

"Do you think maybe you should slow down?" Leanne suggested, hesitantly.

Nikki would have told him to stop working himself into the ground, or she'd stop him herself

Leanne wasn't Nikki. She was the exact opposite, which was why he was dating her, he reminded himself as out loud, Wade said, "This was the last one. I was only doing it for Christmas."

"Good. You need to take better care of yourself." The way she said it, her words sounded more like a question than a statement.

Cursing himself, he promised, "I'll try," before

hurriedly getting off the phone. He was too damn tired to listen his evil twin berate Leanne for being everything he had decided he wanted in a woman. Or everything he *should* want in a woman.

But, damn it all, he didn't want a Southern belle who hung onto his every word and couldn't make a decision on her own unless it had to do with the job. She even asked him what she should cook when he came over dinner.

What he wanted was an acid tongued transplanted Yankee who would tell him to go to hell before she'd offer to come and cook breakfast for him on her day off.

"Damned fool," he told himself softly as he settled back against the couch.

*****

Nikki stood in the shadows of the alcove, watching the festivities with weary eyes. Everybody at Kirsten's party was having a blast, save for Nikki. She could only think of one place she wanted less to be. Home.

Shawn had told her yesterday that he'd seen Wade going out with a woman he vaguely knew from the hospital. A pretty young nurse that Nikki remembered all too well. Leanne Winslow had been the one holding her hand when she woke up briefly in the ER after her accident. When she had asked about Jason.

Coal black hair, porcelain smooth skin, eyes the color of the midnight sky. She had been kind and comforting in the ER and the few times Nikki had encountered her since then, she had always been sweet and concerned, asking how she was. Mother Teresa in the flesh that was Leanne. There was something almost ethereal about the woman

She would be a prefect mother to Abby. A perfect wife for Wade.

Now that is a cheerful thought…

The third man of the evening to approach got within three feet of Nicole before she noticed. Turning her icy eyes his way, she gave him her most obnoxious glare, hoping he'd get the point. The invisible wall of ice she had around her didn't seem to even faze him.

Nikki accepted the offered champagne flute only to set it down untouched on the elegant Queen Anne table behind her. He hardly noticed

He was too drunk to notice. He didn't notice the way Nikki was edging away from him, didn't notice the look of utter distaste on her face. All he noticed was a streamlined body in a crushed velvet dress of crimson and the pouting, sulky mouth.

As he backed her farther into the corner, he also failed to notice the flash of temper that sparked in Nikki's eyes.

But he did notice the cold champagne that was flung in his face when he slurred out an invitation to go find an empty room somewhere. That offer was accompanied by a none too subtle grope.

As he sputtered and swore, Nikki moved around him, moving quicker than she had in weeks. She dodged dancing couples and gaily laughing groups of people.

All around people were celebrating. Not

celebrating Christmas, the holiday season or even the weekend.

They were celebrating life.

No wonder she didn't want to be here. She didn't have any life left in her.

Shutting herself in the library, Nikki settled in a huge leather chair over looking the estate and wished she had not wasted the champagne. She could have used a drink.

Her wish was granted when the door opened to reveal Kirsten, clad in a floor length figure hugging gown of sparkling emerald green. A slit that went all the way up her thigh was the only thing enabling her to walk. Without that strategically placed slit, all she would have been able to manage was a shuffle

In her elegant, ring clad hands, she held drinks. A flute of champagne for herself and a Bloody Mary for Nikki.

Nikki accepted the drink with a smile and toasted her hostess. "Hell of a party," she said before taking a drink of the spicy concoction.

"Yes, I noticed your enthusiasm as you threw perfectly good champagne at one of the junior editors. He's being escorted home as we speak. Donald doesn't appear to hold his liquor all that well." She tossed Nikki a catty little smile before adding, "He's swears up and down you propositioned him and then when he accepted, you threw your drink at him. You little tramp." Kirsten settled herself against the desk and took a delicate sip of champagne as she studied her friend.

Nikki's only reply to that was a snort.

Nikki looked like hell.

Some might think the weight loss was an improvement. She now had the model thin look that was so popular, particularly in New York. The hollowed cheeks made her eyes look larger and the rich material of her dress clung lovingly to her torso before ending in a flirty little skirt inches above her knees. The dress, deep red and flattering to her svelte new figure, actually belonged to Kirsten. It had been altered only the day before.

Kirsten's attempts to take her shopping had failed, even though she knew very few of Nikki's clothes fit her any more. And she owned nothing that could be worn to Kirsten's annual holiday bash at her parents' house in Long Island.

Not that she really wants to be here, Kirsten thought wryly. Hell of a compliment. She was boring her best friend out of her mind.

Of course, Kris had known this party would hold no interest for her.

No. This wasn't an improvement. Kirsten saw only despair in that face, pain in those sad eyes. That sleek body was a result of her appetite fading into nothingness. Nikki didn't look slim and sexy. She looked ill.

Nikki forced herself to eat regularly, but she couldn't down more than a few bites out of any meal.

"Is your dad upset that you're not going home for Christmas?"

"A little. We'll celebrate when I go home in January." Nikki drank again, emptying the glass and setting it aside as she shifted her body to face Kirsten.

"Have you set a date? Got your ticket?"

"Yes, mother. I'm going home to face the music."

Kirsten shook her head and sighed. "Nik, you're welcome here as long you like, but we both know you're miserable. You're going to be miserable anywhere until you put this behind you. And you can't do that here."

"I'm aware of that," Nikki said, her voice quiet. "I just need a little more time."

"Time isn't going to help this. If you'd put it to rest, it would, but not until then. You hardly eat, you hardly sleep. You walk around looking like a damned zombie." Kirsten sat her champagne flute down with a snap and moved closer. "You have got to either let him go or go back and fight for him. But this has got to stop. Or you're going to end up the way you did five years ago."

Nikki lowered her lids slowly over her shadowed eyes, tipping her head back to meet Kirsten's angry glare. "I'm not that bad off."

"Yet." Kirsten started pacing back and forth, her heels sinking into the thick piled carpet.

Where had the anger come from? she wondered. Nikki was hurting, Kirsten knew that. She had reason to. She wasn't sulking over nothing.

But Kris desperately feared this was just the beginning of another downward spiral.

That thought not only angered her, it frightened her as well.

"You're not that bad off yet, but you will be. Before much longer, you'll be in the hospital again, hooked up to IV's, tubes running this way and that.

Your dad is going to be sitting there, begging you to fight and I don't think you have much fight left in you, Nicole. He's already come home once to find somebody he cared about dead. He wasn't able to save your mother. He doesn't deserve to lose another woman he cares about."

Swallowing the lump in her throat, Kirsten paused long enough to blink away the tears burning her eyes, "Damn it, Nik. He isn't worth this, Nik. I don't think any man is, but if he's worth this much grief, then why aren't you fighting for him?"

"That's easier said than done," Nikki murmured, her voice thick with tears. She failed to notice the angry and frightened tears that glittered in Kris' eyes. "And he doesn't want me. There's no point."

Wrong words.

"No point," Kirsten repeated slowly, her cat green eyes narrowing.

"No point? So you'll just mourn yourself into the grave this time?" Kirsten snapped, whirling to face the younger woman. "That's where you are headed this time, little girl. Your heart can't take the kind of abuse you heaped on it last time and I'm not talking about the emotional heart. Damn it, it's a wonder it didn't give out on you last time. It can't take that strain again, Nicole Kline.

"It's been five years since you pulled yourself out of that hole, and you're still popping Lanoxin every day. You will never be able to stop taking those drugs, Nikki. They are your lifeline, and one more little injury to your heart could kill you. It will give out if it's put through much more strain, Nikki. You're going to end up having a heart attack or worse.

"And you don't have Jason to latch on to this time. He's not here this time to keep you going."

"I'm not that far gone. I'm still perfectly healthy—"

"Bull shit," Kirsten said succinctly, her voice hard, sharp as shards of broken glass. "You're a damned mess. Over *him,* a jackass who slept around on you, one that had two women knocked up at the same time. He got some woman pregnant one night, drunk out of his mind, angry over a fight he started. Doesn't that strike you as kind of stupid, being that upset over it? How many times have you told me about how angry you were with your mother when she put up with this kind of shit from your father? Why is Wade any different?"

Nikki didn't answer, she just stared Kris with haunted eyes.

"I can't believe you waste your time and your love on such a pathetic bastard, Nicole. Not just once, but twice. You're letting him put you through hell all over again. I can't help but wonder how many others he's got on the sly while he's been chasing you. Why do you even bother with him?"

Quietly, Nikki said, "Wade isn't like that."

"Oh, the hell he isn't," Kirsten replied, slashing at the air with a sharp gesture, rings flashing fire. "He's a no good, lying, cheating, hick bastard who wouldn't know a good thing if it bit him in the ass."

"I love him, Kris. He's not a bad man," Nikki snapped, her own eyes narrowing this time.

Kris managed to suppress the pleased smile as she

snapped, "Then dammit, go back and fight for him. He spent months chasing after you. Do you think he'll give up that easily?" That spark of anger settled her a little. Nikki hadn't shut down quite as much as she wanted people to think.

"He's seeing somebody else," Nikki reminded her, the hollow ache in her chest spreading. "He's found somebody else."

Kirsten snorted. "So he up and got married already?"

"They're dating."

"Oh, the sacred covenant. Dating." Sarcastically, Kirsten said, "And here I am encouraging you to go break up this happy union. Oh, wait a second, this is the man who got another woman pregnant while he was engaged to you. Oh, yes. He's definitely a man who honors his commitments."

"If he's dating somebody, it's because he's lost interest in me."

"You left," Kirsten said, spacing each word out slowly. "You've been gone more than three months. He might think you're not coming back, so he's probably trying to get on with his life. Hell, your dad said he's been asking about you all over town. He even had the nerve to approach those lunatic brothers of yours. *That* right there shows how desperate he is. If he could afford it, he'd probably be hunting you down."

"I doubt that. You didn't see him that day, Kris. He's fed up with me"

Kirsten rolled her eyes. "He's a *man,* sweetie. When men don't get what they want when they want it, they pout. That's how men are. But they get over it." Kneeling in her dress wasn't a wise thing to do, but she did it. Emerald green silk stretched but held as Kris caught hold of Nikki's hand and whispered, "You need to go home, baby. He's got to be worth fighting for, or you wouldn't be such a mess"

"And if he doesn't want me?" Nikki asked, her voice ragged. She clenched Kris's hands tightly as the tears welled up in her eyes and spilled over. "If I go back and he doesn't want me, what do I do then?"

"You'll go on," Kris whispered, freeing her hand and brushing back the younger woman's tousled hair. Her eyes were swirling masses of pain. If this was what love could do to you, Kirsten wanted nothing of it. "Honey, you'll just have to go on. You're strong, stronger than you think. You'll be just fine.

"But," Kris said, smiling softly. "I don't think that's going happen. He loves you, has loved you for years. He isn't going to give up that easily."

A soft, muffled cry came from Nikki and Kris shifted, wrapping her arms around her, whispering, "It's okay…just let it go." She stayed there as the sobs ripped out of Nikki's throat. The storm passed quickly and Nikki passed a hand over her eyes, smearing already ruined make up. Sheepishly, she hugged Kirsten. Then she sat back and heaved a ragged sigh. "I haven't told him about Jason. If… if he wants to try this one more time, he's going to have to know about his son."

"Damn it, Nik." The words came out on a huffy sigh and Kris passed a hand over her elegant chignon. "Why haven't you told him yet?"

Grimacing, Nikki said, "Stubborn. I kept telling myself I didn't want him back, that my past wasn't any concern of his. I guess I figured if I told him, that I'd forgiven him and was ready to try again. And…" Her voice trailed off again as Nikki stared past Kirsten's shoulder, her eyes distant.

"I was scared to," she finally admitted. "I still am. I…I don't think I can take being hurt like that again, Kris. It'll destroy me."

"He hurts you again, I'll destroy him," Kris promised. "But something tells me that he'd sooner chop off his arm than hurt you again. If he was the jerk I wanted him to be, he wouldn't have hung around as long as he did when you kept being a cold little bitch to him."

"You don't know the half of it," Nikki murmured, dashing the back of her hand over her eyes. Then she eyed the black smears on her hand. "I'm a mess."

"I've told you that already," Kirsten reminded her. Gingerly, carefully, she got to her feet and heaved a sigh of relief when she did so without hearing material ripping. "I don't know why I chose this dress. I can't even sit down in it."

"That's probably why you chose it. You like seeing eyes pop out." Nikki gave a weak watery smile as she rose to her feet as well. "The person who designed it must have been a man. They don't think of things like that. But you look great in it."

"I've been told several times tonight that I'd look better out of it," Kirsten quipped, flashing a smile at the younger woman. "I know I'd certainly feel better out of it." She slid a sideways look at Nikki and asked,

"What about you?"

"I don't think it matters to me one way or the other, but for propriety's sake, you ought to leave it on," Nikki replied, her voice droll.

"I meant, do you feel better?"

"No," she replied honestly. "But I will."

Chapter Eight

January fourteenth dawned sunny and cold in New York City. Nikki boarded the plane with her sunglasses in place, her hair shorn once again to chin length. She'd actually managed to gain back three pounds in the past three weeks. She was actually a little hungry and looking forward to the snack served mid flight.

But half way through the flight the weather turned cloudy and then stormy, and the final fifty minutes of the flight were passed with her closing her eyes against a dreadful headache, clenching her teeth against the nausea that roiled through her. You couldn't have gotten her to open her mouth for food even if you had a crowbar.

Hands cold and sweaty, eyes glassy, Nikki shuddered minutely each time lightning flashed around them, each time thunder rolled through the sky.

The kindly Southern gentleman on her side smiled reassuringly at her and patted her hand from time to time as he worked on his laptop. She wondered if she would ever get over her dread of thunderstorms, of rain.

When the plane touched down, Nikki heaved a sigh of relief, took a deep gasp of air and sent a payer of thanks heavenward, earning a chuckle from the man next to her. "Didn't think we'd make it, did you?" he asked, his eyes smiling from behind thick lenses.

"I just don't deal with real well with storms,

particularly when I'm flying around in the middle of one."

"The trick is to not think about," he offered as he politely held her long leather trench coat for her. "You were thinking about it before it really even started so that made it worse. But we're here, on solid ground."

"Thank God," she said fervently, smiling weakly at him and thanking him before grabbing her carryon and slinging it over a shoulder. "Have a safe trip to wherever you're going."

"You, too, young lady," he said, smiling at her before she stepped into the aisle, joining other disembarking passengers.

Her long leather coat swept her ankles as she entered the terminal, looking for familiar faces. Shawn's face was the first she saw. Or rather, she saw his head as he bent to whisper in the ear of a girl who would stand a good six inches over Nicole. Behind him stood her Dylan, leaning against a pole and gazing into nothingness. Her dad stood to the side, searching the crowd with impatient eyes.

They hadn't seen her yet.

Nikki resisted the urge to melt into the crowd and take off running. Ireland. Australia. Scotland. Any place. The Arctic Circle would be fine.

But she didn't. She was getting tired of running.

Tugged off the loose gray beret, Nikki shifted her way through the flow of people until only ten feet or so separated her from her family. She was five feet away before they recognized her.

Jack's eyes glanced over her absently before drifting away. Seconds later, they returned to her thin face and he sighed, shaking his head in resignation.

The thin sad little waif before them bore little resemblance to the healthy woman who had left. Only the sad eyes were the same. Sadness had eaten away at her literally, until she was just a shadow of herself. Jack doubted she'd weigh a hundred pounds. Violet half moons lay under her eyes and Jack wished that for five minutes, he was alone with the boy who had done this to his little girl. Again. He pulled her into his arms, stifling the second nature instinct that had him wishing for a drink.

"How are you, baby?"

Nikki forced a smile and promised, "I'll be better now that I am home." She hoped she wasn't lying.

Dylan was scowling at her when she turned him. "You look like hell. Doesn't that rich girl in New York know how to feed people?" he demanded. His mouth was compressed to a tight thin line, his eyes narrowed. "You were supposed to come back better, not worse."

"She knows how to feed people, I just forgot how to eat," Nikki told him, her mouth quirking in a slight smile before she moved away, letting him shoulder her carry on.

The animosity between her brother and friend was a long-standing one, one she used to. Kirsten had taken one look at her brooding baby brother and steered far clear of him. Dylan simply ignored her, never speaking more than five words to her unless he had to.

Nikki suspected Dylan had noticed the elegant lady from the first moment he had seen her. *Really* noticed.

She also suspected she knew exactly why Dylan avoided Kris so completely. Kris had only been a junior editor when she met him the first time, but she was far more successful than he would ever be. He was a street punk from West Louisville, she was a classy educated businesswoman.

And if she knew her brother at all, the fact that he had what could be considered a crush on her that wouldn't go away only added fuel to the fire.

She arched a brow at him, unable to keep from wondering how long those two would avoid each other. The inevitable would happen sooner or later. Under her patient stare, Dylan scowled and repeated himself, "You look like hell."

Then he hugged her close, and Nikki sighed, relaxing for just a minute. But then he straightened up and stared down at her with shrewd, knowing eyes. "You didn't outrun it, did you?" Dylan asked quietly, studying her shadowed eyes. "But I don't guess you expected to."

"No. I guess I didn't," Nikki agreed, turning away from him and introducing herself to the Amazon who stood hand in hand with her baby brother.

And as she spoke to the sweet natured girl who handled her brother like an old pro, she fought off the feeling of dread that was rising within her.

She was home.

It was time to pay the piper.

*****

Christmas Eve

Wade climbed out of the ambulance, his shift over. He didn't have to be at work until five a.m. three days from now. He had time to spend with his daughter and parents. And Leanne.

And his memories.

Cursing, Wade shoved the thought of memories out of his head as he trudged over to the car after exchanging good byes with J.D.

After supper with his family, he was taking Leanne home. His father, very subtly, of course, had offered to watch Abby for as long as they were needed tonight. And Leanne couldn't have been much more obvious about what she wanted under her Christmas tree.

Her invitations had been subtle, timidly issued, but there nonetheless.

And Wade couldn't make up his mind whether he wanted to take her up on it. He was tired of waiting, tired of being celibate, tired of the only relief he had being his fist. It had been over two years since he'd been with a woman.

I'm not a little kid, damn it. If I need a woman, I ought to be able to have one. And not feel guilty about it, he seethed in silence.

God above knew, as did Wade, that if he played his cards right, he could have Leanne in bed beside him at night, cooking his little girl breakfast in the morning. God above knew his little girl needed a mother.

Wade needed a wife.

But his body was cold at the thought of going to

bed with Leanne. That dynamite body rose only causal male appreciation of a fine female form. Kissing her was pleasant, but Wade got more satisfaction from even thinking about kissing Nikki. And she was beyond his reach.

He had never been more indecisive, more confused

And he had never been more lonely.

Getting Nikki out of his mind was hard, but he was working on it. She had obviously let him out of hers easily enough. Never mind that he still dreamed of her, night after night, he thought as he started the truck and flipped on the windshield wipers to clear the drifting snow from the windshield. The sky was winter white and an inch of fluffy white snow lay on the ground.

Never mind that Nikki was the first thing on his mind when he woke up and slipped into his mind the minute he let his guard down. He was dating. And he enjoyed being with Leanne. She was sweet, smart, drop dead gorgeous, and looked at him as though he was some kind of hero, instead of a something disgusting that had crawled out from under a rock.

Wade congratulated himself on how well he was doing as he turned onto the main highway. So what if Nicole Kline had moved up to New York. She probably had a fancy ass boyfriend up there, not that Wade cared. Some limp-wristed bastard who ate canapés, and drank champagne for breakfast.

Wade Lightfoot did not need Nicole Kline.

He might want her, but he didn't need her. If he woke up at night, still able to taste her on his lips, so what? Didn't most men think fondly of their first love?

Fondly my ass, his evil twin insisted. Wade tuned that mocking voice out of his head as he slowed for a stoplight. The snow was starting to fall heavier. He was getting over her, and doing a good job of it.

And he just might take Leanne up on that invitation tonight.

*****

Then again, maybe not.

Wade rested his chin on top of Leanne's head, his eyes wide open. She was pressed against him, wearing a dress that would have demure if not for the body that wore it. A soft, musky perfume rose from her warm flesh and she had offered to let him come and toast the holiday season.

Wade couldn't think of any place that could be more uncomfortable than where he was right now. He didn't want to be there

And he was fooling himself. He wasn't ready to go to bed with this woman, and he probably never would be. So he forced a smile, bussed her mouth gently and said, "Not tonight. I've got a busy night ahead of me. And you have to work in the morning."

So now he was sitting in front of the fireplace, alone, assembling the toys from hell that all children seemed to want from Santa Claus. Wade was viciously wishing the fat elf would show his face and put these damned things together. A half-empty beer sat next to him and several more waited in the fridge. He certainly wouldn't make it through the night if he had to be completely sober.

His father had offered to help, but this was a parent's job.

And, as always, he was doing it on his own.

Outside, the snow continued to fall. It was, all in all, the picture perfect Christmas Eve. If only...

Wade closed his eyes and let his head fall to rest on his drawn up knee, the socket wrench falling from his hand. *If only I wasn't such a first class fool.* God only knows how he could have spent this Christmas, if he hadn't lost his head back in the summer.

If he hadn't let Nikki wrap herself around his heart so tightly, he might have had Leanne with him.

But he couldn't have Nicole. And he didn't want anybody else.

Now he understood why holidays were so depressing to some people. Loneliness always seemed to magnify itself at this time of year. And even though he had much to be thankful for, he was finding a hard time remembering any of it.

He was tired of fighting off his memories, of subduing his imagination and his sorrow. Why in the hell shouldn't he think of her? When he got right down to it, he knew he was only lying to himself when he expected to get over her.

Was she spending tonight with somebody?

No. She's alone, just like you are.

She shouldn't be. She'd been alone for the past five years. She didn't deserve to keep being alone, but he couldn't find it in him to wish she was spending it with somebody she cared about, who cared about her. *Selfish bastard,* he whispered to himself. *You can't have her but that doesn't mean she should have to be alone because of it. After all, you are the one who screwed things up.*

Without even realizing it, Wade drifted off into sleep.

Nikki.

She was sitting in a window seat, overlooking a night sky filled with glistening Christmas lights for as far as the eye could see. The city wasn't one he knew well. He hadn't ever been there, but millions of people knew it from just the skyline…

New York.

Face tipped back, her eyes closed, tears streamed down her pale cheeks. And as he watched, she opened her eyes and turned her head away from the picture outside her window.

Her face was thin, hollow shadows beneath her high cheekbones. And as she stood, a thin silk chemise showed a body that was pared down to little more than muscle, flesh, and bone. She moved past him, so close he could have touched her. In fact, he tried, but his hand just drifted through her wrist as she walked by.

And he started to drift away.

But before he was completely gone, he heard the softly uttered words.

Damn you, Wade.

*****

Damn you, Wade.

His eyes snapped open and his jerked his head up, staring all around him. The toys, fully assembled for the most part, shone shiny and new in the firelight. His beer, lukewarm, still sat half empty at his side.

Staring into the fire, he remembered the dream.

It hadn't just been a dream

Just as it hadn't just been a dream when he had fallen asleep in the lounge at the hospital years ago just a few days before Jamie had killed herself. He had known before it had happened.

Nikki was miserable.

And again, he was to blame.

He couldn't seem to stop making her miserable.

Let her go, a small voice whispered inside his head. *She deserves a little bit of happiness in her life, somebody who doesn't make her miserable just by existing.*

Hell. He remembered the utter despair on her face as she rose from the window seat.

She would be coming home soon enough. This was her home, not New York. She had come here in refuge five years earlier, and she would come back once she had time to settle herself. And what Wade needed to do was let her go before she came back.

When she did come back, she needed to see that he had moved on with his life, that he was accepting her wishes.

I'm not going to go up there, demanding she give mt one more chance. I need to apologize, and let her know I'm ready to move on with my life, like she wanted in the first place.

And once she saw that he wasn't going to keep intruding in her life, she could finish healing. She had told him, time after time, that she was just learning to live again and he had ruined it all by showing up and chasing her back inside herself.

Once he was out of her life, she could resume her life, without him.

And eventually, she'd find somebody who made her happy.

The thought sickened him, knotted his stomach and made his vision go red.

But the past five years of her life had been miserable. He had broken the spirit of somebody who he had thought too strong to ever break.

The least he could do was let her go.

*****

Leanne gazed at him over softly glowing tapers, her eyes smiling shyly into his. Soft violin music played over discreetly hidden speakers and ubiquitous waiters answered ever wish before it could even be spoken.

January was almost a memory now. Christmas was past. And Wade had been set to testing his resolution to put Nicole in his past. She was back in town. Had been for nearly two weeks. He hadn't seen her yet, but would eventually.

He knew he had to convince her, and himself, that when he saw her he was completely done with her. As though there was nothing between them.

And if the thought made him want to howl, he just reminded himself he was doing it for her. He felt noble for the most part, letting the love of his life go so she could be happy. Settling for a woman who was, at best, a pale second. Not that Leanne would ever know that.

The woman who would be his child's mother would deserve the very best he could give her since he wouldn't be able to give her his heart. Wade smiled at Leanne automatically as he walked himself through the night, step by step. Abby was spending the weekend with her grandparents. The scene at home was set.

If he was suffering from a few qualms about this, it was only natural. His first marriage hadn't been a dream come true.

But this would be different.

It was for the best, for everybody concerned. Leanne would have the family she so desperately wanted. Wade would have a wife and hopefully, the loneliness that surrounded him like a cloak would lessen. Abby would have a mother who adored her instead of ignored her.

And Nikki would understand that she was free.

Wade was giving himself a much repeated pep talk as they waited for their meal. He had just taken a sip of the wine Leanne had sweetly asked he try when he looked up and saw her.

His throat tightened, his stomach clenched as though he had just taken a particularly viscous sucker punch.

Nikki.

She walked past, about twenty feet away, her head bent as she followed the hostess around the corner. His eyes landed on her family, and he cursed the sense of relief that rushed through him when her realized she wasn't here with a date. Or a lover.

A cocky little beret sat atop curls shorn to chin length, her long leather coat swept her ankles as she disappeared from his sight.

Wade nearly choked on the excellent wine as he automatically inhaled at the sight of her. A fist closed around his heart and he could have sworn he smelled the subtle alluring scent of lotion slicked flesh. Blood pounded in his head and muscles tensed.

He had been deluding himself.

Maybe he could let her out of his life, but never out of his heart. And he could never let another woman take the position that should have hers from the first, that would have been, if he hadn't been such an ass

She was his first love, his only love.

And if he couldn't have her as his wife, he would never take another.

A gentle cough had him looking up to see Leanne studying him with sad, wise eyes. Thick lashes briefly shielded her dark blue eyes as she lowered her wine glass to the table with hands that shook slightly. Her mouth trembled once before firming as she asked, "Is she the one whose memory I'm competing with?"

Wade remained silent, closing his eyes, as he tried to calm his racing heart. She was back, after more than four months, she had really had come back home.

"I wasn't sure if that was the Nikki that Abby kept talking about all the time, but I guess I have the answer to that now, don't I?" she murmured, crossing her hands in her lap. "I didn't know you two had met. Looks like you've done a little more than that."

Wade murmured something, what he didn't know. He stared into his wineglass, at the deep red liquid as his mind raced and chased itself in dizzying circles. The flickering candlelight only added to the effect, making his head spin as blood roared in his ears.

"Was it love at first sight?" Leanne asked, watching him. "Or did you know her from before she moved here?"

"Yes. And yes," he whispered, his voice slightly hoarse.

"I see," Leanne replied, her eyes stating clearly that she didn't see at all.

She wanted to know. It was written all over her face.

And he wanted, *needed,* to tell somebody. Five years had passed and nobody but him knew the whole of it. He had been ashamed to talk to any of his old friends, and Lord knew he couldn't talk it over with his best friend. That had been Nicole, and he had lost her. He had hurt her, broke her heart. His parents weren't viable candidates for purging his soul either.

Hadn't he kept quiet about it long enough? If nothing else, maybe telling it out loud would exorcise her from his heart and soul and he could let her go, the way he needed to.

"I…met Nikki before I got married. I've known her for over eight years," he said, his voice rusty sounding. His hand clenched tightly around the fragile stem of the wine glass before he made it relax. He loosened the tie at his neck, released the top button of his shirt.

"Eight years ago," Leanne repeated. "She would have just been a kid."

Wade snorted and said, "I don't think she was ever really a kid, not like we were." He took up the wine glass, tossed it back and wished it were something stronger. And the words started to pour from him. The meals were served, but hardly touched, as he told of the first few awkward dates, and the furious fights. The final fight that had Wade destroy what was most important to him in the world.

"I don't even remember it," he whispered, his voice sounding slightly shocked, puzzled. "It just doesn't seem right that the event that ended up destroying every thing I had been dreaming of for three years passed without me even knowing what happened. I don't remember her showing up at Zack's, or her taking me home. I don't know if I asked her in or if she just barged in. And I don't know if I started it or if I was just too drunk to refuse her."

He paused, frowning into his empty wine glass. "I sure as hell don't know why I let it happen. I never thought of her like that, never. She was just...Jamie, the little girl I had grown up with."

He told her about the last night when he had told Nicole about what he had done, how that revelation had ripped his heart from his body. Of the months of depression that followed, depression that was relieved only by the arrival of his newborn daughter.

"I don't regret Abby. I couldn't. She's everything to me," Wade said, his harsh face softening as he thought of her, that sweet smile, the mischief that glinted in her eyes, her unfaltering love. "I didn't know it was possible to love somebody like that. But to get my daughter, I had to lose Nikki. Had to hurt her"

Leanne listened in silence as he told her about Jamie, how his wife had emotionally slipped away from him and how he hadn't been able to help her, hadn't cared enough to do it.

"She killed herself, you know." His voice was conversational, his eyes bland, showing little emotion. He could have been discussing the weather. "Took a bottle of sleeping pills and never woke up. A few days before she died, I was napping in the lounge at the hospital. I dreamed of her doing that, but I didn't think anything of it. I was always having really odd dreams. But I came home one day after picking up our daughter and we found her mother laying on the bed, wearing a pair of blue silk pajamas somebody had given her at her bridal shower. Her hair was fixed and she was wearing make-up. She even had gotten a manicure and pedicure .

"She didn't leave a note," he rasped, his eyes burning now, with anger, guilt and shame. "She didn't have to; I knew why she had done it.

"And when all was said and done, I was *relieved.* I was tired of trying to help her, tired of listening to her cry about how rough she had it, sitting at home day after day. Tired of her pretending Abby didn't exist. I just didn't care."

It was late, over an hour had passed since he had see Nicole enter the restaurant. And in halting tones, he was speaking of the fight that last day on her mountain, the one that had sent the woman he loved away.

And when Wade finished, he sat back, looking at the woman he had hoped, had planned, would take Nikki's place. How in the hell had he even thought it would work? He'd been trapped in one loveless marriage already. And he had almost walked right into another one.

"I went to her house about a week later, to apologize and see if I could salvage anything. But she was already gone. I kept waiting, certain she would be back. I had this little speech all laid out in my mind. I went up four or five times a week that first month, but she was never there. Her father wouldn't tell me one damn thing, and her brothers would just as soon rearrange my face as look at me"

He leaned back in his chair and rubbed the back of his neck, closing his eyes against the tension headache that had formed ages ago. "I kept waiting for her to show up, so I could apologize. I had no right to demand a damn thing from her, no right to say what I did. I had to apologize," he rasped, staring into the understanding eyes across from him. "I had to. It was eating me up inside. But I never got the chance."

Finally, he fell silent, staring at the melting candles. His untouched meal lay cold before him. The perfect night he had planned lay in shambles. But he should have known better.

Leanne opened her mouth to speak and then closed it, pursing her lips and staring blindly into her wineglass. Wade realized he had hurt another woman he cared about, but he didn't know what to do about it.

Finally, after eons of silence, Leanne looked up at him and forced a smile.

"Not much for the relationship thing, are you, Wade?"

"No." His eyes dropped, unable to look into those dark blue eyes, seeing the hurt she was trying so hard to hide. "Leanne, I'm sorry. I never—"

"Wade," Leanne interrupted. "Don't, okay? No real harm done. And I was asking for it, anyway. I could tell you had somebody else in your heart, but I just kept pushing it. I kept telling myself you'd get over whoever it was, but I ought to know better. Love isn't like the flu. It isn't something you can get over."

Rubbing his heart with the heel of his hand, Wade muttered morosely, "It's more like a cancer. The incurable kind."

Leanne chuckled softly. "I don't think it's always that bad, Wade. You've just had a couple of rough roads. Maybe it'll get better."

Yeah. And maybe there is a blizzard raging in hell right this moment, Wade thought dourly. But he didn't say anything.

Shortly after that, they were outside heading to Wade's truck. "I guess I'm kind of surprised to see her back here," he said as he helped Leanne into the truck. He remained at the open door, staring thoughtfully into the night. "She must like New York for her to stay there so long. I halfway expected her to stay there for good. There sure as hell isn't much to hold her here."

Frowning, Leanne shot him a look. "She's lived here for almost five years, Wade. She's made her home here. Her family's here. Her little boy is buried here." She wasn't looking at him as she fished around for her seat belt. Her words were delivered in an almost offhand manner.

It might have been comical, the way he froze in mid-action. His hand hovered an inch from the door. The ground seemed to drop out from under him and time stood still. Frozen in place, he attempted several times to work his mouth, but found his couldn't speak.

Little boy

Little boy

Wade hadn't heard her right. Before his vocal cords could relax enough for him to speak, Leanne gave him a questioning look. "Are you okay?" she asked but he couldn't hear her voice, he only saw her lips move.

"What..." his voice wasn't even a whisper. He cleared his throat and tried again. "What...did...you...say?"

Leanne stared at him, aghast. Her creamy complexion paled, twin flags of red riding high on her cheekbones. There was no way. He had to have known. But his poleaxed expression, the gray cast to his skin, said otherwise. "You didn't know," she murmured, her eyes wide and confused.

"Didn't know what?" he asked, but before she could reply, voices intruded. Like a wolf scenting wounded prey, he whirled, eyes narrowing as a slim figure moved across the parking lot. "Didn't know what?" he repeated softly, staring at Nicole as if just that alone would tell him what he wanted to know.

Nicole came to a halt, thirty feet away, her eyes colliding with his. They rested on him, then on Leanne for a brief moment before she turned away.

"If you aren't going to tell me, then I guess I'll go ask her," he said, his voice sharp.

"This isn't the right time, Wade. Damn it, I thought you knew. I'm not the person who should be telling you," Leanne said softly, her eyes locking on his as she caught his arm.

"You're right. The right time would have been *months* ago," he snarled, jerking his arm free. "And she should have told me." He started in the direction Nikki had headed.

"No," Leanne argued, releasing the seat belt and jumping from the truck. She was forced into action as she remembered the desolate look on Nikki's face moments earlier. The look would haunt her until the day she died. Much like the look that had been on Nicole's face when Leanne had revealed that Jason was gone. She caught up with him when he was half way to where Nikki and her family had parked. Seizing his arm, she put all her weight into slowing him down.

"Damn it, Wade. Let her go."

"Tell me," he said once again, his voice whisper soft.

A car door slammed shut and Leanne's head whipped around, following the taillights of a classic Mustang. Gone. Nikki was gone. She breathed a sigh of relief then turned her head to Wade, wishing to God she had never laid eyes on him.

As she remained silent, shifting awkwardly from one foot to the other, Wade cupped her shoulders, drew her closer to him. Leaning down, he repeated a second time, "Tell me. Now, Leanne. Or I'll chase her down and have her tell me."

Leanne shrugged away his hands, turning away from him. The cold winter wind blew across the parking lot, cutting through her coat like it wasn't there. It settled deep inside her, making her feel as though she would never be warm again. The bitter hot taste of guilt welled up in her throat until speech was nearly impossible.

Finally, she softly said, "I met Nikki in the grocery store a couple of years ago. She had this little boy with her." Her voice trailed off as she remembered those wide innocent brown eyes, that sweet laugh, silenced forever.

Wade's were sharper than shards of glass as he caught hold of her chin, forcing her to look at him. "I haven't seen a little boy. I've been here for *months* and I've never seen him"

Leanne closed her eyes, shook her head. "You aren't listening," she whispered, her voice breaking. "I saw her again about two weeks after that. This time in the ER. She was comatose. One of her brothers was with her and he was pretty banged up but nothing serious.

"And her little boy was in the morgue. He was killed during a storm when a drunk driver ran them off the road by her dad's home."

Wade wasn't even aware that Leanne was still speaking. The tragic story fell on ears that didn't want to hear. All he could think was that someone else had touched Nikki, held her in the night, loved her. While he had scorned the touch of his wife, clinging to his memories of Nikki, she had been with another man. She had given herself to somebody else, given what was *his*.

She had borne another man's child, probably that faceless high society bastard he had imagined her with. He could almost see it. Some rich New Yorker had met up with her when she hit it big, had wined and dined her, taken her to some penthouse, laid with her on silk sheets.

His stomach revolted at the thought, acid burning bitterly at the back of this throat. But somewhere inside, he clung to hope. Maybe…

His vision faded to gray before coming back into sharp focus, the edges gone eerily red. "You take me to the grave," he rasped, shoving Leanne toward the truck. "Now."

Chapter Nine

JASON CHRISTIAN KLINE
BORN MAY 11, 1995 DIED SEPTEMBER 2, 1996
Beloved Son
'I'll Be With You Always, Until The End of Time.'

The date was all wrong. Only by a month, a handful of weeks, but it might as well have been six months, or a year. She hadn't even waited a damn month, if that. Wade ran it through his head, hoping against hope. But it wouldn't work out. Pregnancy lasted nine months. That last frantic coupling in the woods couldn't have done it.

It had happened after that. And that meant the child couldn't have been his.

Not even a damn month.

Her voice hesitant, soft, Leanne asked, "When... when did you two break up?" The little boy had had dark hair, dark eyes, but that was all she could remember. She had only seen him once.

Bitterly, Wade replied, "Not soon enough. She didn't wait very long though, a month at most."

She had gone straight to another man and yet she had been punishing him all this time. "Bitch," he breathed out, hands clenching and unclenching, a vein throbbing at his right temple.

All the times she had pulled back, had thrown Jamie in his face, rushed back at him. All this time, he had thought she had been mourning what they had lost, had been too afraid to get involved or feared of being hurt. She had been mourning, all right, but not over him. She'd been mourning the loss of some guy's brat.

And his little girl. She had done the unforgivable, she had hurt Abby. The cool answers, the distance she had insisted on keeping between them, the reluctance to talk to her, touch her; it had all affected his baby, even though Abby had tried hard not to let it show.

He conveniently forgot the warnings she had issued, how many times she had tried to get him to leave her be. *Sooner or later, you'll realize I'm not who I used to be and I'm not somebody you want to be around. Certainly not somebody you want your daughter around.* She had been warning him but he hadn't listened. His subconscious played those words over and over.

But they were drowned out by the louder refrain of his bruised heart and pride. It kept replaying other words she had spoken.

I can't look at you without thinking about Jamie. About what you did.

And she had gone and done the same damn thing.

She would pay, damn it. For every time she had twisted his heart inside his chest, every time she had put even a flicker of hurt or disappointment in Abby's eyes, for every slur she had made against his wife.

He hadn't even realized he had spoken aloud until a palm smacked up against his chest. He almost didn't recognize the livid face practically nose to nose with his. Leanne's voice rang out in the quiet cemetery as she shouted, "Pay? *Pay?* Damn you, she has paid! She lost everything she held dear. That little boy was her entire life and he's gone."

"My little girl is my life," Wade rasped. "She hurt her. She called my wife a whore, then turns around and does the same damn thing. She treated Abby like she had the plague, treated me like dirt. But she had gone out and done the same damn thing."

Leanne was practically shaking with anger, and with shock. She couldn't believe what she was hearing, or what she was seeing. The hard cold face of the man before her was someone she didn't know. Wide-eyed with disappointment and disillusionment, she bitterly whispered, "You cold hearted bastard. That little boy was her reason for living. I took care of her after the accident. She was in a coma for two weeks. And when she woke up, she was empty inside. There was *nothing* there.

"You think about how you would feel if the reason you had for living was suddenly ripped away," she whispered, her own heart aching at the memory of those grief stricken, desolate eyes she had faced, eyes that haunted Leanne day after day. "*Ripped* away, not stolen like you were taken from her. He didn't abandon or leave her, but was ripped away for no reason. Everything just suddenly gone, with no hope of ever getting it back.

"She's never completely healed from it. Her grief damn near killed her," Leanne said roughly, trembling inside from the force of her emotions. "*She had to bury her own child, Wade.* That is a price no parent should ever be asked to pay."

His fury deafened and blinded him. In his mind's eyes, he could see it all so clear. Nikki in bed with another man, Nikki heavy with child, Nikki loving that child. The love he had wanted her to give to Abby, she had given to another child while refusing them.

It gnawed at him like a cancer, sickened him, crazed him.

Leanne's eyes burned with tears, her voice thick as she asked, "I'm not getting through to you, am I?"

He would rip that woman into shreds.

Eyes boring into hers, he advanced on Leanne and whispered, "This never happened, Leanne. Do you understand me?"

She looked fragile, but she had always thought herself to be stronger than she looked. Refusing to be intimidated, she scoffed, "Oh, yeah. Right. Like I'm just going to pretend that you haven't lost your *ever loving mind*"

"That is exactly what you are to do. And I'm thinking clearer now than I have in months," he said, raising his arms to brace against the large memorial behind her, caging her in.

"You don't even know what happened back then," she whispered.

"I know more than I needed to know. She got herself knocked up, the same way Jamie did. And she's got the nerve to go badmouthing my little girl's mama. Making me feel like scum. Treating my daughter like a leper.

"But that doesn't matter," he whispered into her ear, voice silky. "Because this doesn't concern you. And you aren't going to go telling her a damn thing. Because if you do, I'm going to remember those secrets you've been confiding in me. Remember how easy I am to talk to, how trustworthy I am?"

Her face paled. Good Lord. He wouldn't.

"Now the hospital knows about that baby in

Lexington was some kind of fluke. That you weren't to blame. But to the uninformed public, they might start to have second doubts about it."

He would. *Idiot. Fool. Why did you tell him?* she screamed at herself, her mind racing. Because she had thought she knew him, could trust him.

She didn't know he had been obsessively in love with somebody else. "She doesn't deserve to be broken again, Wade," Leanne pleaded, making one last feeble attempt. But he was right. She would say nothing. She had rebuilt her life after a tragic accident. She couldn't lose it all.

"Think about it, Leanne. The hospital would feel pressured into letting you go on a leave of absence - they might even ask you to resign."

It was then that she discovered that she wasn't as strong as she had thought she was. Besides the obvious, there was another major difference between her and Nicole Kline. Nicole had lost everything but she overcame it, proved her strength. She was no coward.

Leanne, on the other hand, most certainly was. She wouldn't dare pick up a phone and breathe so much a word of warning to Nikki. Tears filled her eyes, her chin dropped. And she nodded.

Wade smiled coldly.

At the sight of that cold, triumphant smile, she turned away, blindly heading for the gravel road. It was less than a half-mile to where she lived. It was cold and dark, a moonless night. If Leanne was lucky, maybe *she* would be hit by a drunk driver and put out of her misery.

Guilt and fear gnawed a hole in her belly. And she cringed at the thought of her own weakness. She had just sold out a defenseless woman.

As his mind chased itself in crazy circles, Wade watched distractedly as Leanne walked away from the cemetery, head bent against the chilly wind. He grew vaguely aware that it was late, dark, cold. He couldn't let her walk home alone.

He got in the truck, gunned the engine. Pulling up with her less than two blocks away, he rolled down the window and snapped, "Get in."

She ignored him, staring straight ahead. Wondering how she could have been so wrong about a woman.

"Get. In." he said slowly spacing the words out as he tried to rein in his rage once again.

She slowed and stopped. Then she turned her head in slow motion and spoke, her voice eerily distant. "I just sold my soul to the devil, buddy. But that doesn't mean I have to ride with him. I don't want to ever see your face again, Wade Lightfoot.

"And I pity that little girl of yours," she added. "She's going to grow up to be as heartless as you are."

And then she started walking, resolutely ignoring the truck that followed her home as she mentally kicked her own ass every step of the way.

*****

Blind fury fueled Wade, kept him running for the next few weeks. The house was placed on the market and he gave his two weeks notice. His old job back in

Louisville had been promised to him and they would stay with his folks until he found a new home for him and Abby.

All the while Wade tortured himself with images of Nikki and the father of the baby. He didn't think about the boy, didn't think of the tiny little grave on the hillside. Didn't think about the accident that should have killed her as well.

The accident report. He shouldn't have had an acquaintance in the police department track it down. It had almost lessened his resolve. It had been frank, brutal, frightening. Truck overturned twice, tumbled down a thirty-foot embankment. Snapped a little boy's neck and nearly blinded his mother. Both Nikki and Shawn had worn their seatbelts, Jason had been secured in his seat. None of that had mattered.

Wade refused to think about that piece of paper. It was just words strung together. He didn't think about it, or about what he was doing.

He wasn't sleeping much. It showed in his bloodshot eyes but nowhere else. While sleep gave his so called better half a chance to argue the wrongness of what he was doing, it also gave him a chance to see her twisting naked on sheets with someone whose face wasn't clear to Wade.

The lack of sleep wasn't bothering him much. Anger had a fuel all its own.

*****

The house was silent, save for the hum of the printer. A stack of paper, nearly four hundred pages thick, sat next to the laser jet. She sat back in her chair, feet propped on the desk, her mind carefully blank.

Nikki was tired, exhausted clear to the bone tired, weak, bleary minded tired. Her muscles ached from a two-hour wood chopping stint the day before. And the day before that, she had ridden her bike over the cold winding roads for several hours. Her face was chapped from the biting wind and it had taken hours to feel warm again.

The woodpile outside her house was unbelievably large. Nikki stocked in enough wood to last through several winters. And she had put more miles in on her bike the past four weeks than she normally did all summer.

She learned that Wade was dating Leanne Winslow. The night in the parking lot of Tonito's loomed large in her mind at the worst times. And she had heard rumors from Cheryl, Shawn's girlfriend. Her father owned the only jewelry store in town. Wade purchased a diamond solitaire from there about a week before Nikki had seen them at the restaurant.

It hadn't taken very long to replace her. It stung her pride, wounded her heart.

Nikki forced herself to get up and walk into the kitchen. Conscious of the wisdom in Kristen's words, she made herself to eat a good meal at least once a day, even if she didn't want it. Though she had gained another four pounds, Nikki was aware that she was still too thin. The cardiologist had not been pleased, to put it lightly. Her hipbones jutted out, and she could count her ribs simply by looking the mirror.

She was now on a high calorie/high protein diet.

And that damned doctor had told her if she didn't put on at least a pound every week within the next month, he was putting her on a liquid dietary supplement. Nikki's lip curled at the thought. No way was she drinking that crap she'd had to feed to the residents of the nursing homes she had done her clinicals at, while still in nursing school at U of L.

So she ate the damned food. And hated every tasteless bite.

Nikki was a ghost of her former self and knew she ought to be ashamed she let this happen again. But she simply couldn't work up the energy to care.

But she wouldn't put herself in the hospital again. Never again.

Later, as the sun rose to its zenith, shining down a thin watery winter light, she sat at the table, staring outside without seeing anything, eating a sandwich piled high with ham and tomatoes. She ate the awesome chili her dad had made and sent home with her, and never tasted it.

It all tasted like sawdust to her, but it had for weeks. Months.

He hadn't called. Hadn't spoken to her the one time she had seen him in the store. Not that this was a bad thing. Nikki wasn't sure she could handle it. She was far too fragile. Seeing him with another woman had hurt her even more than she expected. Part of her insisted once she recovered from the shock of that, she would do what she had come home to do.

But another part knew that if she approached him, and he rebuffed her, it would destroy her stubborn determination to keep going. She knew she wasn't as strong as Kirsten said she was. She would, once again, lose the will to live. And she wouldn't have Jason to keep her going.

And for some reason, if for no other than just sheer stubbornness, Nikki didn't want to just fade away again. Maybe the pain would go away, but then again, so would she. She had never been a quitter, and she didn't want to start now.

But something would have to give, and soon. She couldn't keep going on in this limbo forever.

Chapter Ten

Nikki's black Bronco came to an abrupt halt when she took the final curve to her house. Wade's truck sat blocking the road and he was leaning against the hood, hands buried in the pockets of a beat up leather jacket; one she had bought him their second Christmas together.

He still has it.

Blinking away the tears, Nikki shifted the Bronco into park and rolled the window down as Wade approached. She had been home nearly six weeks and this was the closest she had been to him since that awful day late last summer.

The cold wind blew through the window, whipping her hair, stringing her eyes. It was blocked when Wade leaned against the door, propping his elbows in the window frame. He was silent for a long time, studying her.

"Hey," he said quietly. The words he had rehearsed left him when he got his first good look at her. *Dear Lord. She looks like a war refugee.* She was thin, unbelievably so. Her cheeks were hollow and her hands that gripped the steering wheel were pale and fragile looking. Her eyes looked unnaturally dark in her wan face.

Sourly, Wade decided her high society boyfriend in New York must like his women scrawny.

Angry as he was, it wasn't as hard as he would have liked to make his voice sound hesitant and uncertain. Pleading. "Nikki." He cursed himself when his voice faltered of its own accord. His throat was tight as he said, "How… how've you been?"

"Well enough," Nikki replied. Wade didn't like just how easy, how steady her voice was. How could she sound normal when he was a mass of fury and pain inside? "And you?"

"Awful," he said bluntly, hating that it was true. Hated that just seeing her made his wounded heart feel better.

"Is there—"

"Will you—"

They both spoke at once, and then fell silent. "You first," she offered. A slight smile edging up the corners of her mouth.

Wade took the chance, not wanting to give her an opening to slip up the hill, into her house, away from him where she could lock the rest of the world out and remain hidden in her fortress. He steeled himself and reminded himself he had a job to do. Something that had to be done before he could get on with his life.

"I want to talk with you. Can you come for a ride with me?" he asked. Half of him shouted, *Say Yes!* while the other half begged, *Say no. Don't let me do this to you.*

Nikki shrugged and looked away. "You're welcome to come on up," she said, reaching for the gearshift.

"I'd rather you come with me. I…" Letting his voice trail off, he gazed at her with hot eyes. "I really don't need to be alone in that house with you, Nicole. Not just yet."

He didn't tell her that he didn't want to be in that

house. A house where she had raised her son. A house where she had probably welcomed her son's father, her lover. A house where he had never been welcomed.

Blood rushed to her face as he stared at her, and he could all but feel the heat that was rushing through her body as she shifted on the seat. She was going to refuse. Wade could see it in her eyes. Telling himself he had to convince her, he gave in to the urge to touch her, just brush his hand across her cheek. He was just trying to get her to go with him that was all. If he satisfied this crazy urge to touch her, so what?

So soft, he wondered. So cool, silky. "Please," he implored, willing to beg, if that was what it took.

Her eyes widened before flickering shut. Without moving, she seemed to arch closer, against his feather light caress. And then as if somebody had turned off a light, she shut down, locked herself back in.

"All right," she said quietly. "I can't be gone long though. I've got a lot to get done."

He backed away without answering. "I'll follow you up," he said softly. And then he turned on his heel.

Soon. In a few more days, she would be out of his life. And hopefully out of his heart.

He certainly would not be in hers. She was going to hate him, very shortly.

The very thought twisted his guts, tightened his throat until he could barely breathe. Scowling, he reminded himself it didn't matter if she hated him.

But he knew he was lying.

He frowned as she climbed out of the Bronco. His

eyes locked on her slight figure, clearly outlined by navy leggings. Why in the hell had she lost so much weight? Whoever in the hell he was - and Wade had no doubt that there was a he - he must like his woman all skin and bone.

Wade couldn't help but wonder if it was the father of the baby. Maybe she had been in New York with him all this time. Maybe...

With a growl, Wade halted that thought before it could fully form. Nikki had come to a halt outside his truck and was eyeing him uncertainly, her purse slung over one shoulder, hands tucked into the pockets of her trench coat. Wade forced a smile that felt as though it would crack his face as he swung back into the truck.

She moved slowly, tiredly. He doubted she was eating enough to keep a bird alive.

Well, her appetite would be roused over the next few days. He would take her to bed until she couldn't take him any more. He intended to mark her, brand her as his, so that for the rest of her life, she would never be able to look at another man, for want of him

He would use that sleek body until he had her out of his system.

And then he was going to walk away.

*****

Nikki eyed Wade, her uneasiness growing by leaps and bounds. It had merely been a seed when she had climbed into the truck. Wade wouldn't hurt her physically and she had taken everything else he had dished out. She would be fine.

But they had been driving for well over two hours. And Wade hadn't made a single sound other than a noncommittal grunt from time to time. As the highway sped on by, she forced herself to speak. "Wade," she said, striving for a light tone. "I know you are a man of few words, but this is a record even for you. How are we supposed to talk when you won't even open your mouth?"

Wade merely sent her a sidelong look she couldn't decipher and drove on.

"Wade, what's going on?" she asked flatly, crossing her arms over her chest as he turned off the main highway onto a side road.

"I figured we needed to clear the air," he finally said.

Minutes passed and he said nothing else, so Nikki sighed and again spoke. "Is there some reason we can't do that in Monticello?" she prodded.

By now they were on a road that was little more than a gravel path and he didn't take his eyes off of her as he drove on. "I didn't want to do it in your house. Too easy for you to kick me out there," he said, shrugging his shoulders.

He fell back into silence, without another word. But there was something in his eyes that bothered her, something that had her belly drawn into a tight knot, one that got tighter with every mile that passed. Silent, she stared out the window as he followed that country road, taking another one that spiraled upward.

They were in the mountains now. Through the occasional break in trees, she could see the Smokies, soaring into the sky, their peaks shrouded by low hanging clouds.

Stifling a shiver, she leaned back in the seat, wishing she had listened to her gut when it had insisted she not go with him.

And fighting off the fear that she really hadn't had a choice.

*****

Out of the corner of his eye nearly an hour later, Wade watched her shift in the seat. Her face had become paler and paler as they drove further. They hadn't seen a car in nearly two hours. This rutted dirt road would eventually end some twenty miles ahead, if he were going the right way.

If she sat up much straighter, her spine was going to crack from the strain. With a resigned sigh, he edged his truck as far off the narrow road as he could, turning up the heat before turning to face her. It was twenty degrees out and the nearest town was more than seventy miles back. One thing was certain, she was stuck with him until he decided otherwise.

With one arm draped across the steering wheel, the other across the back of the bench seat, he looked at her. Again, it struck him how wan she looked. She looked weak, fragile. In all the time he had known her, she had never looked like that; he never thought she could look like that.

But she did. She looked as though a breeze would knock her down. The emptiness in her eyes pulled at his heart and the words seemed pulled from there as he whispered, "Damnation, I've missed you."

Startled, Nikki turned her head to look at him. Her wary eyes skittered away and she shrugged as she said softly, "I don't know why. You said yourself, you were tired of waiting around for me."

Looking sheepish and sorry wasn't as hard as it should have been. "We need to talk about that," he muttered. Reaching out, he trailed his finger down her cheek before hooking the back of her neck and drawing her closer. He closed his eyes and breathed in her scent.

That unforgettable scent drew him, lured him closer, tempted and taunted him. He counted to ten, then twenty as he reached for control

Then he buried his face against her neck, basking in her warmth and softness. Control never seemed further away. "But we'll talk later," he muttered and dragged her across the seat to drape awkwardly across his lap.

Expecting her to go rigid, to say no.

But she didn't. She went willingly, almost eagerly into his arms, her body shuddering violently as it came in contact with his. He instinctively realized she wouldn't back away this time

Slanting his mouth across hers, he released the frustration and yearning that had been building for weeks, months. Years.

Whimpering deep in her throat, Nikki arched upward, straining against him. Her arms locked around his neck, her hands dipped into his hair and fisted.

With a few quick economical motions, Wade

divested her of her jacket and flannel shirt. Her slight weight was ridiculously easy to maneuver as he shifted, repositioned her so that she sat astride him, the steering wheel at her back.

When he touched her, a gasp fell from her lips, and he watched as her eyes lit from within. That sleek ivory flesh felt so soft under his hands, so warm.

Greedy, he buried his hands in the short curls at the nape of her neck, arching her mouth up to his.

Through the thick cotton of his sweater, he felt her nails biting into his skin. A hungry little whimper fell from her lips as he traced a line of kisses down her neck, raking the sensitive skin there with his teeth.

"Wade," she moaned, and he felt her entire body shiver under his hands. His cock ached and throbbed, and as she started to rock against him, he thought he'd leap right out of his skin.

"Damn it," he hissed, lifting her slightly, moving away from that sweet, hot heat between her thighs. Through the thin silk of her bra, her nipples beckoned, hard dark little circles that he was dying to have in his mouth again.

He was having a hard time focusing on his plans when she was plastered against him, her mouth hot on his, her tongue dancing in his mouth, her body wrapped around his like a kudzu vine. Cursing the tight confines of the cab, he twisted and shifted until she lay beneath him.

Her hands clutched at his shoulders, her hips rocked against his. Wade swore he could feel the heat of her right through their clothes. Too many clothes. Wrenching away, he drew to his knees to remedy that.

The silk and lace of her bra opened at a flick of his hand, the cups falling aside to reveal round firm breasts with rose brown nipples already erect. Rolling them between his fingers, he watched though slitted eyes as she arched up, panting. Giving into the urge, Wade lowered his head to nip and suck and suckle until she was mewling beneath him, whimpering deep in her throat.

He tore at the laces of her hiking boots until he could tug them off, then he reached for the waist of the slim fitting navy pants, pulling them down with quick impatient jerks of his hands.

As he revealed her sleek body to his eyes, he stopped and stared, hardly able to recognize this thin, pale woman to the lush body he had loved in the past. Pale flesh, concave abdomen. Wade gazed at her, torn between lust and disbelief. He could count her ribs.

Bitterly, he reminded himself that girl didn't exist any more. Probably never did. Hooking his fingers in the lacy front panel of her panties, he jerked hard, shredding the fragile material, tossing it aside.

Levering himself fully clothed over her, Wade cupped her face in his hands, covered her mouth with his. Kissed her deeply, stroking the sweet hollow of her mouth as she wrapped her arms around him and held him close.

Closing her eyes, Nikki basked in the warmth of his body, shuddered at the slow teasing strokes of his hand as it stroked from armpit to waist and back again. On each stroke, it wandered lower, fingers searching, seeking, gentle.

A direct contrast with his hard determined mouth

as it pressed one biting kiss after another to her mouth, her neck and her breasts. Her breath caught in her throat and her lids drifted partly shut when he caught one pearled nipple between his teeth, bit down gently, then swirled his tongue across, easing the slight hurt.

Stroke after teasing stroke, he circled around her nipple now, nipping at the underside, blowing a cool puff of air across it, nuzzled it while lower, his hand stroked closer and closer.

His hands became greedy, demanding

Rough denim rubbed against the tender flesh of her inner thighs, rasped sensitive nerves as he shifted slightly to give that roaming hand easy access. One long callused finger parted her, slid across the damp portal while his thumb flickered across the hardened pebble of flesh.

"Wade," she gasped, her hands reaching for his, tugging. Her eyes were nearly blind with need, her weakened heart pounding in her chest, strong and sure.

Nikki's eyes fluttered open, locked on his intent face. His eyes glittered fiercely, his jaw tight. And she shivered. She recognized his touch, her body recognized his, but she didn't know this man, this hard faced, grim stranger.

Something cold settled low in her belly, warring with the heat. A flash of fear fluttered in her chest. She was deeply aware of the feeling that something wasn't right, something was off.

Unconsciously one arm raised to shield her body while the other went out, her hand pressed to his chest, whether to stay him or drawn him close, she didn't know

A muscle spasmed in his cheek and he slid his hands over her thighs, draped them over his. "Wade," she whispered, distraught, nervous, almost afraid.

His eyes locked on hers, dark and relentless. And angry, she thought. Determination oozed from every pore of his body and she was certain he meant to do this, whether she was willing or not. He was intent on something he seemed to need and she had ceased to matter.

And then he buried his face against her neck, held her tightly against him. His voice nearly breaking, he asked "Don't you want me any more, Nikki?"

Wade didn't recognize his own voice, the need in it. He only knew he had to do this, had to have her. He couldn't live another minute if he didn't mark her, brand her as his and erase the touch of another man's with his. If he didn't ease the ache that had been building for five years. God, she had to want to him. He would die if she stopped him.

He didn't hear the need, but she did. It roared through her like a tornado, destroying all resistance

Beneath him, her arms closed around him, shielding him against something she couldn't see, but sensed. Her eyes closed. *Not want you?* she thought desperately. *My God. A day hasn't gone by that I haven't wanted you.*

She didn't even realize she had spoken out loud but Wade heard her words, heard the truth in them, and shuddered. He stiffened, his eyes tightly closed as her words echoed in his mind. The absolute sincerity in her words, in her eyes soothed a thousand myriad hurts, and caused a million more to take their place.

She'd gone to another man… Like a freight train, one thought after another rammed into his head, a hard fist of nausea closing around his stomach until he thought he would vomit. Another man had seen this, had touched her like this, felt the wet tight embrace of her body.

Hands that had unconsciously gentled went hard as unspoken pleas turned to demands. Covering her body once more with his, Wade moved closer until his sex nudged her damp flesh. One hand moved to guide him in while he propped his weight on the other elbow and, with one heavy thrust, he buried himself inside her.

She flinched, arching up against him with a weak whimper, her eyes wide and dark as the sharp discomfort bordered on pain. Her body recoiled from the rough, sudden invasion.

The movement didn't slow him, didn't deter him. She was wet and hot, but his entry was difficult, for her tight flesh resisted him. She was wet, hot, and hungry…but her sheath was so tight…He flexed his hips, pushing deeper until he was sheathed to the hilt. Her flesh rippled around his, alternately clenching and relaxing. As her muscles worked to accommodate him, he wondered at it. *She's so tight.*

And one thing was certain. Whatever she had been doing in New York, she had not been with another man.

Her eyes opened slowly, her lips parted as she took rapid shallow breaths. She stared up at him, her face flushed with need.

"Are you okay?" he asked roughly, forcing his body to wait. At her nod, he dipped his head, planted a sweet gentle kiss on her damp mouth. Weight braced on his elbows, he began rocking against her, his thrusts slow and gentle. With each steady thrust, her body opened, relaxed, welcoming him instead of resisting. Silky hot tissues gripped his sex as he pulled away, hugging him tight as he buried his length back inside her.

Raining kisses over her face, he crooned against her ear, coaxing, praising, pleading. "You feel so damn good, baby" he whispered.

Beneath him, she tossed her head back, staring at him. He shuddered as she wrapped her legs around him, holding him tight, as though she never intended to let go. And he was holding back. Tossing her head back, she held his eyes, arched up, trying to take him deeper, but he stilled her movements by pinning her hips with his own

Wade's body tensed as she clamped those silken little muscles around his cock, released, then did it again. "Wade, please," she whispered.

"Easy," he crooned in her ear, using one hand to hold her still as he pulled back, nearly withdrawing. "We've got a lot of time to make up for."

And slowly he entered her. Gave her an inch, then pulled back. Slid a little deeper that time, not so deep next. All the way in this time, then so far back only the tip of his head remained within her. Clamping a tight rein on his lust, he filled his sight with the picture she presented. Eyes dark with passion and need, lips swollen and red from his, legs spread wide to receive him. Dipping his head, he asked, "Do you want me?"

"Yes," she gasped when he nipped at her neck.

"How much?" he demanded, shaking his head to clear his vision.

"More than anything," she whispered, reaching down to cup his buttocks, draw his hips more firmly against her.

He caught her hands, pinned them beside her head. Then he slowly rotated his hips against hers, ducking his head to suckle at her breast. His voice was muffled as he asked, "More than everything?"

"Yes," she whispered. Over the length of her body, he stared up into her eyes as she arched her hips to his up, taking him in just the slightest bit deeper. "More than everything. It's always been like that."

"Always?" he repeated, lifting his head and resting his chin between her breasts as he stared at her.

She opened her heavy lidded eyes, stared into his. Those soft hazel eyes were open and naked with her need. "Always," she whispered.

"Always," she repeated, softly. "Even when you were no longer mine."

Shaking, he sank deep within her and hooked his arms under hers, cupping her face in his hands as he gently took her mouth. He held his body still within hers as he loved her mouth endlessly. Her inner muscles rippled around his shaft and he pulled back. His tongue stroked over, plunged deep, withdrew from her mouth to nip her lip, nuzzle her face and then he pulled back slowly.

Wade ran searching eyes over her face and landed on the faint scars at her left brow. And they reminded him. Deliberately, he dredged up hated thoughts of her with another.

It gave him strength, control, reminded him of why he was here. He wanted her to know, she had to know, what it felt like to have your heart shatter within you chest. She had to know. And he had to make her feel it.

But it wasn't easy. She flexed around him, her sheath like hot wet silk. He eased deeper, slowly inch by inch, until he rested against the gate of her womb. Slowly withdrew, eased back, pulled back until they were nearly separated. Remembered how empty he once felt, how his heart had fallen to pieces. Shattered.

He thrust hard and deep, held himself there and asked, "And what about when you were no longer mine?"

His heart froze within his chest as those beautiful eyes flooded with tears. It resumed beating, then, fast and furious as she reached up, cupping his cheek in her hand. Brokenly, she whispered, "I've always been yours."

He shuddered, unable to move as her words rippled over him. Wade felt his throat close, threatening to choke him and his heart swelled so that his chest ached as badly as his sex.

Instead of shattering her, she had shattered him. Looking into those tear-drenched eyes, he saw the truth there. Whatever had happened in the weeks after she had left him hadn't changed how she felt in her heart.

In her heart, she was, and always had been, his.

And this pointless game of domination seemed

childish. Shamed, he hung his head as her words whispered over in his head and heart.

"You always will be," he promised, cupping her hips in his hands, and driving himself home.

His hips pumped, harder and harder, until he was lifting her on the seat with each thrust. She pulsed around him. Arched up, her pebbled nipples came in contact with his chest, leaving trails of sensation. The base of his spine tingled and he felt his testicles drawing in tighter to his body.

Harder and harder, he moved, tightening some coil deep within. In a broken litany, Nikki whispered to him, *"not enough...please...love you...Wade..."*

The words made little sense aloud, but he understood, adjusting his position so he could slide his hands between her thighs, circling his thumb around the tiny bud of nerves, edging closer and closer, until with one sudden movement, he pressed down hard, firm.

A sharp startled cry left her lips, echoing through his body like a jolt of lightening, while her snug channel clamped tight around his sex, her flesh becoming even hotter, wetter as she screamed out his name.

She convulsed around him, sinking her teeth into his shoulder just as he emptied within her. A low groan left him as her hips pumped against his, her body trembling. His body jerked as he withdrew and plunged deep one last time, held himself there as her body milked his.

Damnation.

Chapter Eleven

Nikki slept quietly, curled up against his side. The rough ride didn't disturb her, nor did the silence of the man next to do her. She was unaware of his indecision, of his dilemma as she enjoyed the first sound sleep she'd had in months.

Wade felt her warmth against his side as he steered the truck over rough, uneven terrain. She slept as peacefully as Abby did at night. The way he hadn't slept in years.

What in the hell am I doing out here? he wondered

His shattered heart and bruised pride were calling out for something. She had played him for a fool and that was simply how he saw it. She had purposefully led him to believe there was no other man in her life, had claimed that even when her eyes were black with passion just a short while ago in the cab of this very truck.

Hell, he could still smell the musky scent of sweat, sex and woman in the air. *Her* scent still clung to him, stirring his flesh even as he damned himself for wanting her so badly.

He had never known her to be a hypocrite, but how could she condemn Jamie and then go out and do the very same thing?

Could he live the rest of his life, knowing she had given away what had been his? Knowing that she scorned the mother of his child for doing something Nikki herself had done?

Did he want all the times he had seen the light in

Abby's eyes extinguished by a cool word or look to go unpunished? Nikki hadn't ever been cruel, but Abby's sweet, childish attempts to befriend Nikki had all been ignored, and Abby had sensed in her heart that Nikki rejected her.

No. Steeling himself, locking his jaw, he told himself, *You have to do this.*

He pulled up in front of the cabin some twenty minutes later. It was cold out already and the sun hadn't even started to set. He shook the sleeping woman awake, instead of kissing her awake, the way he wanted to. He couldn't give in to the urge to cuddle her close, hold her tight.

Wade would learn to live without that. He would have to.

*****

Nikki came awake slowly, reluctantly. Damn it all. She didn't want to wake up. Her sleep had been peaceful and dreamless. Her body was warm and relaxed, sated.

Her mind, however, was puzzled. Her eyes scanned over unfamiliar territory and a frown wrinkled her brow. She looked over the see Wade staring moodily at the front of a little cabin.

"Where are we?" she asked, her voice husky from sleep.

She barely heard his terse reply, for her eyes had fallen on the clock. It was nearly six. They had been driving for four hours. Well, not all of the time had been spent driving, she realized, a dull flush creeping up her neck.

It faded quickly though, as she climbed out of the truck. His answer had just sunk in, enough for her to grasp what he had said. But she must have misheard.

"Exactly what are we doing in Gatlinburg?" she asked, pulling her coat closed over her chest. Damn it, it was cold.

He paused in the middle of unloading boxes from underneath the truck bed cover. His eyes were solemn, his mouth a tight narrow line. "Settling things," he finally said, after staring long and hard into her eyes for what seemed liked an eternity.

"Why here?" she asked, baffled.

He didn't answer but she didn't notice right away as her mind finally started functioning. Again, she repeated, "Why here?" holding her hands out, palm up in the age-old gesture of confusion.

"Because here you can't kick me out of the house, or walk away from me. Because here your damn brothers can't interfere, nor can anybody else. We're on equal ground here and I'll have my say," Wade said, facing her over the bed of the truck.

"You did that a few months ago," she reminded quietly, remembered pain darkening her eyes.

"That was anger, not me." He took a box from the truck and shoved it in her arms.

Automatically, Nikki took it, dimly noted that it was full of food, while she studied him, trying to fit the pieces together in her head. It wasn't easy; her brain was still addled from sleep and sex. Studying the food, she realized he had planned this. Very thoroughly planned it. Finally, she asked, "Are you saying you're not angry now?"

Unreadable black eyes met hers. Softly, truthfully, he said, "No. I am not angry." He was hurting, he was desperate. He was unbelievably confused, he was insanely jealous, and he was furious. Anger didn't come close to describing what he was feeling now.

He took the box from her, dropped it to the ground, then moved closer until his toes nudged hers and she had to tip her head back to meet his eyes. He cupped her chin in his hand, studying her face.

She stiffened when his fingers traced over the scars nearly hidden at her hairline, but the questions didn't come. His mouth spasmed once before it drew tight into a frown. "We're going to settle this," he repeated, his voice firm. Then he released her, took up a couple of boxes and walked away.

She shivered deep inside.

Why had that sounded so much like 'end this'?

Canned stew and biscuits were on the menu for that night. Nikki sat in her chair, quiet. Wade frowned as she continued to push the food around on her plate. She had eaten exactly four small bites and that had been nearly five minutes ago.

She glanced up at him, caught him watching her. She attempted a smile, but it fell short of being successful as she said, "Dad bought a cabin up here a few years ago. I've never gone to it, but my brothers come out a lot in the winter to go ice fishing or hunting. And Dad practically lives there during the summer."

Wade's only answer was an unintelligible grunt. He continued to stare at her, scowling when she laid her fork down and closed her hands around her glass, staring into it as though the sweetened iced tea held the answers to all of life's problems.

Wade's own appetite was somewhat diminished. Guilt was a living, breathing thing. It had a taste, a feel, a smell to it all its own. It filled his belly until there was no room for food.

He insisted to himself once more that he had nothing to feel guilty about. He was simply settling the score. She was the one who had lied and betrayed.

She's also the one who had to bury her baby, his conscience whispered.

She lied to me, led me to believe one thing while something else was the truth. She betrayed me.

Didn't you betray her first? What did you expect her to do? Join a convent?

Wade forced himself to take a deep slow steadying breath. Now he was arguing with himself. A sure sign of impending mental breakdown. He forced his normally rigid self-disciple into place as he reminded himself he had a job to do.

Forcing the guilt aside, swallowing its bitter taste, he studied her skinny frame.

"You need to eat," he told her as he popped the last piece of biscuit in his mouth. He chewed and swallowed, drank some tea, staring at her the entire time.

A disinterested shrug was his only answer, so he repeated himself.

Her eyes met his and she calmly said, "I'm not hungry."

No. He didn't imagine she was. After damn near starving herself, food probably wasn't even an afterthought for her any more. She looked so pale and tired. Her cheeks were hollow, large half moons bruising the delicate skin under her eyes. The bones of wrists and elbows pushed sharply against soft flesh.

And he'd be damned if he would let her go to waste all because some fancy suit in New York wanted her looking like a scarecrow.

"You can either eat, or I'll shove it down your throat," he offered, shoving his own plate aside.

She merely arched an eloquent eyebrow at him and said, "You do that and I'll just throw it back up. I told you I'm not hungry."

Bluntly, he informed her, "You look like hell. You're pale, exhausted. Your cheekbones stick out so much, it is a wonder they don't cut right through your skin. You look like the poster child for world hunger."

She smiled slightly and shrugged yet again. "I doubt I look all that bad. I eat a good meal on a regular basis."

"Regular as in regularly once a week?" he bit out, narrowing his eyes on her face.

"Regularly as in three times a day…I just don't eat as much as I should. I was just eating about once a day, but I got fussed at. So I eat three times a day, just like a normal person."

Once a day? Wade thought incredulously. *Once a day?* He had seen the amount of work she put into taking care of her home, the wood chopping, the cleaning up of debris left over from the rough fall. He had seen her out cycling the hilly areas around her home. He couldn't imagine the amount of energy she burned on a daily basis. And she was eating once a freaking day?

"Why are you doing this to yourself?" he demanded, shoving his chair back away from the table. "You have no spare flesh on you. You're nothing more than skin and bone. Hell, I can practically see right through you."

Her shoulders moved restlessly as her eyes roamed around the room. "I'm taking care of myself. I just don't ever have an appetite any more. I'm only a few pounds under my ideal body weight. I can't help it that I'm not hungry anymore."

A few pounds my ass, Wade thought. Though she wasn't at all tall, her frame was hardly a delicate one. She had broad shoulders, broad hips. Sturdy muscle and strong bones made up her body. He'd bet his next paycheck she was at least twenty pounds under what she should be.

And it sickened him to think that she might be doing this to herself to please some man. It made him furious to see that damn blank look on her face, as though she were staring through him. As though they hadn't just had explosive sex in the front seat of his truck just a few hours earlier.

Narrowing his eyes, he decided maybe she needed a reminder. Damn it to hell, she wouldn't look through him. Not any more. His eyes focused on her face, then her mouth as he said, "You always used to be…hungry."

Her eyes darted to his, then skittered away as he rose. This cabin, Nikki realized, was damn small. Less than forty by forty. It consisted of a one room that was for eating, cooking and sleeping. A large king size bed took up a good portion of space. Only one bed. A lumpy looking sofa. The tiny little bathroom didn't even have a lock on the door.

He closed in on her, lessening the space between them even as she tried desperately to widen it. His eyes ran over her, mentally removing every stitch of clothing from her hide as he offered, "I'll see what I can do about whetting your appetite. Maybe all you need is some strenuous activity."

"Wade, this isn't exactly what I would call settling things," she said, her voice placating even as her eyes darted about, looking for an escape route that didn't exist. "I thought we were here to talk."

"We've talked. We've settled nothing. Let's try a different sort of communication," he whispered as he walked her up against the wall. "You've run out of room, Nikki. No place left to go." His eyes lit with unholy glee as he added, "No place left to hide."

His voice rasped like a callused hand over smooth silk. A shudder wracked her from head to toe as his arms came up to rest beside her head, bracketing her between the wall and his body. She swallowed and hoped her voice would be steady. "I'm not hiding from you, Wade. If I wanted to hide, I wouldn't have gotten into the truck with you."

"Why did you?" he asked, lowering his head until they were nose to nose, mouth to mouth, his body heat reaching out to warm her from only inches away.

"I thought we were going to talk," she said faintly, arching her head back, trying to maintain a little bit of distance.

"We will. Eventually," Wade whispered,

following her retreating mouth his own.

"Wade—"

He cut her off with a soft, slow kiss that had her blood sizzling its way throughout her body. "We've always communicated so much better when we didn't use our mouths to talk," he murmured as he pulled his mouth from hers, lowering his head to nuzzle at her neck.

As his hot mouth blazed a trail down her neck, Nikki stifled a whimper by biting the inside of her cheek. He moved closer and closer until she was caught between a hard male body and the rough wooden wall at her back.

"Wade," she said, shakily Squirming weakly, against him, she tried to loosen his hold. "Wade, this is not going to solve anything." The last word ended on a gasp as she tried to suck in much needed air.

"Yes," he countered, his voice guttural. "It will. Damn it, woman. I should have done this from the beginning. We get along fine as long as you aren't thinking." His dark head dipped as he spoke, so that the final words were spoken against her mouth. His tongue thrust between her lips, past her teeth, to steal the air from her body.

Hot hands moved down her torso, to her hips, sliding beneath the waistband of her leggings, shoving the material down her narrowed hips. Her boots, still untied from the first time in the truck, fell easily from her feet as he lifted her, pinning her body to the wall with his own. One jean-clad leg came between hers and he bent his knee, bringing it contact with her exposed flesh.

Planting his foot in the crotch of her leggings, he shoved them the rest of the way down, kicking them away in a tangle. His hand came up between them, hooked in the neck of her sturdy button-down flannel. Nikki felt a hard jerk as he rent it down the middle. Buttons went flying as he lifted her up, moved between her dangling legs and closed his mouth around a lace-covered nipple.

Slowly, oh, so slowly, he eased his hold until her weight came down. Nikki gasped as it brought her up against his groin. The rough material of his jeans chafed against the inside of her thighs as she arched her hips and shuddered, trying desperately to get closer.

And then she was. His hand freed his erection from the confines of his jeans, adjusted her position. Wade slowed his touch as one hand strayed to the juncture of her thighs, tested her flesh. "I don't want to hurt you," he murmured.

"Wade," she whimpered, rubbing against him, pleading.

Moisture flooded his hand and hot satisfaction gleamed in his eyes as he petted the slick flesh with a feathery light touch. He shifted, grasped her hips, and filled her as his name fell from her mouth in a rippling gasp. She was still so tight. His hands went to her buttocks and cupped them, as he worked her up and down.

Her legs closed around his hips like a vice while she panted and twisted her hips until with a groan, he buried himself to the hilt.

Flesh slid against flesh, stifled mews of pleasure

and whispered exclamations filled the air. His hips hammered against hers, her hot tight flesh rippling around him. She arched back with a gasp as inner convulsions started, caressing his shaft until he thought he would go mad with the pleasure of it.

With a muttered oath, he pushed away from the wall and stumbled the three feet to the bed. Came down on top of her and thrust violently into her once, before pulling out, away from her clinging hands.

Wade put his mouth against her, tasting the spicy sweet tang of her as she climaxed against his mouth and hands. Then, he rose and stared down at her, his chest heaving, while he waited for her to calm.

Her breathing started to slow, and sense began to gather within her eyes. He wanted to watch her eyes go blind again. He stripped off his shirt, came down on her, mounted her and drove in. Pushing her quickly toward another orgasm, had her hovering on the brink, then changing his rhythm, withholding it from her. He shuddered when she locked her arms around his neck, gasped his name and pleaded with him.

Beneath him, Nikki clenched tightly around his cock, her flesh convulsing, her nails digging into the ridge of muscles at his shoulders. "Wade, oh, Wade, please," she whimpered, her head thrashing back and forth.

"Nobody else can make you feel like this," he rasped against her ear, settling into a hard driving rhythm.

Her hips bucked against his as he thrust against her, driving deep within the wet well of her body. One hand raced down, cupped her buttocks and squeezed, his fingers digging into the soft flesh, the dark crevice. "Nobody," he repeated, thickly

She screamed, her eyes blank, as a massive orgasm ripped through her, leaving her weak and shuddering as Wade, savagely triumphant, found his own release. Closing his eyes, he anchored her hips against his, rode it through to the very end as her body milked his, demanding everything he had to give.

With a shudder, Wade collapsed against her, body numb from pleasure. Mind numb from shock. And his heart was aching.

His name. She had screamed and whispered his name as her flesh had shuddered and heaved around his. And right before a sob had torn through her, Nikki had gasped out, *"I love you"*

Ragged breaths sawing in and out of him, Wade closed his eyes, now in despair.

Because Wade Lightfoot had finally realized that no matter what he did, or what she did, it wasn't the end of things. Nothing would ever completely end things.

Because he would never be free of her.

*****

Eventually, Nikki ate, dressed in the blue flannel with the buttons missing, revealing a pale wedge of flesh every time she shifted. Wade held her close, his face pressed against her hair, breathing her in while his mind raised and spun in dizzying circles.

Damn it.

What in the hell was he supposed do now?

The cabin was dark, lit only by the fire. She was cuddled close to him, warm, soft, everything he held dear. Turning lambent eyes to his, she smiled and her lids lowered slowly, closing, before opening to reveal something that made his blood run hot. As he struggled to find his tongue, Nikki shifted and straddled him.

Her shirt fell away with a graceful shrug of her shoulders, revealing skin made golden by the firelight. As it flickered and danced, highlighting hollows and curves, Nikki skimmed hands up her sides, licked her lips and whispered against his mouth, "I'm feeling… hungry."

He cracked a smile and found his voice as his hands reached up to close around her waist. "I've made a monster," he whispered. "You'll be the death of me." His eyes nearly crossed with pleasure when her talented fingers slipped below his waist, inside his jeans after making quick work of the zipper.

"I can't think of a better way to go," he admitted weakly as she closed her hand around him and she sank to her knees before him, lowering her head until the soft heat of her mouth enclosed the head of his cock.

*****

Hours later, Wade lay wide-awake while she slept curled against his side.

What kind of monster have I become? he wondered.

The red haze that had clouded his mind, and

fogged his vision for weeks, had suddenly and completely cleared, leaving him sick with guilt.

Wade had no claim on her. He had lost all rights the minute he had gone to bed with Jamie.

God above, she had lost her baby. It bore too much pain to think of; he couldn't imagine losing his little girl. He wouldn't have wanted to live.

Who in the hell was he to blame her for anything? To want any kind of retribution? Any imagined slight was nothing compared to the agony she must have gone through. But that hadn't stopped him from wanting to add to it.

Slowly, carefully, Wade rose, slipping from the bed, not wanting to disturb her. She looked so exhausted, needed her rest so badly. Shrugging into his shirt, donning his jeans, he headed for the door, pausing long enough to slip his feet in battered workbooks. Cold air hit his face and chest as he headed for the railing of the tiny porch deck.

What in the hell was I thinking?

If he could have reached his own ass, he would have kicked it from here to Tokyo. Slumping against the rail, he called himself every name he knew, berated himself for being such a fool. Then he repeated himself. Twice.

Nikki had lied to him, by omission, and she had misled him. But she had also warned him to leave her be. And she had meant it. It had all been done out of self-defense, an effort to protect herself from further pain. From letting him cause her any more pain.

She hadn't succeeded. He could remember the agony he had glimpsed in her eyes so often, agony he had ignored.

There was no suitable punishment for what he did to her. He could remember every loathsome thought since Leanne had unwittingly revealed Nikki's secret. With painful clarity, he remembered the shock in Leanne's eyes as he had stood seething over the grave of a dead child. The reality of his own cruelty, his own selfishness and jealousy made his stomach churn with bile.

The memory of Nikki's tight body made sweat rise on his brow, even now. Whatever had happened had ended long ago. She hadn't been with a man in years, maybe not since she had conceived. There was no way she could have been with another man recently.

Again, he stilled as he remembered how she flinched, how her body had tried to retreat from his, and he could still see the flash of pain in her dark eyes when he had entered her that first time.

And then his thoughts turned inward as he thought of the hill by her family's home.

He knew exactly where the crash had happened. Had driven there, climbed from his truck and looked around, not expecting to see anything. But more than two years after it had happened, one could still see the path her truck had taken down the incline. Patches of bareness, branches broken off long ago due to impact with a large object. Metal, steel and earth weren't a pretty combination. He would know, considering how many accidents victims he'd tried to keep alive over the years. Most often, he succeeded, but often enough, he failed.

She could have been killed. It was a miracle that

she and Shawn had escaped with their lives.

Nikki was so lucky to be alive.

And so miserable for being so. She had been grieving for far too long. Hurting over what he had done to her, then hurting because life had ripped her only child from her. She had told him, time after time, that she wasn't strong enough to handle it.

What had she said?

You can't make it up to me, her voice whispered in his mind as he remembered. *You have no idea bow badly I was hurt, how much I lost.*

Nikki was right. He was completely clueless.

They were finished–he knew that. There was no way that they could have a life together, not with all the anger and resentment that swirled in him, despite all his attempts to drown them. She may not know it, would not be expecting it because he had just told her in graphic detail that he wanted her back.

But there was no way he could stay.

Wade was selfish, he was a bastard, a Neanderthal, and he knew it. But it would eat him alive to stay here, trying to make it work, knowing she had been with another man. His jealousy would be like acid, eating away at him until one day, the poison erupted and destroyed everything in its path.

He wouldn't let his own anger, his own jealousy hurt her after this. Not any more.

His emotions were illogical, unjustified. But he knew it was a fact. Not liking it didn't make it any less true. Wishing it were otherwise couldn't change how he felt

A numbness settled around his heart, growing

until it encased his entire body. He could not possibly stay with her now. God only knew he'd hurt her enough already. What else was there left to do but leave her in peace? That was what she wanted to begin with.

*****

Nikki came awake slowly, stretching her body and smiling at the pleasant aches that made themselves known. She didn't know exactly what was going on, but it was looking fairly promising.

Maybe they were going to get that second chance after all.

She hummed deep in her throat as she rolled to her back, hugging the pillow to her chest. Her eyes caught a motion outside and she turned her head.

Wade.

He stood outside, staring off into the distance, his head bent, shoulders slumped, looking utterly defeated. She had only seen him look that two other times. That day he had come to her home after that fight in the grocery store parking lot, over a boy whose face she barely remembered. And that day when she had learned about Jamie and the baby.

Dread filled her.

Nikki sat up slowly, tugging the blanket around her.

Maybe they were going to get a second chance.

But they were going to have to be honest with each other first. Starting with her. Eventually, Wade would find out about Jason. And if he found out from somebody other than her, it would ruin whatever they had made now.

Her pleasure faded to a dim glow as she drew in a shuddering breath. How did one go about telling a man that he had a child he had never known, and never would know? That the child had been killed in an accident years earlier?

Clutching the blanket tighter, Nikki was amazed to discover that beneath the dread, she felt relief. She was scared about his reaction, hated the pain she knew this would cause, but, deep inside, she wanted to do this, had to do this. She wanted to tell Wade all about his little boy and she wanted to grieve with him.

But how did she tell him? How did she explain why she didn't tell him before now?

You're a writer. Finding the right words is what you do, Nikki reminded herself as she slid from the bed and stood.

Hopefully, when it was most important, she would be able to do just that.

*****

"Wade?"

Her voice, soft and sleepy, came to him over the roaring in his ears. Unbelievably weary, he turned his head, to see her standing in the doorway, a thin hand clutching the blanket around her naked shoulders.

His voice rough, he said, "It's too cold out. You ought to be inside."

With a slight smile, Nikki glanced at him, from the bare feet tucked inside boots, to the naked chest revealed by his open shirt. "You're one to talk," she said, smiling at him. Then she held out her hand. "Come inside"

Slowly, his cold hand came up and closed over her warm one. Despising himself, hating himself, but unable to deny the need to be close to her, to be warm, for just a little while longer. He was going to have to be without her soon enough.

He would need this time, to get through the empty years ahead.

Nikki silently urged him onto the sofa, curling her body next to his. Wade buried his face in her hair, breathing her in, his arms locked tightly around her. It wasn't right. How could he have found her again, only to have barriers come between them that would be impossible to break?

"Wade, I think it's time we had that talk," Nikki said, breaking into his thoughts.

He raised his head automatically when she spoke but quickly lowered it again, mumbling something under his breath. Even he wasn't sure what it was he had said.

Quietly, Nikki told him, "There's some things you need to know, Wade. Things I should have told you months ago."

His body went rigid. *Now?* was all he could think. *Why is she going to tell me now?*

Over the pounding of his heart, he realized she was speaking to him, and her words were slow, almost awkward. "I was in pretty rough shape after you told me about Jamie. A part of me died that day and I just lost interest in life. I wasn't interested in eating or writing or reading. All I wanted to do was sleep. So that's all I did for the longest time. I never went back to school, never did anything.

"I ended up selling my book, but Dylan kind of helped me through that. He got me through the mess of contracts, talked to a couple of agents, helped with everything. Hell, he could probably *be* an agent at this point, he's handled so much for me.

"He was so damn proud of me. I wasn't all that concerned about it. When they read the third book I'd written in the *Chronicles* line, they offered me contracts and money on the spot. So I was able to buy Dad and them the house I'd always promised. I didn't much care, but I wanted to keep my promises. Once we moved, all I did was wander around inside those four walls day in and day out." Her voice faded, growing distant as her eyes turned inward. "I was sort of fading away, losing weight, losing myself.

"You had married Jamie and I thought my life was over," Nikki whispered, straightening, gently shrugging his arms away. Keeping the blanket around her shoulders, she rose and walked over to stare out the window.

Wade could picture all too well what she was describing. It was the shadow of the woman he had found on the road several hours ago. Had somebody come along and taken away the loneliness for a little while?

Or God, no, had something else happened? Why in the hell hadn't he thought of that before now? Anything was possible, especially in that hellhole she had lived in. She was so small, and while she could mostly likely hold her own against a lone man, what could she do about a number of *men*?

He shook his head to clear his thoughts she started to speak again.

"I was probably just a few months away from my own funeral. I had stopped eating. I hadn't taken a bath in God only knows how long," Nikki continued, one hand straying up to touch shiny strands of hair. "My hair was so filthy, so matted. I wonder how anybody was even able to tolerate being in the same room with me."

Eyes full of bemusement, Nikki turned to look at him. "And then, the oddest thing happened. It was in the middle of January and Dad came home late one night, drunk, of course. I was sitting on the couch, staring at the blank TV. He started talking to me, blubbering about what a wreck his life was. I said something to him, I think it was, 'That's nice, Dad,' and I got up to go to bed. He shut up and gave me the strangest look.

"The next morning, he was awake and cooking breakfast. I think he had been up all night, telling himself he had just imagined how horrible I looked. But there he was, sober as a priest, and he really looked at me. He didn't say a single thing as he poured every bit of alcohol he had down the drain. Then he started his truck, came inside, picked me up and took me to the doctor. He's been sober for over five years now. I think he realized he was going to need all his wits about him just to keep me alive."

A grim look entered her eyes as she described how pitiful she looked, hair unkempt and gummy from weeks without washing, loose skin hanging off her bones, face hollow. And slowly, Wade began to realize that if she was telling the truth and he knew she was, she couldn't have been out carousing with another man, erasing him with another man's touch.

A niggling little doubt was making itself at home in his mind, darting out of reach any time he tried to latch on to it.

"He dragged me into the doctor's office. I had on an old pair of Dylan's sweatpants and this nasty T-shirt that stank to high heaven. Daddy put me in front of the doctor and told him that he was to get me well, even if it meant being hospitalized. The doctor took one look at me and shook his head. At first, he thought I was just anorexic and talked about counseling and various pharmaceutical treatments for depression.

"I had starved myself so badly, my body was no longer doing what it was supposed to do. I'd developed an arrhythmia because my electrolyte levels were so badly out of whack. My blood pressure was erratic. My stomach had started to atrophy and I had to learn how to eat all over again. And the doctor very bluntly told me that if Dad hadn't done what he did when he did it, if he had waited just a few weeks more, I'd would have been dead, probably from a heart attack. I had damn near destroyed my heart. As it is, it can't function on its own any more." She had wandered over and picked up her purse, pulling out a brown prescription bottle, which she held out to him.

Wade took it, his hand closing convulsively around the brown bottle. Lanoxin. The type of medicine a person could die without. "I'll probably be on heart medication for the rest of my life."

Wade had long since gone cold, was staring at her in some numb kind of shock. She wouldn't have let that happen, not over what he had done. And in a shocked tone, he whispered that to her...

Sadly, Nikki just stared at him and shook her head. "I wasn't me any more, Wade. The girl you knew wasn't there any more. I had let her go, and ended up getting lost inside myself. I couldn't find my way back."

She paused long enough to take a deep shaking breath before meeting his eyes. "And that wasn't all. It was bad enough that my heart was a wreck and my body was about ready to shut down. A complete physical for a woman of child bearing age includes a pregnancy test. They had almost forgotten it, since it was so highly unlikely, considering my condition. But...but they were wrong. I was four months pregnant, Wade."

January...she said January... Four months pregnant...it had happened in August. His heart simply stopped beating. He stared at her, dismayed and deeply shocked, for the longest time. Pregnant. Four months pregnant. "...how?"

"That last time in the woods." She turned away now, resting her forehead against the cold pane of glass while she struggled to speak around the knot in her throat. "By all things logical, there was no reason for me to have carried the baby that long. It was deprived of everything that was so important during the first few months. A miracle from God is the only way I can explain it. I'd lost you, but He had given me something else to hold onto. And that saved my life."

Nikki dashed away a tear with the back of her hand, started to drop her hand and then she paused, studying it, seeing how thin and pale it was, realizing how very weak she had become. How tired. She was doing it to herself again. Grimly, she swore to herself, *No more.* She was nowhere near as far gone as she had once been, but this wouldn't happen to her again. No matter what.

"The doctor strongly advised me to abort the baby. Told me I'd never make it to full term, and if by some slight chance I did, the baby would be severely handicapped and may not survive delivery. He had been starved and neglected when he needed caring the most. He was so small. I didn't even weigh a hundred pounds, but somehow, this little life was inside me, and trying to live.

"A part of you," she whispered, her voice hot and intense. "And that was all that mattered. The doctor told me I was crazy. That having a baby in my condition was suicide. He tried to make Dad see his side. Neither one of us would listen. Dad was ready to support whatever decision I made. We found a doctor who was willing to try.

"Dr. Gray said from the beginning it was likely that I would miscarry at any given time. If I did make it to full term, the baby could die in delivery or be born severely handicapped. And I might not survive the pregnancy. I was unbelievably weak. He wanted to make sure I knew what I was doing, what I was up against. I told him I wouldn't give up my baby.

"So he put me in the hospital right away. He rode

with me in the ambulance, walked me through the admission process. He wasn't leaving anything to chance. I couldn't be upset, couldn't be scared about anything. He explained what the IV was for and supervised it being put in and started. It was for the electrolyte imbalance and the dehydration, to give my body some nutrition while I learned to eat again. Dr. Gray explained the medications to me, the vitamins and digitalis, were to regulate my heart rate. The heart monitor was to make sure the meds were working. Bed rest, he said, was necessary because of how weak I was. I was in a very precarious position and it was nothing less than a gift from God that my baby had made it this far.

"I was in the hospital for two weeks. I gained back four pounds, and my heart rate returned to normal. I had to stay on the medicine, though, throughout the pregnancy. I was out of the danger zone, gaining weight and eating regular meals. But… but my baby wasn't doing so well. He had been neglected during the most important time and he wasn't growing or moving around the way he was supposed to. The ultrasound showed him to be half the size he should have been." Her mouth trembled briefly before firming.

Her next words were cut off with a yelp when hard arms closed tightly around her, like bands of iron. Wade buried his face against her neck, shuddering, rocking her back and forth. *His baby.* Not another man's. *His.* She had been too busy grieving herself to death to go to another man.

Wade didn't even realize she was speaking until

he raised his head, his eyes diamond-bright with unshed tears, and saw her mouth moving. Sorry. She whispered it, over and over, "I am so sorry."

Sorry…?

Wade shook her slightly, his voice low and rough. "Don't you apologize to me. I'm the one who screwed up. It was my fault—"

She covered his mouth with her hand and shook her head. "No, Wade." Her voice was determined and firm. "No. It was my fault. I ended up in the hospital because I let myself wither away. I almost killed our baby. I had screwed up and I was going to fix it."

She leaned forward then, settling into his arms briefly, steadying herself. "We pulled through, somehow. He was born normal and healthy, just a little small for his age. I was a month overdue, while his body played catch up. He was so beautiful," she whispered, her voice soft and lost in thought.

Nikki shifted, turning around so that her back was against Wade's front. He remained wrapped around her, his face buried against her hair, while she continued to speak. "He looked just like you. He was the light of my life. Everything was going to work out okay for me. I bought my own house, and we moved in it the day after he turned six months. Spent our first Christmas there."

Wade closed his eyes, not wanting to hear any more. He knew the rest of the story, vividly, had a nightmare or two of his own about it. But she was determined to finish telling it.

"He would have been just four months younger than Abby," she whispered. "Would have started school next year."

A shudder racked her body from head to toe before she could stop it. Anger edged her voice as she started to speak of the stormy day three and a half years earlier. "Shawn was staying up at the house for a few days. Dad and Dylan were fighting some and he wanted to get away from it. This storm came up.

"We were going to my dad's. I knew better than to drive home in that kind of weather. We were less than a mile away and this car came of out of nowhere. I heard this horrible noise, this loud crash and there was this terrible jolt. Then the world started to spin. I had tried to jerk the wheel to the right, away from the drop off.

"I wasn't able to control the truck." Her voice shuddered and broke, hands clenched into fists. "The bastard hit us again, trying to go around us on the side of the shoulder. The safe side. I lost control and we went tumbling over the hill, broke through the guardrail. When I came to, the rain had stopped. And my little boy was gone."

Once she finished talking, she fell silent and Wade just stood there while his eyes burned and his throat ached from the knot inside it. A hot, greasy ball of shame settled low in his gut. *My son.* Already dead and buried and Wade hadn't even known he existed. He was shaken and confused, angry at both himself and at her. Why hadn't she told him?

It was ironic. He had married a woman he didn't love because she had been pregnant and, years later, he learned the woman he did love had been pregnant as well. It sounded like something that belonged on a talk show.

Do you know a man who left his fiancée to marry a woman he didn't love because she was pregnant with his child? Did this man unknowingly leave his fiancée pregnant?

Wade carefully shifted Nikki aside, not trusting himself to speak. He got to his feet and walked to stare out the window, hands tucked into the back pockets of his jeans. Damn it all to hell.

What am I supposed to do now? he wondered. He closed his eyes and rested his forehead against the cold pane of glass, a weary sigh escaping him. Grief, black as night, swirled within his heart, mixed with impotent anger. What was he supposed to say?

And beneath it all, the anger, the grief, the confusion, and the guilt, he felt relief. It hadn't been another man. He wouldn't have to let her go in order to save her from his own anger.

The grief mingled with happiness, making it bittersweet. He had lost a son he had never known existed. But he would be able to keep her. They could make more children, other sons.

He'd never known this one.

But there will be others, he thought, his mind racing from one thought to the next.

Why hadn't she told him before now?

Why hadn't she come to him when she had learned about the baby? He would have helped her.

Do you really think she would have wanted your help?

No. Probably not.

But why hadn't she told him before now? There had been plenty of times she could have mentioned. *Wade, by the way, a few months after Jamie had Abby, I had a baby myself. He looked just like you.*

He heard the brush of fabric across fabric, then the shift of wooden planks being walked on. Her footsteps were soundless, her heat warming his back from a few inches away. Turning, he stared into her eyes, seeing his own torment reflected there.

"Why didn't you tell me before now?" he asked quietly, keeping tight control of his own anger. It was, after all, rather poetic justice. He had come seeking retribution and had ended up finding out he was his own worst enemy. He was the nameless faceless bastard who had haunted his dreams.

Her shoulders lifted and fell in a weak shrug, the corners of her full mouth turned down in an unhappy frown. "I didn't want you back in my life. I was determined to keep you out of it. I told myself that you didn't have the right to know, even though I knew it wasn't true." Nikki moved away as she spoke, snagging his shirt from the floor and pulling it over her head. It fell quickly to cover her pale flesh and fragile body. "And I tried not to think about it much. It hurt too much. Telling you wasn't going to bring him back, so I told myself there was no reason to put myself through it."

Slowly, Wade nodded, accepting that. He could understand that, even if he didn't like it. He couldn't even imagine how he would have felt if Abby—

He shied away from that thought, focusing on the matter at hand. "I had a right to know," he said quietly, his voice intense. "Regardless of how you felt about me, I had a right to know."

Nikki turned to stare at him, her head cocked, her

shiny sweep of chestnut hair falling across her brow. "Did you really? Legally, yes, you did. But I have to wonder, if I had told you at the beginning, what would have happened? You would have insisted on having your parental rights, visiting privileges. I would have been forced to see you with your wife and your daughter. I was already in bad shape. How right would it have been to put me through that, especially when I did nothing wrong, nothing to deserve what happened to me? I lost everything, Wade. He was all I had. Why should I have shared him with you?"

"Because he was mine," Wade rasped, his eyes narrowing as he moved closer.

"And you were mine. I shouldn't have had to share you with Jamie. It would have killed me to see you with her, can't you understand that?" she demanded, her eyes flashing angrily at him.

"Yeah, well, if you had been forced to share your son, maybe you wouldn't have left Louisville, and maybe he'd still be alive," Wade snapped, catching hold of her and jerking her up against him.

It was a good thing he had hold of her arms, because at his words, she wilted, her body going lax, while she stared up at him out of huge anguished eyes.

Wade could have kicked himself the minute the words left his mouth. There was no way to take them back. Staring down at her, he damned himself to hell and back, but he didn't release his hold on her. She was as limp in his hands as a rag doll, absolutely no strength in her body. Her eyes were dark and wounded.

Carefully, he scooped up her limp body and

deposited her on the couch before moving away, regret burning in the back of his mouth like acid. "I shouldn't have said that," he finally said, resuming his spot back at the window. "I'm sorry."

The silence reigned for what seemed like an eternity. Wade tried to find a way to soothe the most recent pain he had inflicted on this woman but could think of nothing. How could he have said that? He didn't blame her, so why did he say something that would make her think he did?

Wade had to figure out a way to make this better. They had so much they needed to talk about, so many important things, and he had gone and totally bungled things before they could even begin.

He was formulating what he would say, and how to say it, when the quiet noise behind him began.

When he worked up the nerve to turn around, she stood before him, dressed in his shirt and her leggings, her boots laced up. Her jacket was in her arms and she held it to her breast like a shield. "I'd like to go home now," she said woodenly through stiff lips.

"No." The panic that rose up was swift and thick, enveloping his mind and freezing any apologies he had been about to make. Panic fueled the simmering frustration and he lost the ability to think clearly.

"I would like to go home now," she repeated.

Wade shook his head, moving to grab her arms. She stood rigidly under his hands, staring at a point past his shoulder. "Damn it, Nikki. Don't you think it's time we settled this?" he insisted, wishing desperately he could take back the past few minutes. Hell, the past few weeks.

"It is settled, Wade."

"It's not," he argued, tipping her head back, forcing her eyes to meet his. They were empty, blank. Her skin was pale, her face smooth. Under his hands, she trembled slightly, minutely, as though frozen from within. "Don't you think I'm entitled to a little bit of anger here? Maybe one could even expect me to be a bit of a jackass. This is one hell of a piece of news you handed me."

Her lids lowered slowly, shielding her eyes from him while she studied him from under the fringe of her lashes. "I lost my fiancée. That damn near destroyed me. If it wasn't for my little boy, I would have given up. Then, I lost him. Again, I had to rebuild a life for myself, this time alone. The past few years have been more than a bit traumatic for me, Wade. If anybody is entitled to be a bit of a jackass, it should be me."

Now her eyes raised, locked on his. Hot, angry. Softly, she asked, "Tell me something, Wade, what have you lost?"

"I lost you," he whispered, his own eyes dark and haunted.

"Through nobody's fault but your own," she ruthlessly reminded him. "That was your doing, nobody else's. I think I've had more than my fair share of heartache. I certainly don't need you to add to it. I told you about Jason because I thought we were going to give this one more shot. I felt it was past time you knew. I made a mistake and I admit that. However, it has become clear to me that you blame me for making what most would agree was the right decision. You appear to blame me for wanting to raise my son in a place a little safer than where we lived. He could have easily been killed crossing the street or in a drive by shooting. He could have been kidnapped and murdered or any number of things. Would that have been my fault? If it had happened in Louisville, would I still be to blame?"

Exasperated, frustrated, he shook her. "I don't blame you. I shouldn't have said that, but damn it, you threw me off track. How can I be expected to be logical?"

She merely stared at him, through him. From the way she looked at him, he realized she had already dismissed him from her mind. *Not if I have anything to do with it, you haven't,* Wade thought angrily. She wasn't going to spring a surprise like this on him, then stomp off because he had reacted in a less than admirable manner.

"You can't just leave things like this, damn it. It's unfinished."

"Is it?" She turned her head, looking at him this time, instead of through him as she asked, "And how would you propose that we finish this? What would be an appropriate ending for us? Are we going to kiss and make up, act like we weren't the two biggest mistakes on God's green earth? Or maybe we should just shake hands and be friends. How should this story end, Wade? God knows I've tried to figure that out, but I'll have to admit I'm stumped."

"I…I don't know," he answered, helplessly.

Nikki turned away, tossed her jacket down on the couch as she paced the floor. *Damn it all. When are things ever going to be easy for me?* she wondered with resignation. Nothing in her life was ever easy. She stopped at the back door, her eyes roaming sightlessly over the landscape.

She had to admit…it was lovely here, even in the desolate winter light.

Maybe this summer, she would take a few weeks and go stay at her dad's cabin, wherever in the hell that was. If he didn't go and put it on the market, like he had mentioned off and on the past two years.

On the market.

And Nikki remembered a for sale sign that graced the yard of a little ranch house in Monticello.

Slowly, she turned on her heel. Remembering her feeling in the truck on the way up here that there was something odd going on behind those dark eyes. Remembered the odd shuttered look in eyes as he braced himself above her. For a moment then, she hadn't known this man.

What in the hell is going on here? she wondered.

"Why did you bring me up here, Wade?" she inquired calmly, even though there was a burning in her chest. Even though, deep inside, she already knew what was going on. Anger, the kind she hadn't felt in years, was building. She tried to rein it in, but she wasn't having much luck

He stared at her, his dark eyes blank. She knew. She had figured it out. "I think you know why I brought you up here," he finally said, turning away.

"Why is your house for sale?"

He stared out the window, his eyes not really seeing the beautiful cold winter morning. "I'm moving back to Indiana. Abby's not happy here. I'm not happy."

His answer fanned the hot flames that were spreading to engulf her body. "So," she said coldly, glaring at him. "This was... what? One last trip down memory lane?"

"More or less," he replied.

"You went to an awful lot of trouble for a roll in the sack, Wade," Nikki said, her voice ice cold. As she spoke, she turned back to stare out the window as she struggled to regulate her breathing, to reign in the anger. *Stay calm about this, Nik,* she told herself. *Getting mad isn't going to solve anything.*

She was silent a moment longer and then she whirled, her eyes locking on his.

"You son of a bitch!" she shouted, advancing on him until she stood toe to toe with him. Small hands planted against his chest and she shoved with all her strength but was unsatisfied when all he did was stumble backward a step before coming up against the wall.

"I never thought you were a cruel man, Wade, but that was before this little stunt. Did it ever occur to you what might be going on in my head if I were to give in to you?" she demanded, thumping his chest with a clenched fist. "You have been after me for months to give you a second chance. I wanted *us* to have a second chance. That's why I came back from New York. Hell, if I'd wanted some quick and easy sex, I could have gotten that *there.* I come back here, I give in, against my better judgment, only to find out that you just wanted a private farewell party."

"Nikki—"

"Shut up," she said softly, baring her teeth at him in a snarl. "Just shut up." She spun around on her heel, pacing back and froth. "You barged into my life just when I was finally able to think about living again," she muttered. Then she stomped back and rose up on her toes until they were nose to nose. "You tore it apart all over again. You intruded on my privacy for weeks. You interfered with my personal life. You made demands on me you had no right making. You insulted me, my morals, and my integrity. You went out of your way to cause me more pain. You brought me here under false pretenses."

She paused to suck in air, lower her voice. "I could have handled that. I didn't protest or tell you 'no,' when that's all it would have taken to make you stop. I didn't do that, because I wanted you. I wanted to make love with you. But this wasn't about making love. It was about adding one more memory to your hope chest."

Nikki moved away, cupping her elbows in her hands and hugging herself. "Well," she said hollowly, the anger draining out of her as quickly as it had risen. "I hope you enjoyed getting your rocks off. Did you get everything you wanted or is there something we missed?"

"Nikki—"

She held up her hand, cutting him off. Shutting him out. "Just take me home now, Wade. We're done here."

Wade jammed his fists in his pockets, staring at her closed face. She had shut down and locked up, he realized. He wasn't going to be able to talk to her now. He relented with a slight nod, gathering his gear, dragging the rest of his clothes on as she stood and stared out the windows

He knew she wasn't seeing anything. Her soulful eyes were as cold as the air outside, and just as empty.

Where do we go from here? he wondered wearily, shoving his arms into the sleeves of his coat, pocketing his keys.

This trip had definitely deviated from his plan.

I had a son, he thought bleakly

He wondered what the little boy had looked like, how his laugh had sounded.

Grief for the child he had never known, and never would know, ripped through him. He paused outside the door of the cabin. Behind him, Nikki was settling in the truck. He pressed his palms to his eyes and dragged a deep cold draught of air into his lungs. *How in the hell am I supposed to deal with this?*

Hours later, he pulled up in front of her house. "How much longer are you going to keep running from yourself, Nikki?" Wade asked, killing the engine as he stared up at her silent house. Moonlight gilded his features with a silvery glow, casting one half of his face into shadow.

"I'm not running from anything," she stated coldly. "I just want to lead my life the way I choose to do so. I don't want to have to live my life weighing every decision I make, wondering what you'll find to blame me for next."

She tugged on the door handle, only to discover it was still locked. "Let me out, Wade."

He ignored her as he said quietly, "The only thing I do blame you for is choosing to spend your life alone and miserable, instead of taking a chance. I'm sorry, Nicole. I don't know how many more times I have to say that before you can forgive me."

Tossing him an angry glare, she said, "I had forgiven you. More the fool me. I came back here to try to give things a second chance. If I wanted to be alone, I would have stayed in New York. And that's exactly what I should have done. Maybe I should thank you for that little trip to Smokies. It certainly brought me back to my senses."

"Is there anything I can say that would explain that?" he muttered, speaking more to himself than to her. "If you came back to try this again, then why not go ahead and try?"

"Because you proved to me that it would be a waste of my time, Wade. You're not worth wasting any more time on. You were right about that, after all. You are not worth it. No man who does what you just did is."

"What in the hell did I do that was so terrible?" he asked, refusing to think of what he had been planning to do, get her to admit how she felt, and then walk away. "I didn't make you any promises. And you knew my house had been sold. You should have assumed what I was up to." Snagging her chin, he forced her to face him. "And you can't say you weren't willing."

"Why should I lie?" she asked, shrugging her shoulders. "You're right. I was willing. And I should have known better than to think it was all going to end happily-ever-after. But this is a better ending, anyway. Now we both know where the other stands. I know that you've turned into a using, lying womanizing bastard. You know that I've turned into the bitch who only looks out for number one." She tossed him an icy glare and said, "Now, let me out of this damn truck, get off my damn mountain, and out of this damn town. I don't ever want to see you again."

Silently, he thumbed the lock mechanism, all the while, staring at her with sad eyes. As she started to slide out of the truck, he spoke. Unable to stop herself, she froze, and listened. "I am sorry, Nikki. Sorrier than you will ever know. And I hope you're making the choice that's the best for you. The one that will make you happy.

"I hope you don't regret sending me away. We didn't have a choice last time. I took that away from us with my stupidity. We have a choice this time. And it looks like you've made yours." He stretched out his arm, brushed his thumb across her lip.

"Be happy, Nikki. That's all I want for you."

Moments later, her back pressed against the door, Nikki started to shake. Gravel crunched outside as Wade turned his truck around, heading down the mountain. And out of her life.

Be happy.

Did he have to go and say things like that? Things that made her think? Made her doubt her decisions?

Was she doing what was right? What was best?

When was the last time she had ever really been happy?

Had she been asked that question a few days

earlier, she wouldn't have known the answer. Not since before Jason had died, for certain. And maybe not even while he had been alive. In some part of her heart, she had always been mourning Wade.

But now, she knew the answer. For just a few hours yesterday, she had been happy. Peaceful and content, wrapped up in Wade's arms, back before she had started thinking again.

That entire time hadn't been about second chances, but about good byes.

How could he have done that?

She had to give him credit. It had been clever of him to get her in the middle of no man's land, where they couldn't be interrupted, where there were no reminders of the past. He had to have known that all he needed was a little time to wear her down.

And had he ever.

Blowing a lock of hair out of her eyes, she remembered those heated minutes in the cab of his truck. He had all but blinded her with the heat, something she had suppressed, but hadn't forgotten. And again in the cabin, several times throughout the night.

Now the only thing she could think of was that it was highly unlikely that she would ever feel that way again.

She had told him about Jason, relieving herself of that heavy burden that had been weighing her down. She hadn't even realized how guilty she had felt until it was all over. She had expected the anger, had thought herself prepared for it.

She hadn't expected him to blame her, though.

Wearily, she pushed away from the door. In her office, she kept her back to the computer. She couldn't think enough just yet to concentrate on writing. Instead, she selected a book from the shelves, curling up on the couch.

Put him out of your head. Put the entire mess out of your head.

Wise advice, certainly. With an effort, she opened the book and started to read. She hadn't even gotten past the first paragraph when it slipped from her hands and she buried her tear-drenched face in her arms.

Chapter Twelve

Three months later…

A warm early summer breeze drifted past, catching the ends of her hair and tugging at them playfully. As she sat next to the grave, knees drawn up to her chest, Nikki stared at the pale gray headstone.

This was the first time she had come here in over a month. Slowly, she had come to realize that it had become an obsession with her. Forcing herself to stay away had been her therapy. It had been harder than she had expected at first, and then it had been so much easier than she could ever had hoped. The grief that weighed upon her like a stone was lessening, bit by bit, day by day.

Running a hand over the closely cropped grass, she closed her eyes.

Her baby wasn't there. Not anymore. He was beyond where she could reach him and in a better place than this. A place where broken hearts and broken families were unknown, a place where rage, misery and betrayal didn't exist.

With her eyes still closed, she pulled up an image of him, his sweet laughing face as he had toddled though the stream not very far from where she sat, tiny fish darting around his little feet

Over the past few months, since Wade and his little girl had packed up and left, she had come to realize that a person didn't have to be there physically. Jason was still with her, tucked safely inside her soul where he couldn't be hurt.

The memories of his father and sister he had never known were with him.

With a sigh, she rose to her knees, pressed her hand flat to the headstone. Silently, she said her good-byes.

It was time to let go.

And it was time to get on with her own life.

She made her way to the little church. Her Bronco sat parked in front, black paint gleaming under the sun. She paused, one hand resting on the hood as she stared back at the cemetery. A breeze drifted by, bringing with it the unmistakable scent of honeysuckle. Tipping her head back, she drew the air in and smiled.

Saying goodbye didn't hurt as much as she had thought it would.

Something tickled her hand and she looked down. Perched there, on her index finger, was a tiny butterfly. Pale yellow wings marked with traces of blue. Cautiously, she lifted her hand, waiting for it fly of. It didn't. She held it up to her face as her smile bloomed.

Jason.

Vividly, she remembered the picnic. How her little boy had chased after butterflies and found a dead one, one with wings the color of the sun and the sky. The scent of honeysuckle on the air. The pleasure of the early summer sun shining down on them.

He had come back to say goodbye.

Sometimes, she had thought his loss had been so devastating partially because she hadn't been able to say goodbye, had never been able to find the closure she so badly needed. Maybe she had spent all these hours by the graveside, searching for him just so she could say goodbye.

But he had never been there.

Until now.

She could feel him, all around her. Maybe it was her imagination, but at that moment, she heard a deep baby chuckle, smelled the soft scent of his skin.

Suddenly, the butterfly fluttered its wings and took off. As it flew away from her, the final heavy weight of grief fell from her shoulders.

And Nikki finally understood what it was like to be free

If only she been able to do this months ago, she might not have lost Wade.

Smiling a sad little smile, she climbed into her car. She had come to grips with the pain, as she had so desperately needed. It had finally eased. It was still there, but it had distanced itself from her, become more bearable.

She had come to grips with losing Wade.

You simply couldn't have everything in life that you wanted. You just had to make do with what you had.

Shrugging off the memories, she started the truck and headed for home.

The little red light on her machine was blinking. For once, it didn't occur to her to ignore it until the poor machine could hold no more messages. She hit the play button as she kicked off her sandals.

The voice that filled the room was unfamiliar.

At first.

"Hello. I'm trying to reach a Nicole Kline. I'm not

sure if I have the right number." Silence. *"This is Louise Lightfoot. I was asked to try and contact you."* More silence, followed by a deep shuddering breath. As she waited, frozen in dread, listening to that voice from the past, Nikki prayed. Like she had never prayed before. *"My son… Wade…he's been in an accident, Ms. Kline. He was asking for you. He's in…"*

As she named off the largest trauma hospital in Louisville, Nikki's legs folded beneath her. "Please, God," she whispered softly, weakly. "Please, God. Not again." For a few moments longer, she knelt on the floor, folded over, her face buried in her hands as her all too vivid imagination painted the worst possible pictures.

Then she saw Abby's little face.

And shot to her feet.

In less than ten minutes, she was on the road to Louisville, speaking rapidly into a cellular phone she rarely used. It was several years old and dusty. She kept it out of habit more than anything else. This was the first time she used it in months, if not longer.

She listened to the standard tripe handed out to non-family members. Hung up on the bored nurse. Called again, listened to the same crap from a more understanding nurse, who offered to get a family member.

The voice that came on the phone was another blast from the past. Wade's older brother, Joe. "He was hit by a drunk driver on the way from work a week ago. We've been trying to track you down ever since. He was…he was asking for you when they brought him in. It was touch and go that first night.

They didn't think that he would make it. Mom finally got in touch with your dad earlier today but he wouldn't give her your number. She called back again later and your brother gave her your home phone number."

Nikki stored that little piece of information to deal with later and asked the question she hated to ask. "How is he?"

"Unresponsive," Joe said quietly. On the other end of the line, he pressed his thumbs to his eyes, closing out the harsh hospital lights. "He fell into a coma about two hours after they brought him in. He took a few blows to the head. We, ah, we don't know…we don't know if he's going to come out of it or not."

"The doctors?"

"They keep saying we have to keeping hoping for the best, but you can tell they're losing faith that anything will happen. There's no physical reason for the coma." Miles away in Louisville, Joe stared in silence at the still body that lay on the bed. Hooked up to various tubes and lines, Wade was barely recognizable. "It's been a week, Nik."

"He's gonna be fine," Nikki said, her voice rough. "Talk to him, okay? He will hear you. Tell him…tell him I'm coming."

She could only hope that he really wanted her there.

*****

Wade was floating in darkness. Occasionally, a

familiar voice would break past the thick cloud that seemed to envelope him. Mom, Dad, and Joe. Lori and Zack. It was funny, those two being married. Most often, it was Abby's sweet little voice that called to him, telling him stories the best she could remember. The longer she spoke the closer he came to getting out of the dark well, but always, her voice would start to falter, then tremble and break, and then she was gone, and he was adrift again.

The one voice he wanted to hear, kept waiting for, never came. He thought he remembered calling out for her after… After what?

Had he been in an accident? He didn't feel like it. But then again, he couldn't feel much of anything.

Occasionally, the darkness was relieved by lights. Two different lights. Confused, he would freeze where he was, afraid to move toward either one. He knew what those lights meant, but why would there be two of them? He didn't want to die. He wasn't ready.

Why were there two lights?

Another voice floated to him, soft, female, familiar, but then Wade recognized his mother's voice, and distantly, her scent. Losing interest, he withdrew.

*****

Nikki stood at the foot of the bed, staring at the figure laying limply under white sheets. Not so long ago, she had lain in a bed much like this, in a small country hospital, tubes running this way and that. A thin tube had been inserted through his nose to feed him and the faint outline of another tube led toward a catheter bag. Yeah. She had been there before.

One arm was turned up exposing his inner elbow, where an IV line was secured. Clear fluid fed into the line from a bag hanging at the bedside.

He was thinner, paler. Weaker.

"Are you going to talk to him?"

Slowly, she turned. Standing in the doorway was Abby, clad in a pink top and blue jeans. She had grown, quite a bit from when Nikki had last seen her. With a start, Nikki realized it had been almost a year.

"Yeah," she answered, her voice tight and rusty sounding. "I'm going to talk to him." She nodded politely at Louise, feeling vaguely uncomfortable and ashamed. Wade's mother had always made her feel that way. She held her hand out to Abby and offered, "Why don't we both talk to him?"

Slowly, Abby reached out her hand, leaving her grandmother's side. In her oddly adult way, she said, "I think my dad loves you. He was so sad when we left."

"I was sad, too," Nikki admitted, passing a gentle hand down the inky black hair. Why did adults always think that they were hiding their problems from children? The little kids always knew.

"Then why did you let us leave? We could have stayed, if you'd asked him," Abby whispered, her large brown eyes filling with tears. "We could have stayed"

"Maybe we both needed some time to figure out what we really wanted," Nikki said.

"I know what he wanted. I know what I wanted. We wanted you to be our family," Abby said, her eyes straying to the figure in the bed. "Was it because of me? Didn't you like me enough to be my mom?"

Nikki didn't think her heart could hurt any more than it already did, but she was wrong. "Oh, sweetie," she murmured, pulling the little girl into her arms. "Baby, it wasn't you. It was me. I've been all messed up inside and I'm just now starting to get myself straightened out"

Over Abby's small shoulder, Nikki saw Louise Lightfoot, standing guard. Protecting son and grandchild. Seeing the girl in front of her as someone who hadn't measured up, hadn't been good enough for her son. Nikki reckoned that Louise blamed her for Wade's indiscretion with Jamie. If she had been the type of girl she should have been, Wade wouldn't have strayed. Nikki also knew she certainly wasn't what the older woman had pictured her future daughter-in-law to be. Someone from the wrong side of town, a broken family, hoodlums for brothers, an alcoholic for a father, the daughter of a woman who had killed herself rather than deal with the problems in her life.

None of that counted now. Her hoodlum brothers were reformed, for the most part. Her father was sober and had been for years. Nikki had proven beyond a shadow of a doubt that she was strong enough to deal with anything life may throw at her. They lived in a small town where people liked and respected them.

But even if that hadn't been the case, Nikki knew it wouldn't have mattered.

Wade thought she was good enough. He had wanted her, and God willing, he still did. The little girl clinging desperately to her shoulders definitely wanted her. That was what mattered.

Rubbing a soothing hand over Abby's back, she rose, cradling the little girl against her. Carefully, she settled in the chair by the bed, reaching out and taking Wade's hand. "What should we say?" Abby asked, whispered.

"I don't know. What do you think we should say?" Nikki asked.

With the hope of the young, Abby cocked her head and said, "Maybe we should tell him how little girls ought to have a dog. A real one."

"Wise choice," Nikki decided

Side by side, they talked until their throats were raw and their voices hoarse. Twilight was settling in when Nikki and Abby fell silent. Sleepily, Abby asked, "Do you think he heard?"

"I know he did, honey," Nikki said with a smile as she brushed back the silky black locks of hair from Abby's face.

"Why doesn't he wake up?"

"I think he's kind of lost. It's like he's in a place he doesn't know and somebody went and turned out the lights. He's just got to find his way out. That's why we need to keep talking to him. If he hears us, he'll know which way to go."

With a sleepy smile, Abby said, "He gets lost a lot. He always finds his way back, though"

"He will this time, too," Nikki promised, hoping she wasn't lying.

Abby fell asleep on her lap, her face pressed against Nikki's breast, small arms locked around her neck.

From the chair in the corner, Louise sighed and

said, "I wished we could have explained it to her like that. We didn't know what to tell her." Silence fell again as Louise came and collected her sleeping granddaughter. "I need to get her home.

"Do you really think he heard?" Louise asked, her voice breaking.

"Yes."

"How can you be so certain?"

With a sad smile, Nikki replied, "Because nothing else is acceptable."

Moments later, quiet footsteps followed by the soft click of the door, and then Nikki was alone with Wade. Pressing her lips together, Nikki reached once again for his hand.

"Wade, it's me," she said, forcing her voice to be level. "Buddy, you need to wake up. There are people here who need you. Your little girl. Your folks." In a whisper, she added, "Me.

"We went and messed things up real good, Wade. But that doesn't mean we can't straighten them out." Her voice broke and she clenched her hand tightly around his. "Damn it, Wade. Don't do this. I can't lose somebody else. You've got to come out of this." Tears fell down her cheeks and she leaned forward, laying one arm around his waist, resting her face against his belly. "I love you. I always did. Sometimes I hated myself because I couldn't stop. But it's a part of me, like breathing, like writing. I can't live without you. I can live with you not wanting me, but I can't do it unless you're out there somewhere."

His face remained still, his eyes closed as she continued to cry against his chest. "Damn you, Wade.

Wake up!"

Her voice faltered and then strengthened as she started to talk to him. She told him about Jason, about the pregnancy, about the short time she'd had with him before she had lost him. "He looked just like you. He was smart and sweet and funny."

She told him about her books, the ones she had written. The ideas that brewed and simmered in her head before she was able to get them down on paper. She told him about her family, how they had straightened out and actually started acting like a family. How Dylan and Shawn had gone from troubled street punks to hotheaded but decent young men.

Through it all, he was silent.

Shifts changed. New nurses came and went. One quietly offered to get her a drink, some food and was told no. Another suggested she get some rest and was ignored. Some of Wade's old friends had pulled strings, talked to a couple of doctors, and Nikki could stay around the clock. She wasn't leaving until he woke up.

Some time near dawn, eyes dry and burning, Nikki released his hand and rose. She wandered over to the window staring out at the sleeping city. In the distance, she could see the Kennedy Bridge and the distant lights of southern Indiana.

Restless, she paced the room. Why wouldn't he wake up?

*****

Silence swarmed all around him and Wade

wanted to scream with frustration. Where had she gone? Nikki?

He couldn't talk, couldn't move...*damn it!* Was she going to walk away again? If she did, he wouldn't even be able to stop her. He should have tried harder last time, should have kept pushing her.

Dammit, where had she gone?

He floundered, hesitating. Two different lights. Which one led the way home, to Abby, to Nikki?

He paused, turning from one to the other. As the silence continued, he made a choice.

*****

Soft sobs filled the room. Nikki still sat at the bedside, her face buried in the sheets by Wade's side. It had been three days. Three days since she had first entered this quiet room. Since that first, she hadn't cried. Until now. Sheer exhaustion and fear had eaten away at her and sometime after Louise had taken Abby home she had simply broken.

"Oh, God, Wade," she whispered brokenly. "You have to come back." One hand clutched desperately at his.

"...cry..."

Startled, she jerked up right, one hand pressing against her mouth. His face was pale, his hand limp in hers. But his sculpted mouth parted. "Wade?" she whispered, almost afraid to speak.

"...don't cry..."

"Wade," she gasped, leaning forward as his eyelids slowly lifted. Then he was staring up at her.

"Please don't...cry..." he repeated, his voice a weak whisper.

"I can't help it," she wailed as more sobs built in her throat. Tears of relief this time, as she huddled at the bedside, his hand clutching hers tightly.

*****

"Did you mean it?"

A day later, Nikki raised her head to look him. Gritty-eyed from lack of sleep, her mind bleary, she asked, "Mean what?"

"What you said"

"You heard me?"

He frowned at her over the tray of hospital food, broth and Jello®. Yum. "I heard you say you loved me. Did you mean it?"

Locking her eyes on his, she simply said, "Yes."

"What do you plan do about it?"

"What do you think we should do?"

It was almost night again. His parents had finally left, leaving them alone. She was nervous and scared and hopeful. He had clutched her hand most the day, as though he feared she would disappear if he let go. "I think you should marry me," he decided, his voice hoarse, both from lack of use and from the feeding tube that been removed the previous night. But his tone was firm, almost belligerent

"Is that a proposal?" she asked, cocking her head as she lazily swung one foot back and forth. She looked casual and relaxed, but her insides were jumping with happiness and hope.

"No," he snapped. "I'm telling you. I proposed once and that was a damn disaster. This time, I'm telling you."

"Telling me?" she asked archly, raising that arrogant eyebrow and staring at him. "Don't you think this is something we should talk about?"

Catching the teasing twinkle in her eye, he tugged her hand. Willingly, she came down to cuddle against his side mindful of the tubes and wires still restraining him. He covered her mouth with a rough, almost desperate kiss. Then he buried his face in her hair as he replied, "No. You spend too much time talking. Haven't I already told you we get along much better if we don't use our mouths to talk?" She smiled and whispered, "I have just one more thing to say." Scowling, Wade demanded, "What?" Nikki lowered her head, nipped his lip gently before turning her head to whisper into his ear.

"Yes..."

Other Great Titles From Triskelion Publishing

Sexylips66 by Dakota Cassidy Coming in March

"Your lips are puuurdy..."

Those are the words in one of many e-mails that greet Callie Winston, divorced and a columnist for a hip California magazine, when she decides to do some research into online dating for an article she desperately needs to boost her readership. Callie's in danger of losing her job to the younger and hipper set. She's prepared to fight fire with fire, date by lame date, until she gets the scoop. So Callie submits a profile to an online date site called Heavenly Hookups and hits the new millennium dating scene with a warrior cry and a pair of lips that apparently, have caught the attention of a man or two, or eight-hundred to be precise...

Who knew the single men of the world were so freakin' desperate for a date they'd contact a thirty-eight year old, divorced, not so runway model thin columnist? But they do. By the droves, and in the masses of e-mail Callie receives, lies one Brian Benson.

Brian Benson, military lifer, is at a crossroads in his life when he sees Callie Winston's profile on Heavenly Hookups. His attraction to her picture is not only volatile and instantaneous, but sends Brian on a quest to find out if there's more to life than guns and jungles.

But Callie is scarred and bitter from her divorce and she doesn't want a real date anyway. Just a guinea pig or two for her column, but Brian touches a place in her she thought long dead and happily buried. It leaves Callie on a limb that precariously shakes her solitary foundation and gives her hope she doesn't necessarily want or need in her single existence.

Brian Benson wants Callie Winston at all costs and there isn't much he won't do to get her...

The Curse of the Midnight Star
The Discovery by Lynn Warren
Available Now

Jack and Lynsee head into the middle of the Louisiana Bayou to investigate a missing person's case that seems to have turned into murder. As both are experienced agents, they expect some resistance from the locals, especially in a place where legends and superstition abound. They are even prepared for the tension that comes from being in close proximity to each other but absolutely nothing prepares them for the other things that they encounter.

Voices in the wind, men who leave no footprints, images, dreams and a gravesite that is one hundred years older than the one for which they are currently searching, soon have Jack and Lynsee convinced that the legends surrounding Scarlet Oak Manor may be more than legend. Neither believes in the supernatural but as it becomes apparent that something very strange is happening at the manor and that it has no logical explanation they are forced to and look at things not so logically.